DIRTY JUSTICE

SPECIAL WEAPONS & TACTICS 5

PEYTON BANKS

"You are nothing short of my everything." –

UNKNOWN

1

"This can't be happening." Ronnie Floyd groaned. "Please, please, please. One line. One line only," she pleaded while sitting on the floor of her bathroom.

She prayed to the good Lord above. Every promise she could think of from going to church more, to donating food to the homeless spilled from her lips. She was willing to do whatever He required of her, if only the pregnancy test sitting on her counter displayed a single line.

She ignored the coolness of the tile beneath her. Ronnie leaned her head back against the wall with her eyes closed.

Everything was going to be okay. No matter what. She was a big girl and would handle whatever the future held for her.

Sitting forward, Ronnie blew out a deep breath. She snagged the test and froze in place.

Two lines.

She grabbed the box and reread the directions for the fourth time. Maybe she had misread it. Or maybe she was tired and her eyes didn't see the words correctly.

"Two lines is a positive result," she uttered in disbelief. "Shit."

She was pregnant.

Ronnie was going to be someone's mother.

Panic consumed her. She tossed the test in the trash and ran a shaky hand through her dark hair. Her heart raced while her breaths grew shallow and short.

"It's going to be okay." Her voice sounded hollow even to herself.

What the hell was she going to do?

Well, she knew one thing she wasn't going to do was sit on the floor and wallow away in tears.

This was the era of the modern woman. She was strong, had a steady career she loved, and she knew who the father of her child was.

With her eyes closed, she blew out a deep breath and tried to will her racing heart to slow down.

She wouldn't have to do it completely alone. Her

one-night stand a couple of months ago was a trust-worthy guy.

He was sexy, intelligent, carried a badge...oh, goodness. Sarena was going to kill her.

Sarena MacArthur was married to the sergeant of the Columbia SWAT officer who had knocked her up. Her friend had warned her about the guys, and that they had some unwritten code about relation-ships. Even though it would seem some of them were breaking it for love.

Ronnie had slept with Brodie, a member of Mac's team, and he was her baby daddy.

She giggled at the term. Never in a million years would she have thought she'd be a baby momma.

It had been two years since she had been with a member of the opposite sex, and apparently this was what happened when the dry spell got broken.

That night had been totally worth it.

She couldn't help it. Brodie was an amazing guy. They had been harmlessly flirting with each other since the day they had met. Sarena and her husband hosted the team over at their house quarterly, and Ronnie was always invited.

She would go and was pretty cool with all the guys, but there was something about Brodie. He was smart as hell, built, and looked good in nothing.

She rubbed her face and tried to think.

Should she tell him?

Slapping her forehead, she shook her head. "What is wrong with me. Of course I have to tell him."

First, that would be wrong if she didn't. Second, they saw each other often enough that she wouldn't have an excuse not to.

How would she explain a growing belly and no partner around?

She stood and reached for the other three pregnancy tests and threw them away. Each of them had the same result—pregnant.

Flipping out the light, she made her way to her living room. She plopped down on the couch with a groan.

Welp, this type of situation would normally call for wine, but she officially couldn't have any alcohol for a while.

What did people who didn't drink do in these types of situations?

She was truly stumped and couldn't think of an answer.

The doorbell ringing startled her.

"Who the hell is that?" she muttered. She glanced at the clock on the wall to find it was a little after ten in the morning. Pushing off the couch, she walked to the front door and peeked through the peephole. She found Sarena on the other side. She unlocked the door and pulled it open. "Hey, girl."

"Hey, bestie!" Sarena grinned. She practically skipped into the house without waiting for Ronnie to invite her in. Not that she needed an invitation.

Ronnie rolled her eyes and shut the door. "It is too early for all this."

"What are you talking about? It's a beautiful day outside," Sarena exclaimed.

Ronnie followed her best friend into the living room.

She took a seat on the couch and glanced over at the window. The weatherman had called for temperatures to be down in the forties, and there was no sight of the sun.

Her friend must have slipped and bumped her head.

Ronnie and Sarena had been best friends since their sophomore year in college. They had met in nursing school and had been lab partners. They had immediately hit it off and become life-long friends.

"Why are you so bubbly?" Ronnie scowled. She wasn't ashamed to still be in her jammies at this time in the morning. It was her off day, and she was going to take advantage of it. She pulled her blanket off the back of her couch and wrapped it around herself.

"I can't just be happy?" Sarena giggled.

Ronnie eyed her friend suspiciously. She must want something.

"I need coffee. Do you have any made?"

"No, but help yourself and make me a cup, too." Ronnie yawned. She readjusted herself on the couch and tucked her feet underneath her.

Sarena left the room, and banging came from the kitchen. Ronnie turned her television on and flicked through the channels. She wondered if she should tell Sarena now or wait until after she'd been to the doctor.

Her friend would be understanding and would no doubt support her. Sarena was like a sister to Ronnie.

Finding nothing on the television, she lowered the volume just so she could have a little white noise.

Ronnie reached for her e-reader to find something to read. With the shocking news that she was pregnant, she needed to escape reality for a few hours. She browsed through the countless amount of books she had on her device while listening to her friend sing off-key in the kitchen.

Something was causing her friend to be extra happy this morning.

"Your nose is always in a book," Sarena announced, returning to the room.

Ronnie glanced up and zeroed in on the two mugs of coffee in her hands.

Ronnie took hers and put her device down on her lap. Sarena sat on the end of the couch near Ronnie's feet. They sipped their coffee in silence for a moment.

Okay, she's killing me with the suspense.

Ronnie set her mug down on the table before her and turned to her friend. "Okay, spill it, woman. There is something you are not telling me. What's up?"

Sarena took another sip of her coffee and smiled. She was bursting at the seams and sat her drink down.

"I'm pregnant!" she screamed.

Ronnie instantly found herself hollering with her friend. She flew across the couch to Sarena. They engulfed each other in a hug while laughing and crying at the same time.

She ignored her current situation because she was truly happy for her friend. She hugged Sarena even harder while tears ran freely down her cheeks.

Ronnie liked to think she had a big hand in getting Sarena and Mac together. It had been she who had coaxed an unsure Sarena over to Mac's house in sexy lingerie hidden under her trench coat. If one were to ask Ronnie, if it wasn't for her, Sarena and Mac would have never got together. Well, they might have eventually, but Ronnie helped speed along the process.

Mac and Sarena were the perfect couple.

"When did you find out?" Ronnie asked. She sat back and took Sarena's hand in hers. She wanted to know all of the details.

"We've known for a while now. I just had this superstition of waiting until I was out of my first trimester," Sarena said. She tightened her grip on Ronnie's hand. "You don't know how hard it has been not being able to tell you."

"That's okay." Ronnie smiled. She had a secret of her own and she was dying to spill it, but she would wait. She'd see the doctor to confirm and then she would tell Brodie first before she told anyone else. She was already dreading telling her parents and her siblings. Not that she was ashamed of being pregnant, it was just that she'd have to admit to having a one-night stand with a cop. "So how have you been feeling?"

"I've been sick as a dog." Sarena grimaced. She reached down and ran her hand along her slight pudge. "It's like clockwork. First thing in the morning I have an appointment with my toilet."

"Oh, I'm sorry." Ronnie rubbed her friend's hand. She hadn't had any symptoms and considered herself lucky. The only thing that alerted her to test was the absence of her monthly visitor. It had been a couple months since she'd had one, and it was supposed to arrive this week. "How did Mac take the news?"

Sarena's face lit up at the mention of her husband. "He's been a nervous wreck."

"Mac? Nervous?"

That man was the epitome of former military and SWAT leader. He had a gruffness to him and a bark that made everyone listen. He was well-respected, and Ronnie had a difficult time imagining him being anything but the tough sergeant.

"Yes, the man has been hovering over me more than normal. I mean, I love the fact that he holds my hair while I'm throwing up and makes sure I'm hydrated, but I swear, Ronnie, I'm almost to the point where I want to run and hide from my own damn husband."

They shared a giggled. Ronnie pictured what Sarena just described and laughed even harder.

"You know the man is overprotective of you."

Everyone knew that. The man had risked his life to save Sarena. Her friend had been kidnapped, and Mac, along with the SWAT team, had gone to the extreme to save her. If that didn't show how much Sarena meant to him, then nothing would.

"I know, but I can walk from the bathroom to our bedroom. He doesn't have to carry me." Sarena leaned her head back against the couch.

Ronnie chuckled and shook her head. That sounded like something Mac would do.

What Ronnie wouldn't give to have a man love her as much as Mac loved Sarena. Their relationship was like one of those in her favorite romance novels. Ronnie had read enough of the books to recognize the real-life version when she saw it.

A book could be written about the MacArthurs.

Brodie's face came to mind. She shivered with the thought of everything they had done to each other. Even when they'd seen each other after that night, he'd wink and smile at her just like old times. She had promised herself just to indulge one time in the sexy cop, but it was so hard to keep her hands to herself when they were around each other.

Ronnie and Sarena reached for their mugs and continued drinking their delicious brew Sarena had made. Being nurses, coffee was a necessity. It was the only way to survive a busy day at work. They both worked at the same hospital. Sarena was the assistant manager in the emergency room while Ronnie was an ICU nurse. She floated between the different ICUs and the emergency room. Occasionally the girls worked together.

"What do you need from me?" Ronnie asked.

"Well, you know I want you to plan the baby shower. Please?" Sarena's eyes grew wide as she tried to put on her best begging expression.

"Who else would be planning it?" Ronnie gasped playfully. She rested her hand over her heart. "I would have been disappointed if you chose anyone but me."

Excitement filled her. This would give her something else to think about than the little bun growing in her oven.

"Mac and I had dinner over my parents' house last night and were able to tell them and Harden about the baby."

"Harden is in town?" Ronnie asked.

Sarena's brother was a SEAL currently still serving. It was rare for the elder Rucker child to make an appearance.

"Yeah, it was perfect timing. He had come home to visit our parents, so we went over there for dinner."

"How is Harden and Mac getting along?" she asked quietly.

When Sarena had been kidnapped, her brother didn't appreciate it happening on Mac's watch.

"The tension between them isn't too tough. They of course behave in front of Mom and Dad. But Harden is going to have to get used to Mac since not only am I carrying his last name, but his child now, too." Sarena laughed. "What's funny is the two of them are alike in so many ways."

Sarena was correct. Both her brother and husband were Navy men, alpha and extremely stubborn.

"I'll start brainstorming. Anything specific you know you want?" Ronnie asked. She already had a few ideas flying about in her mind. This was going to be fun.

"We have to find out whoever catered Deana's baby shower. The food was amazing."

"No problem. Matter of fact, I'll snag Aspen and Deana to help."

"Don't forget to include Myles' new girlfriend, Roxxy," Sarena said. "She's fun and she's going to take us out to a shooting range. You have got to come with us."

"Hell, yeah. Count me in."

2

Brodie pushed his shades to the top of his head. They sat in place, buried in his thick dark hair. Sweat glistened on his forearms. Training day was never a walk in the park. To be the best, every practice, they went hard. In order to be prepared for the unexpected in real-life situations, they had to train as if they were in one.

This belief had saved the lives of each member of SWAT at least once.

Brodie followed Iker and Zain over to where Mac stood, poised, with his arms folded against his chest. The SWAT sergeant's mouth was drawn in a firm line. Mac was difficult to read at times.

The former Navy SEAL led their team with a firm grip along with their co-sergeant, Declan.

Brodie came to stand with Iker and Zain. He glanced around and took in all of his teammates. Each of them were dressed in their full black tactical gear, covered in sweat and grime. His gaze landed on Jordan Knight, the new member of the team.

Adding a woman police officer to the team was like giving the guys a little sister. She fit right in from the first day. Each of the guys were protective of her as if she were blood.

After all, she bled blue just as they did.

"So, Jordan." Myles nudged her with his elbow.

The big man dwarfed her, and the slight motion caused her to lose balance and stumble into Declan. She grinned and pushed him back. Myles was like a brick wall and didn't move under her shove.

"Go for the knees." Iker chuckled.

"Damn, what did your momma feed you?" Jordan grumbled, feigning as if she were the one hurt. Her nervousness was fading.

Brodie knew exactly what she felt like. It wasn't that long ago that he was the new man on the block. Myles had taken him under his wing, and Brodie already knew he was going to help Jordan out as much as he could.

"Just good ol' home-cooked meals," Myles

teased. "What I was about to say, is that there's a little wager going on."

This was news to Brodie. He wanted to hear this. Normally when the guys were tossing out bets, he was in on it.

What the hell?

"What kind of wager?" Jordan's eyebrows rose.

"Since you are the newest member, you have to challenge the last new member." Myles grinned and glanced over at Brodie.

Brodie released a groan. He had hoped the guys would have forgotten about their new recruit challenge. They had been so busy with calls and training Jordan that Brodie had hoped their little games would be overlooked.

"Are you shitting me? We're still doing that?" Brodie ran a hand along his jaw. He was met with the prickly stubble of unshaven skin.

Iker slapped him on the shoulder and grinned. "Oh, don't think it slipped our minds."

Even Mac was smiling.

He was in trouble.

"What am I missing?" Jordan asked.

"Each time we get a new member on the team, the newbie has to go against the former newbie in a challenge," Declan explained, trying to hold back a laugh. He cleared his throat and nodded to Myles.

Brodie stepped forward in the circle of their team. Jordan shrugged and came to stand before him.

It was always a friendly challenge, but the loser paid a hefty fine.

"So what's the challenge?" Brodie smirked. He looked her up and down playfully. She was about five and a half feet tall. He could take her.

Jordan narrowed her eyes on him.

"And don't go easy on me because I'm a girl," Jordan warned.

Snickers went around.

"We wouldn't dream of that." Zain snorted.

"Hell, naw. You run with the big dogs, you're going to be treated like one," Iker said.

He and Zain shared a fist bump.

"Challenge will be held two Saturdays from today, as long as there are no calls," Declan said.

"The two officers will don their full gear and will run the gauntlet," Myles said. He walked slowly around Brodie and Jordan who were in a stare-off.

Brodie had to hand it to Jordan, she was one tough woman and a hell of a policewoman. He knew her background and respected her.

But Brodie was an Army man, and six years of his life was given to serving Uncle Sam. The Army had ingrained hard work and perseverance in him. Once his time was complete with the Army, Brodie had joined the Columbia Police Department. It was at the suggestion of the captain that he joined SWAT in his first year. A position had become available due to an officer retiring.

The gauntlet, he could do it with his eyes closed.

Whistles and shouts filled the air.

"Do you two accept your challenge?" Myles asked, coming to stand next to Brodie and Jordan. He rested a hand on both of their shoulders.

"I accept," Jordan replied, her top lip curling up in a snarl.

"As do I," Brodie said.

"All right, SWAT. Looks like it's official," Myles shouted. He squeezed Brodie's shoulder before releasing him.

Brodie held out his fist. Jordan's smaller one met his.

It was official and too bad Brodie was going to have to beat his newly appointed sister's ass.

"We have a few announcements to make." Mac motioned for everyone to gather around him.

The air between the team was lighthearted and

relaxed. Challenging one another was just a part of the camaraderie amongst them.

Brodie wrapped his arm around Jordan's shoulders and guided her over with the guys.

"Prepare for one hell of an ass-kicking," he murmured in her ear.

"Ha," she laughed, shoving him away. "You're going down as the one who lost to a girl."

Brodie let out a hefty laugh, watching her move over to stand beside Declan.

This was going to be interesting.

"Not sure if you've heard yet, but Deana had the baby a little early, so Ash will be taking a few weeks off," Mac shared.

"He's beautiful," Myles chimed. Like a proud uncle, he whipped out his phone and pulled up pictures.

The guys laughed as they passed the phone around.

Brodie took the phone from Iker when he came to him. Baby Evan had the fattest cheeks, dark curly hair, and appeared perfect.

He couldn't wait for the day he'd become a father. He'd had a great upbringing. He and his brothers were close to their parents and each other. He was the youngest of three boys. His brother,

Ander, was a fireman while Zayden was a cop. Their father served in the Army and had been ecstatic that one of his boys went into the Army.

For Brodie it was some of the best years of his life. He had joined a band of brothers he would consider family for the rest of his life. He was still in contact with most of his old squad. Some had moved on to private security, a couple were federal agents, and a few did off-the-books consulting.

"One last announcement," Mac said. He raised his hand to silence everyone.

Brodie handed the phone to Myles.

The group focused on Mac whose face relaxed into a wide grin.

"Sarena and I are expecting."

The group went wild, hooting and hollering. Everyone converged on Mac, hugging and clapping him on the back.

Brodie offered his hand to Mac. He drew him in for a manly hug. "Congratulations, Mac. That's amazing."

"Thanks, Brodie," Mac said, stepping back.

Sarena and Mac were an awesome couple. Seeing the two of them together, one would know they were in love.

A slight twinge twisted in Brodie's chest.

Flashes of Ronnie's smile came to mind.

Brodie swallowed hard and moved back from his sergeant. Mac turned to Zain who was congratulating him.

Fuck.

If Mac found out he'd had relations with his wife's best friend, he was as good as dead.

"Drinks tonight to celebrate," Declan said.

"I don't know if I want to keep drinking with y'all," Iker joked. "I might catch whatever bug is going around."

"Same." Zain shook his head. "Every time I turn around, someone has fallen in love."

Brodie smiled watching his teammates high five. Brodie shook his head. The guys were right. Something was in the air or the water. Four of his SWAT teammates had gone from single to deep in a relationship.

Well, if that were the case, Brodie couldn't wait for his turn.

It would be nice to have someone to go to, someone to share the burden of life. What he wouldn't give to come home after a hard shift and have someone there who he could pour out his troubles to or even just rub his back.

The memory of Ronnie's dark-brown eyes

staring up at him while he was braced over her came to mind.

She was coming to mind frequently. He was tempted to call her. He had been eyeing her from the moment they had first met.

She was funny, smart, and beautiful. She worked with Sarena at General Hospital as a nurse. She always made him smile, and he was comfortable around her. They'd seen each other a lot since she was the best friend of his sergeant's wife.

All the more reason why he shouldn't have touched her, but he couldn't help it.

She was so damn sexy.

"We are going to work on entry drills a few more times. We're going to work on them until we feel we've perfected it with our new member," Declan barked, clapping his hands. "Let's make sure Jordan feels comfortable."

Brodie walked over to Jordan once they were dismissed.

"How are you feeling?" he asked.

She smiled and shook her head. Her dark hair was pulled up into a ponytail. She was a pretty girl with smooth brown skin and big brown eyes. All the guys had already vowed to not let anyone near her.

"Nervous. I just don't want to mess this up." Jordan slid her shades on, hiding her eyes from him.

"We have your back. We'll work with you until you feel comfortable. Even in the field, we would never let someone falter."

They walked alongside each other toward the BEAR vehicle that was used when they went out on a call. It was an armored van that housed everything they would need.

"That's good to know. I wouldn't want to let the team down."

"Even coming from the Army, it was nerve-racking learning a new team and trying to fit in. But these men, I wouldn't trade any of them for all the money in the world," Brodie admitted.

"Everyone has been amazing and helpful. I'm thankful to be welcomed. A woman on SWAT, you don't see that much." She chuckled.

"Of course we would have. It was time for new blood, and you were perfect in your interview." Her being a woman hadn't crossed his mind. All he needed to make sure was that whoever joined the team was a hard worker and trustworthy. They put their lives on the line every damn day. Man or woman, that person needed to be able to cover his six.

"I know but I just feel like..." She paused and looked around.

"What's wrong?" His interest was piqued.

"Maybe it's nothing, but I just feel like some people in the precinct look at me different. I get weird vibes." Jordan shrugged.

Iker's head whipped around, his gaze narrowing on her.

"Weird looks from who?" That man had the hearing of a wolf. He moved to stand on the other side of Jordan. He folded his arms in front of him.

"Don't say anything," she pleaded. "Maybe it's because I'm new."

"Don't worry about them." Iker glanced over at Brodie.

It had been two weeks since Brodie broke the news of the identity of the mole. They were just biding their time. Myles had come under attack while visiting his girl, Roxxy. Men had been sent to take Myles out while he was away from Columbia.

By the time Brodie and the others arrived, Myles, Roxxy, and her parents had everything under control.

It was then he was able to start piecing things together discovering who was the one leaking information to the Demon Lords.

"All right, SWAT. Let's go," Mac called out.

They moved into the BEAR with Declan shutting the door. Mac gave a few taps to the wall near the driver's door to signal they were ready to Zain.

Brodie prepared himself mentally.

Practice as if in a real-life situation.

He cleared his thoughts and brought his face mask up to hide his features. Each member had their own preference on how they wanted to be outfitted, but the one thing that was definitely the same: SWAT emblazoned across their chests.

The air in the truck was tense and silent. Weapons were brandished while they waited to emerge and storm the building.

The BEAR rocked as it drove to their destination. Within a minute, it slowed down.

Brodie's muscles tensed. He was the entry man. The first who arrived at the building and jammed open the door.

The BEAR halted.

"SWAT. Let's hunt," Mac's chilling voice broke the silence.

Declan threw open the door and hopped out with Brodie first. Gripping his Glock, Brodie focused on the building and began the march toward the door. Without looking, he knew his team would be behind him in a single-file line. Their movements were that of a well-oiled machine.

He raced up the stairs to the door. He slid his weapon in the sheath on his thigh and pulled his battle ram from the hook on his pants.

He glanced over his shoulder.

Six cold gazes were on him. With a nod, he turned back and gave one good swing.

The hammer slammed to the door. It knocked it off the hinges. He moved to the side while his team flew into the house.

Damn, he loved his job.

3

Chairs in physician's offices were always hard and unwelcoming. Ronnie shifted in her seat to try to find a comfortable spot, but there was none. She blew out a sigh and tossed the magazine she was browsing into the basket on the floor that housed quite a few.

The reading material was all geared toward the expectant mother.

They could have at least had something else in the mix. What if a woman was here for other gynecologic issues that didn't have anything to do with pregnancy?

Staring at the ceiling, Ronnie tried to get her heart to stop racing so fast. She inhaled sharply and let the air out slowly.

Waiting was going to kill her.

Ronnie already knew the physician was going to come in stating the results were positive. She'd taken about ten tests, and they each said she was pregnant.

Finally, Ronnie decided to pull up her big girl panties and call her doctor for an appointment. Due to a recent cancellation and knowing the secretary, she was able to be seen right away.

A knock sounded at the door.

"Come in," Ronnie called out.

The door swung open, and Dr. Thompson breezed into the room with a wide grin.

"How are you, Ronnie?" Dr. Thompson asked. She took a seat in the chair before the computer. She logged in and brought up Ronnie's record.

Ronnie took the time to study her doctor. Dr. Thompson was a beautiful African-American woman with dark-almond skin, dark hair streaked with a few grays. It was left loose and was styled in a bob just below her jawline.

"I'm doing well, Doc. How are you?" Ronnie crossed her legs and turned slightly to the physician. Deep inside, she hoped all ten of those tests were wrong, but in reality, she knew the possibility of that happening was low.

"I'm good. My daughter got accepted to Spelman

College." The doctor's face lit up at the mention of her daughter. Dr. Thompson was a proud momma at the moment.

"Oh my. How exciting." Ronnie clapped. She remembered the day she had first got her acceptance letters from college. It was a big deal, and her parents had been so proud of her accomplishment. "I'm sure you are so proud of her."

"I am. She has worked so hard, and it was her first choice for college." Dr. Thompson crossed her ankles and swiveled in the chair to face Ronnie. "So tell me. When was your last menstrual cycle?"

"I'm not sure. Two months ago?" Ronnie's voice ended on a shriek. She tucked her hair behind her ear. "Ever since I stopped the pill, it went back to the abnormal pattern."

Ronnie had been celibate for the past two years, and it was pointless to be on the pill. Yes, it gave her a benefit of having her monthly flow routinely, but Ronnie had come off it. Now she really couldn't remember when the last time Aunt Flo had visited.

"Okay. The test of course came back positive. Let's do a transvaginal ultrasound to see how far along you are. We can just go down the hallway where I can do it today."

"Sounds like a plan," Ronnie replied. Her heart

did its weird dance again at the thought that she would officially see her little bean.

"Good. My nurse will come grab you in a second. I'll go make sure the room is not occupied by one of my partners."

Dr. Thomson exited. Ronnie leaned her head back against the wall. Her heart ached slightly. She was going to see her baby for the first time and she was by herself. It would be nice to share this with someone.

Brodie.

Would he be happy to learn that he was going to be a father?

She knew nothing really about his family life. She'd heard he had two brothers, but that was about it.

What kind of upbringing did he have?

Were there any diseases that ran in his family that she would need to know about?

The nurse in her wouldn't allow that part of her brain to shut off.

She rested her hand on her stomach. If she didn't know better, she would say she had a little pudge.

Or it could have been all the food she had been eating at work. Patients and their families were always showing their thanks by dropping food off to the nurses. That was the downside of nursing. Most shifts were so busy that she couldn't sit down for a proper lunch. She tended to graze the entire twelve hours. That wasn't good for her.

A knock at the door drew her attention.

"Come in," she replied.

The door opened, and Dr. Thompson's nurse walked in with a kind smile.

"Hi. Dr. Thompson will be ready for you in a minute. Please remove your clothes and put this gown on. It ties on the side." The woman demonstrated before handing it to Ronnie. "You can leave your socks and bra on."

"Thanks." Ronnie nodded.

"Just peek your head out the door when you're ready." The woman smiled again and disappeared out the door, shutting it softly behind her.

Ronnie stood and disrobed. She folded her clothes neatly, chuckling while hiding her undies in between her jeans.

Why did women do that?

Ronnie was about to have a probe inserted inside her vagina. Who cared what underwear she wore?

Laughing, she put on the robe and tied it on the side just as the nurse showed her. Ronnie opened the door and stuck her head out.

"Ready?" The nurse glanced up from the computer. She stood and waved for Ronnie to follow her.

She padded down the hallway and entered a darkened room. The nurse helped her get on the table and ensured she was comfortable before leaving.

Ronnie sat, fiddling with her hands while waiting for the physician. Her heart refused to calm down. It had a mind of its own. She blew out a deep breath.

She still hadn't told anyone.

Not Sarena.

Not her parents or siblings.

Her older brother would go into full protective brother mode, while her sister would be so excited.

Sarena would be, too, but when she found out who the father was, she may kill Ronnie.

A few minutes later, and Dr. Thompson entered the room.

"All right. Let's see this baby." Dr. Thompson smiled.

She instructed Ronnie to lie down on the bed and helped her into the position she needed. Ronnie rested her feet in the stirrups. Dr. Thompson played a sheet over her legs to give her some privacy even though her entire core was open to the room.

Dr. Thompson grabbed the probe and slid a plastic sheath on it. Ronnie bit back a snort.

That's one helluva condom.

Well, if you would have thought of that with Brodie, you wouldn't be in this predicament.

Dr. Thompson placed some lubricant on it and turned toward her.

"Just relax. The gel is going to be slightly chilled. Our warmer broke." Dr. Thompson offered a comforting smile.

"I'll be okay." Ronnie nodded.

Dr. Thompson spread Ronnie's labia and gently inserted the probe inside her. With her free hand, she hit a few keys on the computer before turning the screen toward Ronnie.

"Oh my. You're further along than you probably thought," Dr. Thompson exclaimed.

Ronnie internally groaned. She remembered the night.

She'd had sex with only one person in the past few months. She had been slightly tipsy, and he had been a very willing participant.

The doctor hit a switch, and the sound of the baby's heartbeat filled the room.

Her baby.

Ronnie blinked, the tears falling down her face.

She glanced at the computer screen and saw her little baby floating around. She slid her hand down to her belly.

"Let's get some measurements, and I'll get you some pictures."

RONNIE SHUT the door to her car and sat back in the seat. She grinned, unable to contain her excitement. She snagged her purse and took out the few photos the doctor had given her. She stared at them, tears blurring her vision. They slid along her cheeks, but she didn't care.

Her lips turned up into a smile. Already, she was in love with her baby. Her child was perfect. Measured a little on the large side, it had two arms, two legs, a protruding belly, and a big head.

Laughter burst from her.

It was too early to tell the sex. That would happen at her next ultrasound appointment that was scheduled in six weeks.

"What am I going to do?" she sniffed.

What she did know was that she was keeping her

baby. There wasn't any doubt about it. She carefully placed the pictures back in her purse.

Ronnie decided to drive to her parents' house. She needed to speak with her mother. She wasn't sure if she were going to spill the beans yet, but being around her mother would comfort her.

Ronnie hit the 'start' button and shifted her car into gear. She wiped her face and let the memories of that night come forward.

"A joint baby shower?" Ronnie laughed. She sat in the back seat of Mac and Sarena's SUV. She shook her head in disbelief. Times had certainly changed. It used to be where a baby shower was just for the women only.

But it would seem Ash and Deana were the modern couple and invited everyone for their celebration.

"It'll be fun. You should see the things Mac brought for Ash." Sarena glanced back at Ronnie.

They arrived at the house, and the party was in full swing. The couple knew the baby was going to be a boy, so the theme was cops and robbers.

Just too cute.

Deana and Ash were beaming.

Sarena had been right. The gifts the guys bought were nothing she would have expected. Normally the couple would receive bedding, clothing, diapers, and anything else they registered for at their favorite store.

The SWAT men took it above and beyond.

Ronnie had never laughed so hard in her life. Brodie and the guys had a ball with the notion of outfitting their teammate for fatherhood.

Ash got all the things a new father would need.

A chest carrier—SWAT-style, with a new father badge.

Matching SWAT dad and son baseball caps.

A dad survival kit. A dad's Doo Doo diaper kit, DILF t-shirts.

And the best present of all?

A powerwheel truck with SWAT painted along the side for the baby.

There was plenty of food and drink for everyone. The flirting between Ronnie and Brodie went past the shy, friendly point. There had been touching, teasing, and lots of innuendos.

Ronnie sat on chaise on the back porch enjoying the warm South Carolina air. Most of the guests had started to leave, and she was appreciating the quietness of the outdoors.

The door opened, and Brodie stepped out. His face lit up when he saw her.

"Here you are," he murmured.

He came over and sat next to her. He stretched his arm out along the back of the seat. Her breath caught at the closeness of him. She could smell the scent of his cologne floating through the air. It made her want to close the gap between them so she could rest her face in the crook of his neck.

"You all right?" he asked.

She glanced at him and nodded. "Yeah, just wanted to get some fresh air."

His fingers absently played with the strands of her hair. A shiver went down her spine.

"I missed you in there." He jerked his head toward the house.

"Did you?" she murmured.

His fingers grew bolder and slid down to the base of her neck. He gently traced little circles on her skin. She bit back a moan it felt so good.

She glanced down at her watch. It was getting late, and she was sure Sarena wasn't ready to leave. Since Ronnie had ridden with them, it looked like she was leaving when they were.

"Am I boring you?"

Her eyes flew to him to find a little smirk on his face.

"No." She laughed. "I was just checking the time. I rode with Mac and Sarena. Guess I'll be staying until the last guest leaves."

"If you want, I can take you home," he offered. His hand was now massaging her neck.

She stared up into his hooded eyes.

"That is, if you're okay with being alone with me in my truck," he teased.

She bit her lip and threw caution to the wind. It had been a long time since a member of the opposite sex had touched her. Not that there hadn't been guys trying.

She had just been picky on who she chose to be intimate with.

Brodie was downright sexy. Tall, muscular, and he had the clearest blue eyes she'd ever seen.

She had read thousands of romance books and decided if those heroines could be bold, then she could, too.

Sliding next to him, she closed the gap between them.

"Only if you don't mind being alone with me." She batted her eyes playfully.

He grinned and pushed off the chair. He turned and offered her his hand. She took it and allowed him to help her up.

She feigned as if she'd tripped and fell into him.

Mighty God above.

His body was ripped with hardened muscles. Something pressed against her stomach, and a slight whimper escaped her.

"Is that your gun, Officer?" She raised her eyebrows at him.

He rested a hand on the small of her back to hold her in place.

"Don't worry, Ms. Floyd. I'm very proficient with that weapon."

Her core clenched.

Yes, she would allow Brodie to take her home.

They entered the house and said their goodbyes. Sarena had almost looked relieved that Ronnie had found a way home. With the promise to speak with her later, Ronnie followed Brodie to his SUV.

Being the gentleman that he was, he helped her into the cab. He smiled at her before shutting the door.

Ronnie's heart raced.

The drive home was filled with laughter. With tears running down her face, Brodie kept her entertained with stories of him and the team.

Ronnie leaned her head on the rest and stared at him. He was extremely handsome, and she was attracted to him. From the moment she'd seen him, she always got little butterflies in her stomach when he was near.

They arrived at her house, and she didn't want him to leave. He shut off the car and faced her.

"Do you want to come in for a nightcap?" she asked. Ronnie prayed she didn't sound corny asking. Was that still a thing?

Brodie stared at her without a word.

Her heart slammed as she waited for an answer.

"Absolutely," he murmured. He opened his door and exited the vehicle.

Ronnie blew out a deep breath. Brodie came to her side and opened the door, again helping her from the truck.

He silently tailed her up to the door. Her heart pounded as she slid the key into the lock and pushed it open.

Ronnie stepped inside and flipped the light switch on. Brodie followed her in. She shut the door and swirled around to find Brodie standing close to her. Without a word, he pushed her up against the door and covered her mouth with his.

4

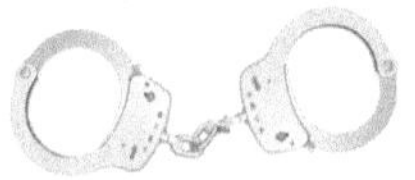

"Mom, I don't know what you did to this food, but I swear you put a little magic in it." Ronnie flopped down on the couch, tucking her feet underneath her.

"I agree. Been saying that for almost forty years now." Her father chuckled. He pushed back his recliner to allow the leg rest to lift.

"You two are a mess." Her mother, Jackie, giggled. She sat on the opposite end of the couch with a big grin on her face.

Ornell and Jackie Floyd had been married thirty-nine years and were still in love. The two provided a great foundation of what love should look like.

Ronnie grew up in a home where she was close to not only her siblings, but her parents. She was the middle child and often teased her parents that she was the one who got forgotten. Her brother, Junior, the eldest, always had attention, and then of course, her sister, Rowan, the baby, demanded it.

Ronnie was the one child who had been independent and quiet with her nose stuck in a book.

Her father flipped the channel and stopped on *Jeopardy*. It was a show they loved to watch and would try to outsmart the contestants and each other.

"Dad, turn this up." Ronnie motioned to the television.

He raised the remote while hitting the button.

The intro to the show came on. Jackie tapped on Ronnie's foot to get her attention.

"Are you going to tell us the real reason you are here?" Jackie cocked an eyebrow at Ronnie.

She had arrived at her parents' house unexpectedly. Not that she needed a reason or invite to come over. She just needed to be around her parents. Their hugs, laughter, and her mother's good food were just what she needed.

"Do I need a reason to come over?" she asked.

Ronnie had decided she wouldn't tell her parents yet. She was going to speak with Brodie first.

He deserved to be told first. Once that was done, then she would tell her family and Sarena.

"Of course you don't. But something's off about you." Her mother stared at her.

Ronnie shrugged and played dumb.

"I don't know. I was missing my mom and dad." She grinned.

"All right. You know I'm always concerned about my babies. If something's bothering you, you better tell me."

"Yes, Mom," Ronnie replied.

Her mother rubbed her knee before settling back.

The three of them were engrossed in the television show. It was an intense game tonight. All three contestants were good and barely missing answers.

"You eat the red stalks of this plant; the green leaves are toxic," Alex Trebec read.

"Hell, I don't know that one," Ornell murmured. "Anything with toxic leaves, we shouldn't be eating in the first place."

"Dad!" Ronnie laughed. "Rhubarb!"

The contestant in the lead buzzed in. "What is Rhubarb?"

"That is correct," Alex responded.

"You got it wrong." Her father chuckled.

"I did not!" Ronnie screeched. Laughter spilled from her as she sat forward.

"You didn't say 'what is.'" Her father pointed at her.

Ronnie slapped her hand on her forehead. "Really, Dad?"

"Your father's right. It would have been wrong had you been on the show," her mother chimed in.

Ronnie rolled her eyes. Her parents always had to correct her. She wasn't on the actual game. She could shout out the answer.

Ronnie grinned and leaned forward. She was going to get the next answer correct.

The *Jeopardy* way.

"Colorful cities for five hundred, Alex," the contestant said.

"This former mining town was Colorado's territorial capital," Alex read off.

"What?" Ronnie shook her head, unsure. Maybe she wasn't going to be answering the question.

"Don't know this one," her father grumbled.

"Me neither." Jackie sighed.

Apparently, none of the contestants knew the answer.

"What is Golden," Alex stated. He faced the

camera. "We'll be back after a word from our sponsors."

"Learn something new every day." Her mother laughed.

"I guess so." Ronnie had never heard of the town and was unfamiliar with mining history. She knew nothing of Colorado except it snowed a lot.

Ronnie yawned. She had been at her parents' for a few hours and should get ready to go home.

"You staying over?" her father asked.

"Not tonight. I'm going to head home once the show is over," she said. She unfolded her legs and stood. Her bladder was calling for relief. "Be right back."

The pressure let her know she had waited too long. She flew out of the room and headed down to the half bath that was located near the mudroom.

She did her business and stood before the sink while the water was running. Turning to the side, she assessed herself.

She didn't look pregnant.

But she knew it wouldn't be long before her belly announced itself. She pushed it out as far as she could and rested her hand on the slight pudge.

"Momma loves you so much already, peanut," she murmured.

Ronnie finished washing her hands and returned to the family room.

Tomorrow, she would call Brodie. This wasn't something she could just tell him over the phone. Maybe they could go out to lunch. She didn't think inviting him back over was a good idea.

But hell, it wasn't like she could get any more pregnant.

Yup, she'd invite him over for lunch or dinner and break the good news.

You're a daddy.

"DO WE BRING IN THE CAPTAIN?" Brodie asked.

"The true question is, do we bring in Jordan?" Myles replied.

Brodie, Iker, Zain, and Myles stood around Brodie's SUV in the parking lot of the police station waiting for Mac and Declan. They shared a glance between each other. They had just returned from a mission, showered, and it was time to leave. Thankfully, this one had been quick, and the bad guy had surrendered immediately.

Brodie loved those types of missions. No one got

hurt. There would be no mountain of paperwork if he shot someone. Just a clean raid.

"You think they will be much longer?" Iker asked.

"They stayed back to speak with Jordan," Myles said.

Brodie took out his phone to check the time. It was a little after nine at night. Not bad. He'd only been at work since seven that morning. That was the downside of SWAT. He loved what he did, but their team was one of the busiest in the state. From common raids to aiding the FBI or sheriff's departments. They got pulled in all directions.

"Why don't we go out for drinks and a bite to eat? I'm famished." Zain patted his washboard stomach.

Brodie's rumbled, too. He could go for a good meal.

"I say we bring Jordan up to speed. Let her choose if she wants to be involved. She's one of us now, so I don't think she should be in the dark," Brodie said. He kept his voice low, not wanting anyone else to hear their conversation.

"That's true. Demon Lords won't care that she's new to the team. The fact that she has SWAT on her chest makes her a target," Iker growled.

So far Jordan was a solid team member, but they

couldn't leave out the other part. She needed to know what team she had truly joined. Danger surrounded them at all times, and she would have to keep her eyes open even when she wasn't at work.

The woman had already picked up on some weird vibes.

Brodie could only imagine who it would have been from.

Grunts of agreement went around the group. The door opened, and the two sergeants walked out. Mac immediately focused on their team. He nudged Declan and pointed to them.

"Again, I say we do this with food and alcohol," Zain muttered.

"I second that motion." Myles raised a hand.

"What are we voting on?" Mac asked.

He and Declan stood before the group.

Brodie quickly brought them up to speed on bringing Jordan in on everything.

"I agree," Declan said. "She's tough and can hold her own."

The door to the building opened again. Jordan came out and paused once she saw the entire group staring at her.

She walked over to them with a cautious look on her face.

"Everything good over here?" she asked. Her gaze landed on Mac. "I'm not fired or anything, am I?"

"No, why would you ask that?" Mac questioned.

Jordan grew more uncomfortable under Mac's gaze.

"It's a little weird seeing you all around waiting for me." She visibly swallowed hard.

"We're a team and we're going out for drinks. You're invited. What say you? Are you down to hang out with us, newbie?" Iker asked.

Her lips curved up in a wide grin. "After my week, let's roll."

"Hear, hear."

Brodie hopped in his truck. They always hung out at the same bar after work when they needed good food and beer. He drove out of the parking lot and onto the street. Traffic was light. He flipped on the radio and found one of the local rock channels.

A slow song came over the airwaves, and immediately it had him thinking of a certain brown-skinned nurse. It reminded him of her. The singer sang about a woman's pretty smile and how much he loved to make her laugh.

That was him and Ronnie. He got a kick out of making that woman giggle and laugh. He stopped at a red light and leaned back against the headrest. It had been a minute since he'd seen her. He reached for his phone. He had her number but had yet to use it. He pulled it up on his screen and paused.

Did he call her now? Was it considered too late?

He thought she was into him.

Mac would probably kill him if he knew he had touched his wife's best friend.

The light turned green. Brodie tossed his phone back in the center console.

He'd call her later.

If they didn't leave the Pub too late, he would call her.

Fifteen minutes later, Brodie arrived at the Pub and parked his truck. He got out and went inside. There weren't that many people out in the middle of the week. The weekends were a different story. Brodie walked through the establishment, his gaze automatically scanning the patrons.

He knew the makeup of the building like the back of his hand. It was drilled into him to be aware of his surroundings.

His team was all sitting at their favorite table in the back. Jordan sat between Iker and Zain. She sat back in her chair with a wide grin.

"How the hell all y'all beat me here?" Brodie scratched his head, laughing.

They turned to him as he approached.

"Driving Miss Daisy here took the scenic route." Myles chuckled, pointing at him.

"Did you stop and get an oil change?" Iker questioned.

Brodie flipped them off and took his seat next to Zain. He loved these guys like brothers. There wasn't anything he wouldn't do for them.

Everyone was here but Ash.

He was there in spirit. He had a new addition to his family, and it was good he was taking some time off.

"We already ordered the drinks," Dec said.

The waitress chose that exact moment to arrive with tall frosty mugs filled to the brim with amber liquid. Mac and Dec helped her pass the drinks out. She quickly took food orders before disappearing.

Mac held up his mug, and silence fell around the table. They all followed suit and raised theirs.

"SWAT, our team is growing. Not only has Jordan joined us, but little Evan is now here. These are two more additions to our family." Mac focused his attention on Jordan. "If you haven't already realized it, you have seven brothers who will do anything to protect you and your family. You need anything, you only need to call one of us and we'll all be there."

"Thanks, guys." Jordan cleared her throat. "It means so much to be welcomed, and same for you. Need something, just say the word."

"We are a close group, and when shit hits the fans, there's no one I'd rather be in a gunfight with," Declan said.

"Hear, hear," the team echoed.

Brodie nodded to her then took a sip of the cool drink.

His two sergeants were right. They were a close-knit group and went through extreme lengths for each other.

Killed for each other.

Went on off-the-books missions to save a loved one.

They had each bled blue for the others, and now their family had grown.

"All right, Brodie. What have you got?" Zain asked, leaning back in his chair.

"Yup." Brodie took another gulp before placing his glass down on the table. "Jordan, I'm going to have to give you the Cliff Notes on the history between the Demon Lords and our team. To make a long story short, the Demon Lords do not like us.

They've painted a red bull's-eye on our chests because we cut them down."

"I've heard. News made it all the way to Atlanta," Jordan replied.

This was a delicate subject, and there were no longer any smiles or joking.

"Now, this isn't your fight. Unfortunately, because you are SWAT, it makes you a target." Brodie leaned forward on the table. "But rest assured, not one man at this table will allow anything to happen to you."

"Damn right," Mac confirmed. Grunts of agreement went up in the air. Mc took a long pull from his mug then continued. "They are scrambling now because of us, and this situation is getting more dangerous. We are being honest and want you to know what you are getting into."

Jordan sat and eyed them all silently.

"You all have made me feel right at home. I truly feel the love, and it is like having seven older brothers," she began. "Back in Atlanta, I didn't get this sense of camaraderie as I have now. You are my team. My brothers. If you are about to go to war with the Demon Lords, then I'll be right there at your side, and if you step in front of me, I got your six."

"Well, shit. See, fellas, we didn't have anything to

worry about," Zain murmured, slamming his empty cup down.

"The Demon Lords were a pain in my ass back in my former city." Jordan took a sip of her drink. "Someone who I considered to be a close friend was gunned down by them. His killer was never found, but I know it was orchestrated by the gang."

Nods of understanding went all around.

Brodie reached for his phone. He opened up a secured app and sent out a file to each of them. Text notifications went off around the table.

"Here's some information I needed to share with you." He glanced up at Jordan and grinned. "I have to admit when you couldn't find your phone the other day, I had it."

"Wait, what?" Jordan gasped. She pulled her phone, shocked before grinning. "This is so cool."

He had snuck off with her phone one day while they were all at the precinct. He had to upgrade her security and connect her with a secured server where he could share encrypted files with her. He felt bad at deceiving her, but it was funny.

"But wait, you all helped me search for my phone. Did you know he had it?" Jordan glanced around the table.

Everyone had the same guilty expression.

"Yeah, we knew, and we sold that shit," Zain said.

They all burst out laughing. They had scoured the locker rooms, break room, briefing room, and the common areas for her phone.

"What are we looking at?" Mac asked.

Back to business.

Brodie took another sip of his beer while holding his phone in his free hand. He glanced around the Pub, and no one was paying them any attention.

"I did some digging around on *him*," Brodie began. "I went deep into his financials, his social media, a background check, and cross-referenced everything. To be honest, I can't find shit. He knows how to cover up shit and appear innocent."

But he wasn't.

They had all seen his face as clear as day on the videotape. He had paid off the thugs who'd hunted Myles and Roxxy down.

"But why would Cruz do such a thing?" Dec asked. "If you are saying he came up clean, there had to be something missed."

Officer Diego Cruz.

He was a decorated cop who had been on the force for a while. He had trained his partner, Max Reeves.

What made a cop turn bad?

"Are you sure he doesn't need money?" Myles asked.

"Does he have a drug problem?" Mac asked.

"Last tox screen he did for the job came back negative." Brodie shook his head, truly puzzled.

The guy had come back squeaky clean. They had all heard of cops going bad. But Cruz didn't fit the mold of those who turned their back on the badge.

"As for needing money? There wasn't anything that would suggest that. He pays his taxes, his credit card utilization isn't high, no student loans, mortgage and car note are current."

"Well, shit." Myles ran a hand along his head. "He don't have an identical twin we don't know about, do he?"

"Nope. No twin." Brodie was stumped, too. "And to do something like this over his partner not making SWAT doesn't make sense. The only thing that is out of the ordinary is he received a collect call from the South Carolina Department of Corrections. Hard to narrow down who that was."

"Demon Lords?" Declan asked. "The prison is crawling with a number of their members, including Victor Huff."

Myles flicked his gaze to Brodie.

Nothing was needed to be said.

Looked like Brodie would need to start digging into the leader of the Demon Lords. Victor, or House as he was known on the streets, was sitting in prison because of every man sitting at this table.

The gangster had boldly kidnapped Ash.

Columbia's finest did what they did best.

Kicked ass.

5

"Hey, Ronnie. How you doing?" one of the EMTs asked.

Ronnie grinned at him. Eric was a regular working for the city. He and his partner, Liam, were constantly bringing patients to the Emergency Department.

"Another day, another dollar." Ronnie waved at them as the guys pushed their empty stretcher toward the open bay doors.

Ronnie walked to the nursing station. She was pulling a long twelve-hour shift today in the emergency department. She was a critical care float nurse for the hospital. This allowed her to work in different units where she was needed the most. It gave her the flexibility with her hours as well. She loved what she did.

Nursing wasn't just a job, it was a calling.

Glancing at her watch, she let out a sigh.

At the moment, her bed was calling her all the way from home.

"Halfway done," she murmured. Usually her shift flew by, but today the time was dragging. "Hey, Mari, anything coming in?" she asked, reaching the desk and standing before the secretary.

Mari looked up with wide eyes.

"Are you insane?" Mari asked. The older woman had been a staple in General Hospital's ED for a long time. She trained everyone from nursing assistants to the emergency room staff physicians. Everyone loved her. Mari shook a finger at Ronnie. "You know you don't ask things like that. You are going to jinx us."

Ronnie laughed and leaned against the counter. Nurses were very superstitious creatures.

One never mentioned the word 'quiet' when talking about the shift. That was almost a cardinal sin and asked for the shit to hit the fans.

And a nurse never asked for extra work.

Most times Ronnie barely had time to go relieve her bladder or eat. Working in critical care meant she had to be on her toes for the full shift because her patients could take a turn quicker than a person could blink.

Today Ronnie had to admit it was nice to have a slow day.

"I was just wondering. I'm up for the next admission and I wanted to grab a bite to eat soon," Ronnie explained.

Mari glanced down at her sheets before looking back up at Ronnie. "Nothing. You're free and clear."

"Great." Ronnie slapped the counter and pushed away. She kept a smile on her face until she turned away. She was dead on her feet. They ached, she was nauseous, but yet hungry at the same time.

Keeping this secret was getting harder.

She would go check on her patient, then she'd head off to find Sarena.

She strolled toward room eight, the memory of the night Ash had been brought into the ED entering her head. She had been working that night when the SWAT officer had been forced to come get checked.

Ronnie had walked into room eight to find Ash trying to get out of his bed. She'd had to threaten him to get him to sit so she could do his vitals. It was a perk to be the best friend of their sergeant. He had grumbled and settled back to allow her to check his vital signs before he'd demanded a phone.

Having a SWAT officer admitted meant his entire team would be showing up.

She'd come out of the room to show Ash the nearest phone he could use and found Brodie standing at the nursing station flirting with a few of the nurses.

Jealousy had revealed itself.

She was unsure why the desire to stab Tabbi, Heather, and Lori in the eyes for just looking at him was so strong.

He wasn't her man.

She had no claim on him.

He must have sensed her eyes on him. Brodie had glanced in her direction. He'd grinned and strolled toward her. She had become tongue-tied in his presence. It wasn't the first time they had met or spoke with each other.

But seeing him decked out in his SWAT gear had her body going haywire.

Now, entering room eight, it was certainly no SWAT officer there. This time it was a patient who had been sent over from a nursing home with a fever. She was just waiting on a bed to become available on the regular nursing unit.

"Hey, Mr. Garrett. How are you feeling?" she asked.

The patient was non-verbal, but his eyes followed her the moment she stepped near the bed. He was a forty-seven-year-old who had suffered a massive stroke that left him debilitated. He was unable to speak or care for himself. His body was deconditioned and a former shell of what once was a healthy young man.

He released a grunt, and Ronnie kept her smile on her face. She wasn't sure what kind of care he received at the nursing home, so while he was with her, he was going to get the best care possible.

"Hopefully it shouldn't be too much longer before I can get you to a more comfortable room," she continued talking as if he would be able to respond. Ronnie stepped over to his IV pole and checked the fluids that were running. She followed the tubing from the machine and ensured it was still connected to her patient.

Even though he could barely move, some sneaky patients had a way of snagging things they shouldn't.

Everything looked to be working properly and connected as it should.

It was time to turn her patient. Since he was unable to move himself, the hospital had strict policies about turning patients to ensure they didn't develop bedsores.

Ronnie fiddled with the blanket and discovered the sheets underneath him were damp.

"Let me call someone to help and we'll get you cleaned up and smelling good." She dropped the blanket down.

Walking over to the doorway, she peeked her head out and saw Monica heading her way.

"Hey, Mo!" she called out.

The nursing assistant stopped and swung around.

"Hey, Ronnie. You need something?" Monica asked. She was a sweet young girl who was currently in her first year of nursing school. Her face lit up with a smile, and she was always so bubbly and helpful.

Ronnie hated to burst her bubble about the real world of nursing. The girl didn't have a clue how much nursing was going to beat her down.

"Yeah. Can you grab clean sheets to help me change the bed in here?" Ronnie asked.

"Sure. Be right there." Mo jogged away toward the linen cart.

Ronnie went back into the room to start preparing the patient.

"My partner will be here in just a second," Ronnie murmured as she untucked the sheet from underneath the mattress. With her pregnancy, she was going to have to be careful with the lifting and moving of patients.

"I'm here." Mo giggled, flying into the room. Her gaze landed on the patient, and her lips spread into a wide grin. "Hello."

Ronnie bit back a chuckle at Mr. Garret's grunt. It was much lighter than his last one. Looked like it didn't matter if a man could move or talk. They all softened when a young pretty college girl walked into the room. He may not be able to move, but there was obviously nothing wrong with his eyesight.

"Any plans this weekend?" Monica asked.

They rolled Mr. Garret onto his side. Monica quickly handled her part of the sheets and helped guide the patient over toward her.

"Not really. I plan to relax and have some me time," Ronnie admitted. She stripped the bed of the soiled sheets and fixed the clean ones under the patient.

"I heard that Luke Ryan was coming to town," Monica said.

"Really?" Ronnie sure did love her some country music. She was a lover of all genres of music, but country just held a special place in her heart. "Are there still tickets?"

"I'd have to see. My brother will be working security, so I'm sure he could get me extra tickets if need be."

"Check and let me know." Maybe she would see if Sarena or her sister wanted to go with her. It would be a fun night of music and fun.

There'd be no drinking for her.

They finished and got Mr. Garret into a clean hospital gown and fluffed his pillow. He looked like a million bucks after they were done with him.

"Thanks so much," Ronnie said as she peeled her gloves off. She tossed them in the trash then followed Monica out of the room. She stopped by the sanitizer mounted on the wall and put a little in her hands to clean them.

"No problem. I'm going to go get a dirty laundry basket. I'll finish up here," Mo said.

"You are awesome." Ronnie grinned. "I'm off to lunch and shouldn't be gone too long."

"Okay, we can hold down the fort. Enjoy!" Mo waved.

Sarena was ambling toward her with a big grin on her face. Ronnie shook her head at her friend. It was amazing how she glowed. She never was one to say someone was, but one look at Sarena and there was no doubt. She had the pregnancy glow while Ronnie felt like shit.

"I was coming to see if you wanted to grab a bite to eat," Sarena said.

Ronnie arrived at her side and gave her friend a big hug.

"I'm starving." Ronnie sighed. She was also still sick to her stomach, but she knew she had to eat.

It was weird.

Food made her feel better.

She hadn't thrown up yet, just steady queasiness plagued her.

"Let's go. I promised them I wouldn't be gone long," Sarena said.

"I need to let Tabbi know I'm leaving the unit." Ronnie looked around and found the other nurse standing outside her patient's room charting. She ran over to her co-worker and gave her a brief report on her patients.

A few minutes later, she and Sarena were entering the cafeteria. They quickly got their food and found an available table to sit down.

"How's your day going?" Sarena asked.

"Not bad." Ronnie shrugged. She took a bite out of her grilled cheese sandwich before reaching for her ginger ale. Sarena was the assistant manager of the ED. That was one of the reasons she loved working the emergency. "You've must have been busy. I haven't seen you all day."

Sarena rolled her eyes. "The state may be coming, so I've been working on our readiness rounds. I had to go with Karen, the manager of PACU, over to the ICU so we could help them prepare."

Ronnie shivered. She could never work management. There was so much paperwork and administrative things that a regular nurse didn't have to worry about. She loved going in to work to take care of patients then leave to go home.

"Anything you need us to do when I get back to the unit?" Ronnie asked.

"Nah, I had my unit ready. We're just doing practice runs for when the state arrives. We should be in good shape."

Ronnie looked down at her food and realized she was no longer hungry.

Two bites, and she felt too queasy to continue.

Ronnie set her sandwich down.

Sarena's perfectly sculpted eyebrows rose.

Dammit, her friend didn't miss a thing.

"Are you all right?" Sarena asked.

"I guess I wasn't as hungry as I thought." Ronnie tried to act nonchalant with her answer. She offered up a smile and took a sip of her soda.

"I was trying to find a good date for the shower. I loved Deana's theme but don't want to copy."

"If it's a boy, you won't have a choice." Ronnie snorted.

Sarena stared at her, then they both burst out in giggles. It was the truth. If the MacArthurs were having a boy, then there was no doubt there would be a cop theme.

"What was I thinking. Even if we are having a girl, Marcas will be getting a pink bulletproof vest for her, pink handcuffs, and I wouldn't even be surprised if he gets her a gun." Sarena slapped her forehead and blew out a deep breath.

Ronnie shook her head and leaned back in her seat. She cradled her ginger ale and eyed her friend.

"We'll still have fun planning. Mac will do whatever you want."

"You're right. He will. All I will have to do is poke out my lip and pout." Sarena's grin turned devious.

"Look at you using your feminine wiles to get what you want," Ronnie teased. "I remember a day you when you were scared to walk over to his house in your trench coat."

"You're the reason I'm knocked up now." Sarena tossed a fry at her.

Ronnie had practically made Sarena go to Mac's house. They had been tiptoeing around each other, and all Ronnie did was give them a little push in the right direction.

"Umm...no, you could have used protection. You're a nurse. You know the consequences of unprotected sex."

Ronnie's heart just about stopped.

Boy, was the pot calling the kettle black.

She knew the risk, too, and apparently that fateful night with Brodie had taken away her ability to be responsible.

Ronnie's smile disappeared.

"Can you believe how quick my belly popped out?" Sarena rested her hand on her protruding belly. It was perfectly round and adorable.

Ronnie was slightly jealous of what Sarena and Mac had.

"It's so cute," Ronnie exclaimed.

She was trying to act normal, but again, her friend was too damn smart. Sarena's eyes narrowed on her.

"Okay, woman. Spill it." Sarena moved her empty plate to the side and leaned her forearms on the table.

"What are you talking about?"

"Ronnie, I have known you a long time and I can sense when there is something bothering you." Sarena's eyes filled with worry.

Ronnie exhaled.

Sarena would badger her until she spilled the beans. She might as well come clean now so her friend didn't worry herself. Ronnie would feel horrible if something happened to Sarena.

"Okay, there is something." Ronnie paused. She bit her lip and looked around the cafeteria. There weren't many people hanging around near them. Not that anyone would care about her news except the woman sitting across from her.

"I knew it," Sarena shrieked. She fidgeted in her chair and scooted closer to Ronnie. "What is it, girl?"

Ronnie gazed down at her hands and knew she would just have to say it.

"I'm pregnant."

She was met with silence. Ronnie glanced up and found a frozen Sarena staring at her.

"How?" Sarena asked. She sat back in her seat. "How the hell do you get pregnant by one of your book boyfriends?"

"Sarena!" Ronnie gasped. She reached for her

napkin and tossed it at her. "Do we need to have *the* talk?"

"Nope. I'm good. My husband ensures I know how babies are made." Sarena giggled. "So what I meant was, how did you get pregnant, or should I say, who impregnated you, and why didn't I know you were seeing someone?"

Guilt filled Ronnie at the hurt look on her friend's face. She was just going to have to come clean.

"Well, truth be told, I'm not seeing anyone." Her cheeks warmed at her admission. "It was sort of a one-night stand."

"Ronnie, will you just admit who your baby daddy is?"

"Brodie." Ronnie waited for the news to register.

"Brodie? Wait, Mac's Brodie?" Sarena's mouth dropped open.

Ronnie nodded, biting her lip, unsure how Sarena would react.

Sarena's expression transformed from shocked to devilish in a manner of seconds. "You cougar!"

Ronnie burst out laughing.

Yes, she knew Brodie was younger than her, but only by two years. Technically, that didn't make her a cougar.

"He's not that much younger than me." Ronnie rolled her eyes. Men dated younger women all the time, and no one batted an eyelash at that. There was nothing wrong with a woman getting involved with a younger man.

"Have you told him yet?" Sarena asked softly, her smile disappearing.

Ronnie shook her head. "I just found out. I just haven't had a chance to call him yet."

Sarena reached out and rested her hand on Ronnie's. Their eyes met, and Ronnie knew her friend would stand by her side until the end of the world.

"He's a really a great guy. Mac and the boys all trust him. He'll do the right thing by you."

Ronnie nodded again. "I'm just scared."

"Don't be. Single women have children every damn day. You are one of the strongest women I know, if anyone can do it, you can." Sarena squeezed her hand. "Just think, our kids will be able to grow up together. We can go through this phase in our lives together."

Ronnie returned the squeeze. She was glad Sarena was taking the news well and had faith in her.

"I just need you not to say anything to Mac yet."

Sarena's eyes grew wide.

Ronnie rushed along to continue. "At least until I tell Brodie. I don't want anyone else to tell him but me, and I haven't shared anything with my family yet either."

"Okay." Sarena nodded.

"I'm serious. You know the guys gossip just as bad as women."

Sarena chuckled, tucking a strand of hair behind her ear. "That you are right. If I did tell Mac, I guarantee the entire damn precinct would know by noon tomorrow. It was hell trying to get that man not to shout from the mountains that I was pregnant."

"I promise I'll be calling Brodie soon."

How did one call a man to notify him that he was going to be a daddy?

6

The ride home couldn't go fast enough. Brodie was thankful the gods above were looking out for him and allowing him to catch all these green lights. After working pretty much twenty-four hours, he was glad to be on his way home.

The guys were getting anxious.

Cruz was on vacation and due back to work soon.

It was rare that Brodie got stumped by anything, but he was when it came to the motive behind Cruz's treachery.

Everything he could find on the man didn't shed any light on why he was giving away vital information to the gang.

Someone must be holding something over him.

That could be the only excuse.

But what?

Brodie was determined to find out what it was. Someone could get hurt, or killed.

An informer he had connections with was supposed to be getting in contact with him. Brodie realized he was going to have to go deeper than what would be on common background checks.

He had to go to the streets.

There was a reason a man in blue turned on his own. Brodie refused to believe it was something simple. Was Cruz in trouble? Or was he just a rat from the beginning, infiltrating the elite infrastructure of the police force?

He guided his vehicle onto his street. His home was located in a cozy neighborhood in the suburbs. He had made the purchase on this home a few years ago, and it was his pride and joy. The beautiful yards were what had first attracted him to the area. It was filled with working families.

He had one nosy neighbor who was always trying to fix him up with one of her granddaughters or nieces. Mrs. Thomas was a retired schoolteacher who was widowed. She led a book club that came by her house every Sunday after church. The older women sat out on Mrs. Thomas's porch while reading their books and drinking their 'tea'.

It didn't look like tea or coffee in their cups either.

Brodie had taken up helping Mrs. Thomas and cutting her grass for her on Sunday afternoons.

The few times he'd stepped on the porch, the scent of alcohol had floated through the air.

Brodie chuckled. Drinking and reading. There was no telling what types of books they were reading as part of their club. They always seemed to hide their book covers when he was around.

Pulling into his driveway, he parked the truck in front of the garage. He killed the engine and got out. His body ached, and he was tired, but there was no time to rest.

His stomach let out a grumble as he let himself inside the house. A few lamps were on throughout due to automatic timing. There was no telling what time of day or night he would be arriving home. He was pretty much on all around the clock.

Thankfully, he had showered before he'd left the precinct.

Dropping his duffle bag by the door, he beelined straight for the kitchen. He should have picked something up on the way home, but the fast-food places held no appeal to him.

"What do we have?" he murmured, opening the fridge. He gripped the door while he moved things around. He was famished.

Yeah, maybe he should have grabbed something.

He opened the freezer and took out a microwavable dinner. It wasn't going to be fancy, but it would settle his stomach. He tossed it in the microwave then grabbed a bottle of water from the fridge. His phone beeped, catching his attention.

He glanced at it sitting on the counter.

It didn't ring, so that was good.

It would be his luck that he'd get home and have to turn right around to go out on a call.

Brodie took a swig of his water and picked up the phone.

"Hot damn."

His informer had just texted him. The number was anonymous, but he knew who it was.

Nick, the Prophet, as he was known, had begun working with Brodie about a year ago. The informer on the streets would be thought of as a snitch.

He risked his neck by meeting with Brodie. In exchange for the reliable information, Brodie looked the other way on Nick's selling of marijuana. Brodie had agreed as long as Nick didn't sell to kids and didn't lace the weed with any other drugs.

Brodie responded to the text, asking when and where they could meet. Nick replied with an address and time.

Brodie confirmed the meeting. He hoped whatever Nick found out would shed some light on what was going on.

Brodie closed the text app but somehow opened the photos. He smiled at the first ones he came across. There were from Ash and Deana's baby shower. He mindlessly flipped through them. He glanced up at the microwave which had another minute or so to go.

He stopped at an image of him and Ronnie. A wistful smile appeared on his lips. They had taken a few selfies together that night. They had both been slightly tipsy at the party.

He had to admit, they looked good together.

He remembered this particular moment in time. He had a slight crush on her. He had used the notion of taking pictures together to get her close to him. She'd felt so good pressed against him.

Her wide grin and the twinkle in her eye that gave way to her personality drew him to her. She was definitely someone he wanted to get to know better.

Hell, that night had been one of the best of his life.

They'd gone back to her house after the party, and he hadn't left until the next morning.

The sex between them was out of this world. The way her body had responded to his had him mesmerized. She was a passionate woman, and he had enjoyed devouring every inch of her curvy frame.

His cock grew thick thinking of the feel of her wrapped around him, the sound of her screaming his name and the taste of her.

The microwave beeped, breaking into his carnal memories.

"Shit," he muttered, running a hand through his hair. He needed to get a grip.

He took his meal from the microwave and set it on the counter. He took the film completely off, allowing the steam to escape.

His phone ringing broke through the silence. He froze at the sight of who was calling.

Ronnie.

He glanced up at the ceiling with a grin.

"You're funny." He laughed. Apparently, God had heard his prayer he didn't know he had sent up.

He swiped the glass screen and hit the 'speak' button.

"Hello?" he answered.

"Hey, Brodie," Ronnie's voice came through.

The slight huskiness in it sent a chill down his spine. He leaned on the counter, staring down at the phone wishing he could see her.

"What's up, Ronnie?" he asked. There weren't many times he was uncertain when it came to women, but for some reason he was when it came to Ronnie. She was different than the women he'd dated before. She was classy, had a great career, and had a great sense of humor. She was everything he wanted in a woman.

Hell, she was definitely someone he would be proud to take home to meet his parents.

Whoa.

Where in the hell did that come from?

"How are you?" she asked.

Brodie grinned. Ronnie was a little shy, and he could sense it coming through the phone. He picked up the phone and leaned back against the counter. "I'm doing well. How about yourself?"

If she wanted to exchange pleasantries first, then they would play that little game. She was a Southern woman, and he knew they were always kind and courteous before getting to the point.

"I'm good. Just got off of work and currently trying to find something to eat." He glanced at the dinner, and it wasn't appealing to him. Hearing her voice was suddenly giving him a second wind. "It's funny you should call right now."

"Really? Why is that?"

"Because I was just thinking of you," he admitted.

"All good thoughts, I hope," she responded with a chuckle. "But honestly, I was just thinking of you, too, and figured since you had made sure your number was in my phone I would use it."

He remembered that day. It had been the third or fourth time they had met. He had playfully taken her phone and added his information to her contacts.

A woman would never know when she'd needed a cop friend to call on.

He grinned.

It had been a smooth way to give her his phone number.

Not that she had used it.

"I told you there may be a day when you may need a personal cop friend to stop by," he teased.

Her laughter had his cock stiffening again. He adjusted himself.

He loved making her laugh.

"You did say that." Her voice ended on a hitch. The tone of her voice changed. The sound of her huskiness amplified. It was sending signals to his dick. "I guess you were right."

His heart slammed in his chest.

Shit, he had to go meet Nick.

He was torn. Go get the information that may help crack open this mole situation or go see to Ronnie.

Fuck.

"I have to run out on an errand, then I could swing by," he offered.

He could do both. Meeting with Nick wouldn't take long. The informer couldn't risk being seen with him. After he got the information, he would hurry to Ronnie's. She didn't live far from him.

"I'd like that," her voice dropped low to a whisper.

He bit back a groan and adjusted himself again. His cock was pressing hard against his jeans. He glanced over at the food sitting on the counter and no longer wanted it.

"Have you eaten yet?" he asked.

"No."

"I'll grab something on my way over."

"That would be perfect. See you when you get here."

They disconnected the call. A grin overtook him.

Tonight was going to be a perfect night. He'd get the information he needed about Cruz then end the day with Ronnie.

It couldn't get any better than that.

BRODIE GUIDED his truck up to the destination that was sent to his phone. He pulled to a stop at the intersection. He hit the button to unlock his doors. The location was in the shady part of town. There were plenty of boarded-up buildings.

He glanced around, his eyes taking in everything. He had his weapon resting his lap. He wasn't a fool to go into the dangerous part of town and not be prepared.

He rested his hand on his Glock.

His gaze landed on a lone figure strolling down the walkway between two small houses that appeared abandoned.

They may be, but Brodie were sure they were

crack houses. It was no secret that addicts hung out in abandoned buildings and to score their next hit.

There were a few houses that he and his SWAT team had raided that looked just like the one he was parked in front of.

Brodie didn't take his eyes off the figure. When he emerged into the open, the single streetlight shone on him, revealing it was Nick.

Brodie relaxed slightly but didn't remove his hand from his gun.

Nick opened the passenger door and slid in the truck. He reeked of weed and unwashed body. His dark-brown hair stood up at all directions as if he had been combing it with his fingers.

"Nick," Brodie said in greeting. He tried not to breathe in the foul odor consuming his car. He rolled his window down slightly to air out the truck.

"Go around the corner," Nick said, glancing out the window. The informer was always skittish when they met. He was tied with some bad men, and talking with a cop could get him killed.

Brodie knew that allowing him to sell marijuana was against the law, but at the moment, Nick had given them information that had helped crack down on some bigger drug dealers. It wasn't the best agreement, but weed wasn't their top priority at the moment.

Brodie shifted the truck in gear and did as instructed. He knew Nick was going to have be careful in meeting with him. He drove a block away before Nick held up his hand.

The area hadn't improved but worsened. No streetlights, boarded-up businesses. Brodie kept his hand on his gun as he scanned the streets.

No one was in sight.

"Okay, we should be safe here," Nick said.

Brodie turned to him with his eyebrows raised. Safe?

"Out with it," Brodie ordered. He didn't want to be in Nick's presence any longer than he had to. He would get the information and leave.

"Yeah, so about that cop you're looking in to." Nick sniffed. He ran a trembling hand through his hair.

Brodie wasn't sure what had happened to the man, but from his research into him, he had been an intelligent kid. Had a full ride to the University of South Carolina but had dropped out after getting involved with the wrong crowd.

"What about him?" Brodie asked, focusing on the kid.

"Word on the street is he's deep in the Demon Lords." Nick glanced out the window again. He raised his hood over his head.

"How deep?" Brodie asked. This was news to him. There hadn't been proof, but it was obvious. The gang had always been a step ahead of them. The information they had was something that was only privy to cops. This confirmed that the mole was Cruz.

Giving out sensitive information.

Paying off thugs.

"Waist deep in shit." Nick turned around. "From what I've heard, the big man was gunning for him. After that last raid where they lost millions, they are blaming the cop for not telling them ahead of time."

Brodie released a curse.

"He was one lucky son of a bitch, but I hear he has to make up for it."

"How is he going to do that?" Brodie pushed.

Nick shrugged. "Don't know."

"How did he even get involved with them?"

"How the hell am I supposed to know? I'm not psychic," Nick muttered. He reached for the door handle. "But that's all I know."

"Here." Brodie pulled down the sun visor and took out a few bills he kept hidden. Nick wasn't the richest weed dealer. He handed the money to him. "Thanks for the info."

"Yup." Nick took the payment and exited the vehicle. He stuffed the cash into his jeans pocket as he walked toward an alley.

Brodie blew out a deep breath and watched him disappear into the darkness. Putting his foot on the gas, he drove off, unsure what to make of the information he was given.

It was a start.

But now, he had another meeting where police work was going to have to be left at the door.

7

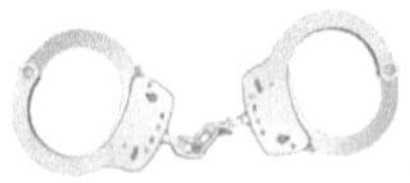

Ronnie breathed in the clean scent of the candles burning in her living room. She had flown around the house making sure it was tidied up and presentable for company. After ensuring her home was spotless, she had jumped into the shower.

Brodie was coming.

The entire time she had been in the shower was spent on figuring out how to break the news to him.

Once dressed, she still hadn't a clue on what to say.

How did one approach the subject of pregnancy after a one-night stand?

Ronnie settled on the couch and stared at her phone. Maybe she could call Sarena to get ideas on how to announce it. She had some experience with this subject. Sarena, on the other hand, was married to the father of her child. They had been actively trying to get pregnant.

Ronnie had been horny with a good-looking guy who had pushed all the right buttons. A night of consensual sex amongst adults, and then he was gone, leaving her pregnant.

A car pulled into her driveway, and the butterflies in her stomach amplified tenfold.

"Here goes nothing," she murmured. Ronnie pushed up off the couch and stood. She walked over to the front door and glanced down at herself one last time. When choosing her outfit, she didn't want to appear too thirsty by wearing something sexy. Nor did she want to appear to be a slob while inviting a man over to her home.

She kept it house guest appropriate.

She had put on a long flowing gray maxi dress with thin spaghetti straps. It was cute and one of her favorite dresses to wear, and it even had pockets.

Her heart skipped a beat when the doorbell sounded.

"Coming," she called out. She gripped the handle and peered through the peephole. Brodie stood on the other side of the door. He turned around when she opened it. "Hi."

She bit her lip and took him in. He wore a dark shirt, jeans, and a pair of shitkickers, the epitome of sexiness.

Her gaze dropped down to the bag in his hand.

Oh, yeah.

She'd totally forgotten he was bringing her something to eat.

"Hey there." He licked his lips.

She felt the butterflies grow stronger.

How the hell is he so damn sexy?

If she didn't know any better, she'd swear her panties just went up in smoke.

"Are you going to let me in? The food is getting cold." He chuckled.

Ronnie blinked.

A giggle escaped her as she held the door open for him and waved him in.

"Sorry. Of course, come on in," she said.

He brushed past her and entered the house. The scent of his cologne hit her. Thankfully, she was holding on to the door and was able to keep herself from falling over.

She was in trouble.

A man smelling that good was always hard to resist.

But she had to be strong.

They had a very important conversation that needed to be had.

"I hope you don't mind that I swung by Big Bull's for dinner," Brodie said.

She laughed, closing the door. She followed him into the kitchen.

"What do you know about Big Bull's?" she asked playfully.

Brodie winked at her while taking the dinners out of the bag.

"Only that they have some good barbecue. I didn't want to stop at a fast-food restaurant. I wanted something good." He snorted.

Ronnie moved around the kitchen grabbing silverware and glasses for them. She placed them down on the island where he was setting their food. She walked over to the fridge and opened it.

"Beer?" she asked, looking over her shoulder. She might as well give them away. She wasn't going to have any need for them.

"Sure."

She snagged one for him and a soda for herself. Ronnie took the chair next to Brodie and handed him his drink.

"You're not drinking?" he asked.

She shook her head and reached for her food.

This could be her opportunity, but she didn't want to ruin a perfectly good dinner. The scent floating in the air was divine. For once, her stomach wasn't protesting at the smell of food.

"What did you pick out for us?" She glanced at him before taking the rubber bands off the Styrofoam container. It had been a while since she had been to Big Bull's.

"I wanted to play it safe, so I got us two smoked chicken plates." A bashful look crossed his face as he opened his container.

"I love their smoked chicken." She smiled, opening hers. Her mouth watered at the scent growing stronger. Brodie was a man after her heart. Mac and cheese and green beans.

He'd done well.

Momma was suddenly famished.

She dug into the mac and cheese and groaned. It was divine. She immediately dove into the green beans and moaned.

Maybe that's what she'd needed all of this time.

The baby must have been wanting a good barbecue dinner. Eating this every day was sure to add pounds to her waist and butt.

She glanced at Brodie staring at her.

"What?" she asked. Her mouth was full, and she

knew better than to speak with her mouth full, but the food was that damn good. She finished chewing and swallowed.

"Nothing." He chuckled. He took a sip of his beer and set it down. "It's nice to see a woman really eating."

"What was I supposed to do when you brought food? Pick at it?" Her eyebrows rose high. What kind of women did he date? She loved to eat and wasn't ashamed to do so. It didn't matter who was around her, she was going to enjoy her food.

He released a hefty laugh and picked up his chicken leg. He tore into it and chewed for a second before turning back to her.

"I don't know." He shrugged.

"I'm not sure who you been feeding, but you bring me good food, it's going to get eaten." She pushed him slightly with her elbow. Ronnie grinned watching him blush slightly. "You've been around me and Sarena long enough to know us black women don't play around when it comes to food."

She giggled as his laughter grew.

"Duly noted," he said while wiping his hands on a napkin.

The chicken was moist and cooked to perfection. She finished it off quickly then reached for her drink. She turned and found Brodie staring at her. He spun halfway in his chair where he faced her.

"What?" She reached for her napkin, sure something was on her face. She wiped her mouth and waited for him to answer.

"Have I ever told you that I love the sound of your laugh?" he asked.

His smile faded while he watched her. The intensity in his eyes grew, and she had to look away. She aimlessly stabbed at a green bean with her fork.

She smiled and shrugged her shoulder.

"I don't think I've ever asked you if you did," she responded haughtily.

"It's infectious," he murmured.

He leaned forward and took her fork from her. He picked up a few beans and mac and cheese and brought it up to her lips. Her heart skipped a beat as she opened her mouth to accept the food.

His eyes darkened when he slid the fork from her mouth. She blinked, realizing he was waiting for her to start chewing.

Ronnie almost forgot how to eat.

Her brain wasn't firing properly.

She didn't know when being fed by a sexy cop became so damn sexy.

But damn.

Her body was certainly responding and paying attention.

Swallowing her food, she cleared her throat.

"What are you doing?" she asked.

Brodie gathered more of the mac and cheese onto the fork. His lips tilted up in a crooked grin. "Well, you seem to be getting so much pleasure from the food that I had to figure out a way to be a participant."

Ronnie froze in place, at a loss for words. He slowly swung her around to face him. He widened his legs where hers could be in the middle of his.

"So, you want to give me pleasure by feeding me?" Her voice ended on a squeak.

Brodie smirked and raised the fork again. He guided it to her lips. This time she didn't open her mouth. She wanted him to answer her first.

"I intend to give you an immense amount pleasure tonight and I want to make sure you have enough energy to maintain your stamina."

Her lips parted, allowing him to slide the fork inside her mouth. She chewed the food, the taste no longer mattered.

Brodie could be feeding her freshly cut grass from her yard and she'd still eat it.

All that mattered was the intense look in Brodie's

eyes, his one hand resting on her knee and her imagination taking over.

Immense amount of pleasure?

Sign her up.

She swallowed and leaned forward, reaching for Brodie. He met her halfway, gathering her to him.

Brodie's warm lips covered hers in a deep, passionate kiss.

Ronnie groaned, wrapping her arms around his neck. His hard body felt so good against hers. She pressed closer to him, unable to get close enough.

He tore his mouth from hers, trailing open-mouthed kisses along her jawline until he met the crook of her neck. A cry escaped her lips as he gently nipped her skin.

Brodie's hand slipped underneath her dress, drawing it up higher.

"Your skin is so soft," he muttered.

Her head fell to the side to give him better access to her. The skin along her neck was sensitive. His teeth slid along the column of her neck, sending a shiver down her spine.

"So warm."

The air in her lungs left her.

He'd reached her panties.

There was no turning around.

Not that she wanted to.

She wanted Brodie.

They would have their discussion later.

His fingers slipped inside the silky material covering her.

"Fuck," he groaned when his fingers met with her slickness.

She dove her fingers into his thick hair, holding his face to her.

"Is this all for me?" He rubbed her swollen clit, eliciting an incoherent sound from the depths of her soul.

She was learning that Brodie had some weird effect on her body. It just went haywire whenever he was around.

"Yes," she gasped.

Brodie lifted his head and stared down at her with hooded eyes. He pushed two fingers inside her while watching her. Her pussy welcomed his invasion. It wasn't exactly what she needed inside her, but it was second best to his thick cock.

Him watching her made her feel wanton.

She widened her legs, offering herself to him. The material of her dress was bunched around her waist at this point.

He balled her panties into his hands and yanked hard, tearing them off her.

She couldn't care less about the material floating down to the floor.

Brodie slipped his fingers from her, and she immediately missed them. He glanced down at his hand. His fingers were coated with her juices.

"Fuck, Ronnie," he murmured. He dropped to his knees before her and raised her legs to rest them on his shoulders. "Hold on, girl."

Ronnie's breath hitched in her throat. She leaned back against the island and held on as much as she could. Brodie wasted no time covering her with his mouth.

"Brodie," she cried.

Her legs clamped on his head as he licked and suckled her clit. Her eyes rolled in the back of her head while she held on for the ride. Brodie's tongue was magical.

She reached out, entwining her fingers into his hair so she could ride his face.

Brodie took his time exploring every part of her. Her head fell back with the pleasure flooding her.

Her hold on him tightened.

His suckling of her clit grew stronger.

She gave in and allowed her orgasm to wash over her.

Her body trembled with the power of the climax. Her cries filled the air.

Finally, she calmed down. All the while, Brodie remained with his head buried between her thighs. He took his time lapping up everything from her. He pressed a kiss to her inner thigh.

Ronnie couldn't catch her breath. Brodie stood and yanked her to him. He took her lips in a bold kiss. The faint taste of herself met her, but she didn't care. Brodie was consuming her.

And she'd give herself to him.

Next thing, she found herself getting tossed over Brodie's shoulder as he marched to her bedroom.

Ronnie did the only thing she could.

Held on.

BRODIE KICKED off his boots and took in Ronnie spread out on her bed. The taste of her still lingered on his lips.

He needed more.

The sounds of her cries while she came on his tongue still filled his head.

He needed to hear more of them.

Hell, he needed to be buried deep inside her.

He pulled out a foil packet and set it on the bed. He watched her widened eyes go to the nightstand. He pushed that to the back of his mind. He wasn't sure why she appeared shocked.

"Take that off," he growled. He couldn't control the emotions traveling through him. If she left it up to him, that dress wasn't going to survive. He reached for his belt and opened it.

"Yes, it might be best if I did this," she replied haughtily.

God, he loved her spunk.

She sat on the edge of the bed and lifted the dress over her head. She tossed it somewhere onto the floor then reached for her bra.

Brodie quickly disrobed, and before he knew it, he was on top of Ronnie.

He couldn't get enough of her. His mouth covered hers in a deep kiss. She kissed him back with the same fire he saw burning in her eyes. Sex with Ronnie was explosive. It was all he had thought about since that one night months ago.

He rolled them over, bringing Ronnie on top of him. He wanted to watch her, take in her volumi-nous mounds swinging in front of his face.

Ronnie's face was flushed, her eyes slightly out of focus.

He loved the sight of her in her lust-filled state.

"What are you doing?" She giggled.

The sound went straight to his dick. It was already painfully hard, and her laughter had it swelling even more.

"This time I want to watch you come on my dick," he said.

Her eyes grew wide. She licked her tongue.

"You shouldn't say things like that," she whispered. She straddled his waist. Her hands rested on his chest. Her dark hair fell forward, creating a cloud effect around her beautiful face.

He settled his hands on her hips.

"Why not?" He guided her forward, allowing him to lick her perky nipple. The chocolate little bud was soft and pliable, and he teased it with his tongue.

Her gasp filled the air as he sucked more of her breast into his mouth.

"It makes me want to do things," she moaned.

He released her and grinned.

"Anything you want to do, feel free, baby." He chuckled. Brodie wanted to see her fully let go. He was going to be here for it all.

Hell, he didn't want to ever leave her side.

He sobered up at the thought.

She was beautiful, sexy, and their personalities were similar.

Whenever he was around her, he just wanted to please her.

Was she the one?

"Brodie."

Even the sound of his name on her tongue drove him insane.

"I'm serious. Grab the condom and put it on me, then have your way with me."

She sat back, biting her lip. He held back a growl. That plump lip was for him to nibble on. She reached over and snagged the foil pack.

Ronnie opened it and gripped him while she slid it on. Brodie had to fight back releasing his load so soon. Her soft hand around him was dangerous. His heart pounded, sending his blood rushing through his veins. He was almost feral with the need—almost craving—to have Ronnie.

Her eyes met his when she was done.

"Come on, baby. I need to feel you around me." He fisted the base of his cock, waiting for her.

Ronnie nodded and lifted. He guided his cock to her drenched opening.

They held their gazes while she slid down on him. She was so damn tight, they had to work slightly before she was totally seated with him, buried deep.

Their simultaneous groans filled the air.

Shit.

Her hot wet sheath was heaven.

She rose then fell down on him. Ronnie's voice grew husky as she repeated her motion.

Brodie kept his hands on her waist, helping her up and down on him. Every movement sent him farther inside her. He gritted his teeth, fighting to keep from exploding.

Not until she reached her climax.

Her breaths were coming faster. She picked up pace. Her breasts were swinging in front of him. He repositioned himself against the headboard.

It gave him the opportunity to taste her pretty breasts while she rode him.

"Brodie," Ronnie cried. She set a rhythm that had them both panting.

He rolled her nipple with his tongue while gripping her ass tight.

"Keep going, Ronnie." He released her breast and took in her flushed skin, slightly damp with perspiration. Her muscles squeezed him, and a curse escaped his lips.

He wasn't going to last much longer.

Watching Ronnie take her pleasure had him captivated. She was the most beautiful woman he'd ever seen. A tingling sensation rippled its way from his balls to his cock.

He was going to come.

Not yet.

Brodie slipped a hand between them. His fingers parted her folds and connected with her clit.

"Yes," Ronnie hissed.

Using his thumb, he rubbed her little bundle of nerves.

Ronnie detonated.

Her nails dug into his shoulders, and she crested. She cried out, throwing her head back.

Brodie gave in, allowing his climax to take over him. The air in his lungs was ripped from him.

He took over, thrusting up while slamming her down on him. He pumped until he had no more to give.

Ronnie fell forward, her head falling onto his shoulder.

He leaned back against the headboard, wrapping his arms around her.

He didn't want to move from where he was.

At the moment, he had everything he'd ever wanted. He was going to have to share with her that she now belonged to him.

Her breaths slowed.

Brodie glanced down and found her eyes closed.

Tomorrow, they would speak.

He couldn't bear the thought of someone else tasting what was his.

8

A distant ringing off in the distance brought Brodie out of his slumber. He stretched, but was held down by a soft, warm body. He opened his eyes and found Ronnie snuggled into his side.

The ringing continued.

Shit.

It was the ringtone he had programmed specifically for work.

He reached over to the nightstand, trying not to dislodge Ronnie from him.

She protested slightly with her lip poked out in a pout. He was tempted to kiss her lips that were still swollen. He didn't have the heart to wake her up. They had only been asleep for a couple of hours.

They had stayed up most of the night rediscovering each other.

He couldn't get enough of her.

Her ample curves called to him. He had taken his time kissing and tasting every inch of her delectable body.

He snagged his phone and answered. It couldn't be good if they were calling at five in the morning.

"Gipson," he barked out.

Brodie settled back against the pillows and drew Ronnie's naked body to his. Her soft breasts pressed close to him. Leaving her bed was going to be the hardest thing he'd ever had to do.

And he'd been through some tough situations when he was in the Army and as a cop, but now, having a good woman lying on him was the best thing that could have happened to him.

Now he had to leave?

Shit.

"There's a shooting involving an officer," Mac's hard voice came across the line.

Brodie instantly grew tense.

"Get your gear and come in."

"Yes, sir," Brodie replied.

The line went dead. Mac wasn't a man of many

words, and when it came to the job, he led with his actions.

Brodie glanced down at Ronnie who was watching him.

"You have to go?" she asked, sitting up.

He swung his legs from the bed and sat on the edge. Running a hand through his hair, he glanced back over his shoulder.

Ronnie leaned back against the pillows, holding the sheet up to cover herself.

"Yeah, there's a situation and we're being called in." Brodie stood from the bed and walked around to the other side. He bent down and gathered his clothes.

"Is everything okay?" Ronnie stood from the bed, dropping the sheet. She went over to her closet and took out a silk robe.

His gaze was locked on her ample ass before it disappeared behind the material. She turned around and faced him, totally catching him eyeing her.

He slid his jeans on and shook his head.

"If SWAT is needed, then the shit has hit the fan," he replied, pulling his shirt over his head. He slid his feet into his boots, not even lacing them up. As soon as he got to the precinct, he would be changing shoes anyway.

Ronnie stood near him, wringing her hands.

The fear was easy to pick up from her.

He moved over to her, taking her in his embrace. With a gentle finger, he tipped her chin up to have her meet his gaze. He didn't want her to worry while he was gone.

"I'll be fine," he murmured. That was a promise he meant. His men were the best, and they looked out for one another.

She played with his shirt, dusting off imaginary lint.

"Just promise me that you won't get hurt," she mumbled.

He bent down and pressed a hard kiss to her lips. "Promise."

He entwined their fingers and towed her behind him. He led them through the house to the front door. They had so much to talk about, but he couldn't leave the team hanging. They depended on him.

Brodie turned to Ronnie. Her big brown eyes met his, and his heart skipped a beat.

Was this what Mac, Dec, Ash, and Myles all went through when they had to leave their women to go out on a dangerous mission? How did they deal with it?

Having Ronnie look at him like this made it hard to walk away. He leaned back against the door, still holding on to her hand. He brought it up to his lips and kissed the back of it.

Brodie had been a patient man knowing the perfect woman for him would reveal herself. The moment Sarena had first introduced him to Ronnie, he had known she was special.

Now after the night they'd just had, he knew one thing.

He wanted all of her.

"Go get the bad guys and come back to me safe," she whispered.

Ronnie pressed close to him and rose on her tiptoes. He met her in a kiss that completely rocked his world. He wrapped an arm around her, holding her tight.

He had to go.

He cursed and released her mouth.

He shouldn't want this woman the way he did. After a night full of passion, he should be spent, but his cock apparently hadn't got the message. It was rock-hard and pushing into her stomach.

"I got to go, baby," he murmured. He dropped a kiss on her forehead and opened the door. "Lock the door and put your alarm on. We need to talk. You and me, later. I'll come by and pick you up."

"We do." She nodded, biting her lip.

Brodie stepped out onto the porch and pulled the door closed. He stood there until he heard her lock the door and arm the alarm. He turned around and took in the quiet neighborhood. Nothing seemed out of place. It was early in the morning, and no one was outside.

Jogging down the few stairs, he hopped into his truck. He hit the button to start the engine and backed out of the driveway. He put it in gear and took off down the street. The cab still smelled of the food he'd brought over.

They had never finished their meal.

He drove down the street and headed toward the precinct. A shooting involving a fellow officer was never good. As he got closer to the precinct the memory of Ronnie's cries echoed through his head. He was going to have to push those memories away.

Going out on a call was guaranteed danger.

One wrong move and he could put not only himself in jeopardy, but someone on his team.

Gripping the steering wheel tight, he pressed down on the pedal.

He was going to have to share with his team what he had found out from his informant.

There was going to be plenty of time for him and Ronnie.

He wasn't letting her go.

Now, he had to focus on what bad guys they were going to have to go after.

"AT 0100 HOURS, there was a domestic violence call from the Osaka Garden apartment complex," Mac began briefing the group.

The entire team was present except Ash. They would have to make do without their team member. He had another two weeks on his leave before he was to return to work.

"Multiple residents of the complex called in complaining about yelling and screaming coming from apartment 1A."

All eyes were on Mac.

They stood out by the BEAR to hear the details of their mission. Brodie glanced around and found everyone with hard glints in their eyes. Each member of the team was focused on Mac. Even Jordan had a scowl etched on her face.

She was definitely fitting in.

Brodie folded his arms in front of his chest and turned his attention back to his sergeant.

"When the officers arrived, the suspect in question was witnessed forcing a female into his car. He then pulled out his weapon and fired on the officers. One officer was hit." Mac's face hardened, and his gaze swept the team. "He then jumped into his car and sped off. Backup was called in, and a small chase began with it ending on the university's campus."

"Why the school?" Brodie asked.

"The suspect, Allen Lucas, is an associate professor in mathematics and apparently had a spat with his girlfriend who is a student of his." Mac glanced down at papers in his hand. "From what we are told, he has barricaded them inside a building on campus."

Brodie rotated his neck, trying to release some of the tension.

This should be a standard rescue and retrieval.

With situations like these, SWAT was called in to ensure there were no causalities.

"Any other questions?" Dec spoke up.

Silence greeted him. They had heard all they needed to hear. Once they arrived on scene, they'd get more information and would take over from the local boys in blue.

"All right, SWAT. Let's roll." Mac's words cut through the air.

They turned and piled into the BEAR. The ride to the university would take about seven minutes.

Mac knocked on the partition, signaling they were ready to go.

Tension was high as it always before a mission. Each member was lost in their thoughts. Brodie tried to not think of Ronnie's big beautiful brown eyes and the flicker of fear that had appeared in them.

Brodie stared ahead and met the gaze of Myles.

"Where were you coming from?" Myles asked.

Brodie rolled his eyes. He had pulled in behind Myles at a light near the precinct. He was hoping his friend wouldn't question why he was coming from the direction he was. His place was on the opposite side of town.

This was not how he wanted Mac to find out he was sleeping with Ronnie.

His sergeant would have his balls.

Brodie wanted to at least wait until he and Ronnie talked. He was laying claim to her, and she needed to know this before anyone else.

"I was out." He shrugged, sensing all eyes on him.

Myles smirked. "With who?"

"None of your fucking business." He chuckled.

"Don't let him bust your balls." Iker sniffed. "He gave up his bachelor card to play house with Roxxy. He doesn't get to hear all of the freaky details of your night."

Snickers filled the cab.

"Thanks, Iker," Brodie snickered.

"You can save all of those nasty details for us single folk when we go out for drinks," Iker said.

Laughter went around.

"Not sure if I want to hear them." Jordan snickered.

"Sis, you may want to close you ears when the men get to talking," Iker joked, elbowing her.

"I don't know. She looks like she has a few tales of her own," Myles teased.

"Y'all are crazy." Jordan shook her head with a laugh. "Let me tell you one thing. You guys could never hang with women sharing stories."

"Is that so?" Iker turned to Jordan.

Brodie was glad the attention was off of him. He glanced back at Myles and found him watching him while Iker hit Jordan with a line of questions.

Myles was a bulldog when it came to his curiosity. He wasn't going to let up until Brodie spilled the beans.

The partition slid open. Zain was driving the BEAR to their location.

"Heads up. ETA two minutes," Zain said.

Laughter and joking faded. The BEAR once against grew tense. They would need to be focused on the mission at hand. A hostage situation could go south at the blink of an eye.

Brodie just hoped the female was still alive.

Soon, the BEAR coasted to a stop. Mac was the first to exit the vehicle. They all followed out and waited for Mac and Declan to speak with whoever was in charge.

There were patrol cars everywhere with their flashing lights. A rope had cut off the media and the public to keep them back at a safe distance.

Brodie's gaze swept the area. Today the patrolmen were keeping the crowd in check. Not that many people were out this early.

"While Mac finishes speaking with Sergeant Harris, we can go over the blueprints of the building," Dec declared, walking back with papers in his hand.

The team gathered around Dec and reviewed the

building's layout. Mac soon joined the group as they devised a plan to safely breach the building.

Once satisfied they had all bases covered, they all prepared.

Brodie pulled his ski mask over his face and tucked his helmet down over it. He ensured his communicator was synced with everyone else. Their mini earpieces were top-of-the-line.

"SWAT," Mac called out. His fierce stare roamed the group. "Let's hunt."

They formed their standard formation when heading toward the building where the professor was housed with the woman.

Situations such as these could go to shit in a handbasket fast.

They had to be careful.

A negotiator had been brought in to get Lucas on the phone. They needed proof the woman was unharmed, which was confirmed.

Brodie led the group. As the entry man, it was his duty to gain entrance to any building. With his battering ram at his side, he knew it would be up to him to gain access to any locked area.

Aiming his firearm up, he swept his gaze over the lawn as they raced across it. The suspect was considered armed and highly dangerous. He'd already shot one officer and there was no telling if he would do it again.

They made it to the front door. Brodie held up his fist, signaling for the team to stop. They blended in with the shadows of the property to make themselves smaller.

Even in their dark camouflage they would be sitting ducks if they didn't stay close to the building. Brodie took a quick peek through the windows on the door.

The hallway appeared clear.

From the intel, the suspect and victim were on the second floor in his office.

Brodie signaled they were clear to enter. He tested the handle, and the door opened. Without having to say it, he knew the team would have his back.

Brodie was the first to enter.

The first floor was filled with administration and a few classrooms.

Lucas had been spotted pacing in his office on the second floor.

The team silently followed close. They all moved in unison with practiced precision. Their footsteps barely audible. This was something they had trained countless amount of hours for.

The tension in the air was heightened when there were victims involved. The goal was to extract the innocent unharmed.

Sometimes they succeeded.

Brodie tried not to think of the times they failed.

With his weapon in his hand, he calmly walked through the hallway and headed toward the stairs.

This was where they would divide. Half the team would take the front stairs, while the other half went up the back.

This fucker wouldn't be making an escape on them.

Mac, Iker, and Zain continued swiftly down the hallway.

Myles, Jordan, and Declan followed Brodie. They entered the stairwell.

"Clear," Brodie whispered.

They crept up the stairs in a single-file line, sweeping the area with their weapons. They didn't want to get caught unawares in such close encounters.

Arriving at the door for the upper level, Brodie paused and rested his hand on the handle.

"We're in position," Mac's growl came through the communicator.

Brodie glanced over his shoulder. Jordan, Declan, and Myles all gave him a nod.

"We are, too," Brodie responded. "Taking a peek."

Slowly, he opened the door. He glanced down the hallway. It was poorly lit with only half of the lights on. Aiming his weapon around, he didn't see anything.

"Dammit, I said to leave!" a panicked voice shouted.

Brodie ducked back inside the stairwell but left the door ajar slightly where he could see.

"Suspect in the hall," Mac's voice came over the coms.

"I didn't want to hurt anyone. The gun misfired," Lucas hollered. He must be on a call with the negotiator. They were notorious for being able to keep the suspects on the phone. Empathy was the draw. The bad guys always wanted someone to feel what they were going through. "Just tell them to go away. Me and Sara just have some shit to work out."

Brodie rolled his eyes.

"We're going to engage with him, while he's away from the girl," Mac's voice came back on.

Brodie widened the door and braced.

This could go one of two ways.

"CPD SWAT! Put down your weapon—"

Gunfire cut off Mac's voice.

Brodie pushed forward without a thought. His team was right behind him. Allan Lucas spun around with his weapon aimed at him.

Brodie didn't hesitate to fire.

His bullet slammed into Allan's thigh. The professor yelled out and crumpled to the floor.

His team flew past him to secure the suspect. Declan had him flipped over and zip tied within seconds. The rest of the team ensured there was no one else posted in the building. They could never be too sure.

"This was all a misunderstanding," Allen shouted.

"Shut the fuck up." Declan patted him down.

Brodie snapped out of his haze and followed behind Jordan who entered the professor's office.

He blew out a deep breath seeing the uninjured female sitting in the chair behind the desk. Tears streamed down her face, but she was alive.

Mission complete.

9

Ronnie pushed her cart down the aisle with butterflies in her stomach. She had to stop at her local Target for a few items and somehow found herself in the baby section.

She paused in front of the receiving blankets and froze.

She didn't know the first thing about what babies needed. Thank goodness for Sarena being pregnant, too. She'd have to speak with her because her brother and sister had no children.

Ronnie paused.

She certainly couldn't ask her sister, Rowan, or her brother, Junior, if they knew since she hadn't told anyone she was pregnant yet except Sarena.

Fear gripped her.

Hell, she hadn't even told Brodie yet. He had texted her that he'd got swamped at work and would be calling her soon so they could get together.

She knew from hanging with Sarena that the life of a SWAT spouse was difficult. Sarena shared with her that she lived in constant fear that something would happen to Mac or any of the guys. They were a close-knit group and considered each other family. Ronnie had been around them enough that she would be devastated if something happened to any of them.

Would she ever be a SWAT spouse?

Or would she only be a 'baby mama'. She never would have thought she would be one, but it didn't matter. She already loved this baby, and if her and Brodie didn't work out, she was sure they would come to some agreement about the baby.

Ronnie bit her lip. Deep inside, she wanted this thing with Brodie to grow into so much more.

If she didn't know any better, she would say she was a star in one of her little spicy novels she always read.

Brodie, the big bad SWAT officer and her a sexy nurse.

Those stories existed.

She'd read them, and they all had a happy ending.

Ronnie Floyd was determined to get hers.

Her gaze landed on a cute little pink-and-gray blanket. It was soft to touch, and she held it in her hands.

She didn't know what she was having, so she put it back. She looked around and found a neutral color. A soft green. Smiling, she placed it against her chest with excitement filling her.

Today, she would buy her first baby items. She tossed the blanket in her cart, strolled along, and found a few other things she assumed a baby would need.

Holding up little socks, she sighed just imaging the tiny feet that would one day fill them.

"Ronnie?" a familiar voice called out.

She spun around and found Deana and Ashton coming her way. Ash was pushing the cart with a baby seat in the basket.

"Deana. Ash. How are you guys?" Her voice ended on a squeak. She tossed the socks into her cart as if they were a hot potato.

"We're good. I haven't seen you in a while." Deana rushed forward and wrapped Ronnie into a tight hug.

Ronnie squeezed her back before stepping away.

"Hey, Ronnie." Ash came forward with a crooked grin. He looked tired and worn down.

She laughed as he crushed her in his arms.

"Haven't had to take care of any of the guys lately at the hospital, have you?" he asked.

"No." She chuckled. "Everyone has behaved themselves and have not had to come to the ED to get checked out."

Ash had been one of her stubborn patients. Thankfully, he hadn't been injured too bad. Just some scrapes and bruises. Like all the men on the SWAT team, he was bullheaded and didn't want anyone to tell him anything.

Not only did she take care of some of the other first responders when they came to the hospital, but the first time she had met Aspen, Declan's wife, she was a patient. Some very bad men had been trying to kill her and had almost succeeded. Aspen had been disoriented, scared, and hurt. Guilt still filled Ronnie on what had happened when she had got off that fateful night.

Those bad men had almost succeeded in killing Aspen.

"What do you have here?" Deana glanced down into her basket. Her eyes lit up as she reached for the blanket in Ronnie's cart. "This is cute. Love the color."

"Yeah, one of the girls at work is pregnant, and we're going to have a surprise baby shower for her," Ronnie lied. She wasn't sure how she came up with the story so quick but was glad it rolled off her tongue naturally.

"That's fun." Deana chuckled.

"Let me see Evan," Ronnie gushed, walking over to their cart.

Ash turned it around so she could see the baby. Evan was one of the cutest babies she'd seen. His round cheeks were chunky, just like they should be. Evan was awake and kicking at his blanket. He took one look at her and grinned.

"Oh my goodness. Look at you," she cooed.

Evan squealed. His large brown eyes locked on Ronnie, and her heart melted.

She couldn't wait to cuddle her baby.

"You want to hold him?" Deana asked, moving to the cart.

Evan began whining slightly. He quieted once Deana placed him on her chest.

Ronnie froze.

Did she want to snuggle and smell a brand-new baby?

Hell yeah.

"Could I?" She reached inside her purse and took out her hand sanitizer to clean her hands. She tossed it back quickly and set her things in her basket.

"He sure likes you." Ash chuckled, running his hand lovingly on the back of Evan's head. "Lately, anyone touches him but me or Deana, and he starts crying instantly."

Ronnie took Evan, cradling him closely to her chest. Her heart raced at the feeling of the little body in her hands.

"Hey, baby," she murmured in a singsong voice. She ran a hand along his back, and he was quiet. "How's he sleeping?"

Deana and Ash groaned at the same time.

"What is that?" Ash asked. He scratched his jaw. "This kid makes a seventy-two-hour shift at work a walk in the park. He has to be part vampire—"

"I think he has his days and nights switched," Deana cut in, laughing. She remained close, watching Evan. She shook her head. "It is amazing how he responds to you. He must like you."

Ronnie grinned. "I have a way about kids."

She did. Not that she was a pediatric nurse, but any time she had to take care of a kid, she went above and beyond to make sure they felt special even though they may not feel well.

"How did Sarena and Mac keep it in so long that they were expecting?" Deana asked.

"I have no clue," Ronnie replied. She glanced down at Evan who was silently studying her. She smiled at him. Little did the tiny chunkster know, he just made her feel completely comfortable about the baby growing in her belly.

She would be okay.

"I'm sure Sarena swore Mac to silence. He's not that good at keeping certain types of secrets," Ash said.

They all shared a laugh. He was right. Ronnie had got to know the brooding sergeant. He was scary at first when she'd met him, but soon he opened up to her and he treated her like a younger sister.

Ronnie breathed in Evan's scent and couldn't wait until she could hold on to her bundle of joy.

"HE HAS to make up for it," Brodie shared with his team.

They had been slammed, and finally the phone

was quiet. Not able to trust speaking in the precinct, they met out in the parking lot near their cars.

"And how is he going to do that?" Mac asked.

"Not sure. Whatever it is, I'm certain it will involve information that will keep the Demon Lords a step ahead of us," Brodie replied.

Official SWAT business was pretty much known by the entire department. When dispatch put out the call it wasn't secretive. Hell, most times it was televised when the news found out.

"Think about it, he could leak information on anyone working Vice and deep undercover," Zain mentioned.

Grunts went around at the notion. Most of the detectives working undercover were classified.

"But who would have access to those files?" Jordan asked. She glanced around at the group. "That wouldn't just be lying around where anyone can get their hands on it."

"The handlers and the captain." Declan sniffed. He shoved a hand through his hair.

"What we need to do is get our hands on a Demon Lord who will talk," Myles suggested. He folded his massive arms in front of his chest. "Someone who will know what Victor is doing. He may be behind bars, but I'm willing to bet money he is still in charge. With everything going on in their organization, someone will rat them out."

Brodie nodded in agreement with his friend. They needed to gather more intel. Something that would help them understand why Cruz was feeding information to the gang.

The door opened from the building, and everyone ceased speaking. One of the patrolmen who must be going off duty headed toward his car. His gaze swept the area and landed on their group. He tilted his head in a nod before getting into his vehicle.

Once he drove off, they turned back to each other.

"Well, it looks like we are going to be hunting Demon Lords harder," Mac said. There was no love lost between Mac and the gang. The previous leader of the gang had kidnapped Mac's wife and held a gun to her head.

"Shouldn't be hard to start picking them off," Iker said. He leaned against his truck with a devious smile. "We start with the lackies who don't know anything about loyalty and want to make a name for themselves. Anything that will knock out their competition to move up in the organization."

"I might know where we can start," Zain offered. "Give me a day or so and I'll get back with y'all."

"Meanwhile, I hear Cruz will be back this week," Mac said.

"I think we may need to look into him while he's away from work," Jordon suggested.

All eyes landed on her. Brodie knew he liked her.

"When he returns, we don't know how he'll be. Away from work we don't know what he's getting into now. Maybe that's why he's off."

"I like the way she's thinking." Iker snickered.

"Jordan. You think you, Zain, and Iker would be up for an old-school reconnaissance?" Mac asked. He stepped into the center of the group. They all moved in closer. "This would be off the books. Captain will have our asses if he catches wind."

"It's been a while since my stakeout days." Jordan shrugged. She eyed Iker and Zain. "Not sure if the boys would be up to it. They look rusty."

"The new girl got jokes." Zain chuckled. He shook a finger at her. "Don't forget the newbie match is coming up."

Everyone laughed. It broke up the seriousness of what they were about to dive into. It wasn't every day that a cop had to investigate a brother in blue.

"Don't worry. I'll kick her ass quick so we can move on," Brodie teased.

Jordan flipped him the finger while rolling her eyes.

"My money is on Brodie." Myles slapped him on his shoulder.

Bets and predictions were thrown out by the group.

The competition had almost slipped Brodie's mind. His gaze met Jordan who promptly stuck her tongue out at him.

He snickered and looked away.

Mac held up a hand. Silence fell as they all waited for their sergeant.

"I expect you all to come up with a plan and get back with us. I'm sure Brodie will have some toys for you." Mac turned to him.

Brodie nodded.

Of course he did.

He would outfit them with the latest of technology that wasn't even out on the market yet, thanks to a friend.

"We're dealing with the Demon Lords, so you know what that means," Declan said. His gaze swept the group. The tension in the air heightened. "Watch your back. They will retaliate if they get word of what we're doing."

Brodie slid a hand along his face.

He didn't have to worry about his family. His father, former Army, was still in good shape and could protect his mother. His brothers could look after themselves as well. He'd still give them all a warning so they could increase their awareness.

There was only one person who couldn't protect herself whom he would need to be careful with. He didn't know what he would do if she drew the attention of the Demon Lords.

Ronnie.

10

"Now who could that be?" Ronnie muttered. She pulled the bag of popcorn from the microwave and placed it on the counter. It was late, and she had planned to chill on the couch and watch a movie.

As a nurse she had a flexible schedule. She usually worked three or four twelve-hour shifts a week, and lately the hospital was cutting back on overtime.

So at the moment, she was only working three days a week. Which she was all right with, because it gave her time to do a deep cleaning on her house.

Her spare bedroom would be converted into a nursery soon. Her heart skipped a beat with the thought of creating a cozy little spot for the baby.

Her body ached, and at the moment, she just wanted to put her feet up and relax.

Also, the cleaning helped keep her mind off Brodie.

It had been a few days since she had spoken with him. She had met Sarena for breakfast earlier that day and shared with her that Mac had been crazy busy with work.

She glanced over at the microwave and saw it was going on ten at night.

Who the hell would be coming this late?

Walking over to the front door, she stood on her tiptoes so she could peer through the peephole.

Her father didn't raise no fool.

She was looking first before just opening her door.

Ronnie blinked.

The object of her desire stood on the other side. Brodie turned and glanced at the hole.

"Really?" she cried out, staring down at herself. She had just got out of the shower and had on her jammies.

A cami and short cotton shorts.

Ronnie leaned her head against the door and chuckled.

What was she worried about?

He has seen everything I've got and knocked me up.

Blowing out a deep breath, Ronnie backed away and opened the door.

"Brodie," she breathed, a small smile on her face.

"Ronnie." His eyes greedily took her in.

Her nipples grew hard and pressed into her thin shirt.

She opened the screen door and stepped back to allow him to enter her home. He brushed past her, his cologne lingering in the air. She inhaled it, and her body immediately craved Brodie.

She closed the door and found herself pushed up against it with a very sexy officer assaulting her lips.

Brodie's mouth moved over hers. She gasped, and he took advantage of the move. His tongue slipped inside, stroking hers.

Ronnie's hands trailed along his hardened body and up to his neck. She dove her fingers into his thick hair as he tilted his head to the side.

Brodie's large hand cupped her breast. The thin cami was useless. She might as well have been naked. He pinched her nipple, eliciting a groan from her. He slid the thin straps off her shoulders and pushed the shirt down, freeing her breasts.

He tore his mouth from hers and trailed kisses

along her jawline before burying his face in the crook of her neck. He nipped her skin then soothed it with his tongue.

"Yes," Ronnie hissed.

She hooked her fingers underneath his shirt and pulled it over his head. A groan slipped from her lips at the sight of his perfectly sculpted chest. She trailed her fingers down the ridges of his abdomen and wanted to follow this same path with her tongue.

Her shorts found their way to the floor, as did his jeans.

Brodie bent down and lifted her. She wrapped her legs around his waist, and he carried her through the house.

"I need you, Ronnie."

"Hurry," she cried out.

He made it to the stairs, but they weren't going to make it to her bedroom. Ronnie's back met the carpeted stairs while Brodie covered her front. She scraped his back with her nails and nipped at his lips.

Brodie's mouth and hands were everywhere. Her body trembled with need. She had never wanted someone so intensely before. This thing between them was unrealistic.

Something she'd only read about in her romance books.

"Fuck, Ronnie," he breathed.

Her hands made it to his boxer briefs and pushed them down. She wrestled the cotton material from his body.

"Brodie. Please," she begged, burying her face in the crook of his neck. She wrapped her arms around him to bring him closer to her.

"Tell me, baby," he growled, raising his head. He pressed a hard kiss to her lips. "What do you want?"

"You. Inside me. Now."

He lined up the blunt tip of his shaft and thrust home.

Their groans echoed together as he sank deep inside her.

Ronnie lifted her legs and locked them around his waist. Their lips molded together while he pumped in and out of her.

Ronnie's pulse raced.

Brodie's strong muscles tensed beneath her touch.

She cried out and bucked against him.

Brodie angled his hips with each thrust, his cock rubbing her clit with the new position.

Ronnie chanted Brodie's name.

The pleasure coursing through her body was almost unbearable.

Brodie continued on, his grunts echoing in her ear.

Her orgasm was growing, racing for her like a fierce tropical storm coming in. Ronnie, unable to take any more, allowed the waves of her climax to wash over her. She threw her head back, a cry escaping her.

Brodie's growl was ripped from him.

Ronnie was captivated by the sheer strength of him. He arched his head back, his climax slamming into him. His hips thrust a few more times before going still, lodging himself deep inside her, filling her with his seed.

Brodie collapsed on top of her. She welcomed his weight, but she sensed he was bracing himself on the stairs to keep from crushing her. Her arms and legs were wrapped around him tight.

Brodie lowered his head to her neck, his warm breath sliding against her skin.

Ronnie bit her lip. She had to tell him.

Tonight.

She wasn't sure where it would leave them, but she had to clear the air between them before things went any further.

Her throat grew dry with the thought that he wouldn't be happy. What if he stormed out? She closed her eyes, praying that it didn't happen that way.

"Ronnie, girl. I swear, I hadn't come over here—"

"I'm glad you did," she interjected. There was no way she was going to allow him to apologize for ravishing her the second he stepped into the building.

"I didn't hurt you, did I?" he asked. He lifted his head and met her gaze. He trailed his fingertips along the side of her face.

"I'm okay. I don't think I can stay here all night." She smiled, arching her back.

The stairs were not the most comfortable, but in the heat of passion, she hadn't even noticed. He chuckled and untangled himself from her. He slowly withdrew from her, and she immediately missed the fullness he gave her.

He stood, and she couldn't help but admire the sight before her. His body was like chiseled stone. His semi-soft cock hung between his legs. She had taken notice of a few tattoos along his body and loved the ink.

He helped her up from the stairs. She leaned into him as he wrapped an arm around her waist.

"This is crazy."

"What?" she asked.

He cupped her cheeks and pressed a kiss to her lips.

"How much I want you. You're all I can think about." He dropped another kiss onto her mouth. "When I'm near you, all I can think about is sinking into you."

Her pulse spiked at his words.

Her breath caught in her throat. "Brodie—"

"I know it sounds crazy, but I only want you." She rested her hand on his jaw, loving the feeling of his shadow of a beard.

"I feel the same," she replied.

"Seriously?" He covered her mouth with his in a deep, passionate kiss.

Ronnie melted to his body, loving how he felt against her.

How did she get so lucky?

Soon, she was going to share with him some news that was going to test their newly formed relationship.

BRODIE STARED at his reflection in the mirror. After he had finally peeled himself off Ronnie, they had thrown some of their clothes back on. She had shared with him that before he came over and basically mauled her, she had planned to have popcorn and watch a movie.

Not wanting to ruin her plans, he had her get the popcorn and movie picked out.

But now after using the facilities and relieving himself, he realized one thing.

He hadn't worn a condom.

They were going to have to talk about it.

He knew he was clean. It had been a while since he'd been with a woman.

Deep down, he knew Ronnie was it for him. He was pretty certain he was halfway in love with her.

Did he want children?

Hell yeah.

He wanted the beautiful wife, two-point-five kids, and a dog. But first he had to lock down his woman.

Ronnie's beautiful face came to mind. She had buried her way into his heart, and he was going to enjoy getting to know her more now that they had agreed they were an item.

He quickly washed his hands and left the half

bath. Walking into the living room, he found Ronnie had put her shirt and tiny shorts back on. She had a blanket, popcorns, and two sodas waiting for them.

"I hope you don't mind action-packed movies about assassins." Ronnie grinned. She looked adorable waiting for him with her legs tucked underneath her.

A woman after his own heart.

"I knew you were special." He chuckled. He slid on the couch and rested his arm on the back.

Ronnie immediately sat next to him and covered them with the blanket. She set the bowl of popcorn on his lap before starting the movie.

He loved the feeling of her pressing up against him.

The movie began, and it was one of his favorites.

An assassin who had retired, but soon had to rejoin the game.

"How are you so warm?" Ronnie mumbled, leaning her head on his bare chest.

"What can I say, I'm just a hot-blooded male." He shrugged.

Her laughter filled the air as she swatted him with the back of her hand.

"You're crazy." She giggled.

"Crazy over you." He brought her close and

pressed a kiss to her lips. He couldn't get enough of her. Brodie had to have another taste of her. His cock was straining at his jeans, ready for another round.

"Brodie, there's something we need to talk about," she blurted out, pulling back away from him.

He stared into her eyes and saw fear and slight panic in her pretty brown pools. She took the bowl from his lap and set it on the coffee table before turning back to him.

"We do." He blew out a deep breath. He took her hand and brought it to his lips. "I just want to let you know that since we are going to be a couple, that there haven't been any other women for a while."

Ronnie smiled and shook her head. "That's good to know—"

"The reason I'm bringing it up is because I forgot the damn condom tonight and I want you to know that I've been tested and clean."

There. He'd got it off his chest.

"I'm clean, too, and there hasn't been anyone in a couple years apart from you." She played with the blanket, not meeting his eyes.

Her hand trembled, and if he didn't know better, he would say she was nervous.

He went on alert.

Something was wrong.

"What is it?" he asked.

Big fat tears hovered on her eyelids.

He released a curse. "What's bothering you?"

Ronnie pushed off the couch and stood in front of the television. She wiped the tears sliding down her cheeks then rested her hands on her waist.

"Brodie, I really like you. A lot." She paused and drew in a haggard breath.

Brodie sat forward, unsure where this was going.

"I like you, too, Ronnie. Whatever it is, just spit it out," he encouraged. If there was something or someone bothering her, he would take care of it.

Tears continued to flow down her cheeks. He was really starting to get worried. He stood from his perch on the couch.

"I'm pregnant."

Brodie blinked.

He couldn't have heard her right.

"What?" He swallowed hard and stared at her. He took a step toward her then paused.

"I'm pregnant," she repeated, softer.

He closed the gap between them and took Ronnie into his arms. He cupped her face in his hands.

"Are you certain?" he asked. His heart pounded at the news.

He was going to be a father.

Ronnie was carrying his child. There was no doubt in his mind the baby was his. Ronnie had said there hadn't been anyone for years, and for as long as he had known her, she'd never brought anyone around.

The tear streaks on her face almost broke him. He didn't know what she was feeling, but he saw that she was guarded as if waiting for his reaction.

"Four home pregnancy tests, a doctor's visit, and a sonogram confirmed it." She rested her forehead on his chest and blew out a deep breath.

He closed his eyes for a brief moment and realized that he was elated. Happiness filled him. He had already had a sense that Ronnie was made for him.

Now if this wasn't a sign, he didn't know what was.

He tipped her chin back up so he could meet her gaze.

"You've just made me the happiest man," he admitted with a grin forming on his lips.

"Really?" She searched his eyes cautiously. "You're not upset?"

He barked a laugh and wrapped his arms around her. He pressed a kiss to the top of her head. He didn't know who he wanted to tell first, his parents, his brothers, or his team.

"Upset with you? Never." He bent down and scooped her up into his arms. If anything, it was his fault. He had never had sex with a woman without protection. There was just something about Ronnie that caused him to lose common sense.

"What are you doing?" she squealed, wrapping her arms around his neck.

He walked back over to the couch and bent down to grab the remote. He shut off the television before stalking over to the stairs.

"Taking you upstairs so we can celebrate properly."

11

Ronnie was still in shock. Brodie had brought her upstairs and made love well into the night. Her body was well-loved, sore in the best places, and a smile was etched on her face.

She was relieved at how well Brodie had taken the news. She had gotten overly emotional down in the living room, unsure how he was going to respond.

It was early in the wee hours, and they had slept on and off since coming into her bedroom. Ronnie should be tired, but she was running on adrenaline at the moment. She leaned into Brodie as he gazed upon the ultrasound of their baby.

He traced it with his finger while he stared at it with awe.

"Is it a girl or a boy?" he asked.

He focused his blue eyes on her, and she bit her lip and squeezed her legs shut.

Down, girl.

That's why you're pregnant now.

"I go in a few weeks for my next ultrasound and I'll be able to learn the sex," she said.

"Can I come with you?" He turned to her like a kid begging to go to a candy store.

Her heart melted.

"Of course," she replied.

He pulled her to him, wrapping an arm around her. Her back rested against his chest. His hand slid down to rest on her small pudge of a belly.

"I would love to have you there."

"I want to experience everything," he murmured. He dropped a kiss to her shoulder. "My mother is going to be so happy. You just don't know how much my brothers and I have been lectured that she wasn't getting any younger."

"Your mom sounds wonderful," Ronnie said. His excitement was adorable. They would have to plan a day for their families to get together.

"I can't wait for you to meet them. My parents will love you."

She covered his hand with hers and let out a sigh.

"I'm so glad that you're happy about the baby," she divulged.

He tightened his arms around her.

"I was so nervous that you'd leave and I'd never see you again."

"Did you seriously think I'm that type of guy?" he asked. He pulled back slightly.

She looked over her shoulder at him and found him staring at her with a serious expression.

"I would never run from my responsibilities. Before you told me about the baby, I had already decided I wanted you."

Ronnie was rendered speechless.

"Well, we weren't careful, and honestly, I was just in shock. First time I have sex in years and I get pregnant." She pushed a wayward strand of her hair from her face.

"I know it's been fast, but I do have feelings for you, Ronnie. I want to be with you." He brought her hand to his lips and kissed it.

"I want to be with you, too."

"Good. We'll figure this out. Together."

Ronnie nodded. She smiled and fought back tears.

"I like the sound of that." She pressed a kiss to his chin.

"How do you want to tell our families?"

"Why don't we have everyone get together? That way we can meet everyone." She closed her eyes for a moment, still unable to believe how smooth this was going. Now that Brodie knew, she was going to have to share with her family. "We can tell them together."

"Sounds like a plan. Come on. I've got to let you get some sleep tonight." He chuckled. "I want to tell them soon, so we need to get to planning."

He placed the sonogram photo on the nightstand and switched off the light. Darkness surrounded them. They shifted down into the bed against the pillows. Ronnie snuggled into his side and rested her head into the crook of his arm.

She yawned and felt the signs of sleep coming for her. She had a warm, muscular man in her bed who was apparently crazy over her and happy that they had a baby on the way.

Brodie adjusted the covers over them, and Ronnie allowed herself to succumb to her dreams.

Right now, everything was perfect.

BRODIE PUSHED ON, his feet eating up the pavement. It was early morning and the perfect day for a run. He was still on cloud nine about the news of Ronnie's pregnancy.

It took everything he had not to say anything to any of the guys at work. Myles had been eyeing him yesterday, but Brodie tried to ignore his teammate.

He was on a five-mile run and headed in the direction of his parents' home. He might as well stop by and speak with them about getting together with Ronnie and her family.

Brodie was sure he would find his father sitting out on the front porch drinking his coffee while his mother was inside putzing around in the kitchen making them breakfast. His parents had been married for thirty-five years and were creatures of habit.

Brodie could set his watch by his father.

The former Army man was a stickler for coffee first thing in the morning while reading the paper.

Rounding the corner, Brodie found Heath Gipson on the porch doing exactly what he knew his father would be doing. He grinned and picked up speed.

"Well, look what the cat dragged in," Heath called out.

Brodie rolled his eyes, running up the driveway.

"What are you talking about. I was just here earlier this week." Brodie came to a halt at the bottom of the stairs. His breaths were coming fast, his skin flushed. He rested his hands on his waist while trying to catch his breath.

"You boys used to come see your parents almost daily," his father grumbled.

His father may be gruff and a hard-ass, but he loved all of his children. The old man was proud of all of them and always made it known. Each of the Gipson offspring served their community. Zayden, his eldest brother, served on the Columbia K-9 unit, while Anders, the middle son, was a firefighter for Columbia.

"Well, I'm here now," Brodie taunted, walking up the stairs.

The old man sat back in his chair with a twinkle in his eye. Clearly, he was just busting Brodie's balls.

"Who are you talking to?" Teri, Brodie's mother, came out the front door. She drew to a halt with a wide smile spreading across her face. "Brodie! Morning, baby."

"Hey, Momma." He leaned back against the pillar, folding his arms across his chest. He wished he had at least brought a t-shirt with him. It was nice enough outside that he hadn't needed one.

"Let me get you a water. You look beat." She spun around and rushed back into the house. Teri Gipson was a doting mother who'd had the challenge of raising three crazy boys. They, like all military families, had moved all over until they'd finally settled in Columbia when the boys were teens.

"What brings you by, son?" Heath picked up his mug and took a sip. "Since you're out for your morning jog, doubt it had anything to do with the call from the other day."

Brodie shook his head. He had called his brothers and father to give them a heads-up that he and his team were going in deeper with the Demon Lords and for them to stay sharp.

"I wanted to speak with you and Ma about something else." His smile disappeared. He hadn't really thought this through and how he was going to tell his parents he was about to become a father. Hell, he was twenty-eight years old and felt like he was sixteen trying to explain the time he'd stolen his father's truck.

"Here you go, baby." Teri came back onto the porch with a bottle of water and a towel. Teri had a way about her that she always knew what he needed without him having to say.

He accepted them from her and leaned down, plopping a kiss on her cheek. She moved on and sat in the empty chair next to his father.

"Are you in trouble?" His father turned serious and leaned forward.

"No."

That garnered a smile from the old man. Without a doubt, his father was already running a list of contacts in his head he could call on to help. That was Heath Gipson. He may yell and curse when they were teens being brought home in the back of a police cruiser, but he went above and beyond to protect his boys.

Brodie took a long swig of the water and wiped his bare chest down, before resting the towel on his shoulder.

"What's going on?" Teri looked between the two of them.

"Brodie said he needed to speak with us." Heath nodded toward Brodie.

Teri turned toward him with wide eyes. Concerned filled her big blues, and Brodie didn't want her to worry.

"I'm not in trouble. I promise." He finished off

the bottle, crumpling it in his hands. "I met someone."

Relief crossed his parents' faces.

"That's good, baby. Who is she, what does she do, how did you meet, when can we meet her—"

"Calm down, Teri. Let the boy finish," his father interjected Teri's outburst. He patted his wife's knee, chuckling.

Teri's cheeks were rosy while a wide grin was plastered on her face. She scooted to the edge of her seat, and Brodie could already see her scheming. It was rare for him to bring a woman around, so the simple fact he was bringing this up, she was probably already planning wedding bells.

Teri Gipson made no qualms that she was ready for grandparenthood.

She was going to love Ronnie.

"Well, to answer your questions, her name is Ronnie Floyd, she's a nurse at General Hospital, we met through mutual friends, and you will be meeting her Saturday night."

"Oh, a nurse. So she's smart, caring, and must have a big heart in order to take care of the sick." Teri sighed. She was already halfway in love with Ronnie.

Brodie thought of Ronnie, and she was all of

those things and more. A small smile played on his lips remembering the last time he'd seen her. He'd had to tear himself from her bed in order for him to leave to report to work.

"She's something special. You will love her," Brodie said.

"Look at him, Heath. He's in love," Teri exclaimed.

His gaze flew to his mother.

In love?

Was he? He wasn't sure. He'd never been in love before. Infatuated when he was a teen, but never in love.

What he felt for Ronnie was strong, and the thought that she was the woman carrying his child enhanced what he felt for her.

"Mom, you are jumping ahead. We just want our families to meet. We've decided to be exclusive and its time y'all met."

His parents shared a glance before turning back to hm.

"Meeting her parents? This sounds serious, son." Heath's eyebrows rose. He sipped his coffee without taking his eyes off Brodie.

"I mean I am getting older." Brodie swept a hand through his damp hair. He didn't want to give away the secret yet. "I really do care for her. A lot. We've known each other a couple of years now and finally decided to act on what was there. She's definitely a keeper. I want all of you to meet her."

"When your father and I first met, he tried to resist me. He was grumpy, harsh, and stomped around with a chip on his shoulder, but all I saw was a big teddy bear that I just wanted to hug." Teri sighed and turned her attention to her husband. She held his hand in hers, entwining their fingers.

"Your mother is stubborn as a horse and wouldn't leave me be. Demanded that I take her out on a date," Heath grumbled.

"And look where we are? A home filled with love, and three boys who grew up into strong men like their daddy," Terri replied. She beamed at her husband.

Brodie was hit with a longing for what they had. He could see him and Ronnie together in the future with a few additional children to go along with the first.

"Soon, our family will start expanding and we'll be the best Gigi and Pop-pop there is."

His father's face softened, his lips curling into a smile. "Well, now that I'm retired, I'd get to spend all the time I missed with my boys with the grandkids.

It would be nice to teach a little one how to fish, throw the pigskin around, and spoil them rotten."

Brodie couldn't hold it in. Seeing his father join his mother in the want to become grandparents broke him. While Brodie was growing up, Heath was gone a lot due to the military's way of life. Not that any of them resented him. Brodie and his brothers were proud of their father. When he was home, he spent all of his time and focus on them.

Their childhood was filled with happiness and love.

"She's pregnant," he blurted out.

"What?" Teri's head whipped around. A scream escaped her lips as she jumped up and rushed to him.

He opened his arms in time to catch her. He groaned at how tight she was squeezing him.

"Ma, I'm wet and stinky." He laughed, trying to keep some distance between them, but she wasn't having it.

"I don't care! I'm your mother and changed your diapers. Sweat is nothing," she cried, her grasp on him getting harder.

He wrapped his arms around her, smiling and dancing in place. He looked over her shoulder at his father who stood and ambled over to them.

"Move out the way, woman, and let me at my son," Heath griped.

Teri backed away, sniffling and wiping tears from her face. He was enveloped in his father's strong embrace.

"Congratulations, son. I'm sure Ronnie is a fine woman, and we can't wait to meet her."

12

"We put that little device you gave us outside the window of his home office," Iker groused, plopping down on Brodie's couch.

The team were all over so they could meet to go over the data that had been coming through.

"Take your boots off and don't touch shit." Brodie walked through the living room.

The last time the entire team was over, somehow one of the vases his mother had bought him mysteriously broke.

Primary suspect was Iker.

"We have our own Martha Stewart in the house," Iker muttered, but kicked his boots off. "And for the last time, I didn't break that damn vase."

Snickers went around the room.

"Whatever." Brodie shrugged. Thankfully, it had been a cheap one his mother had purchased to put flowers in. "There's nothing wrong with keeping my house clean. No telling who's dropping by." He chuckled.

"Any nasty stories you care to share to make all the homemakers jealous?" Zain wagged his eyebrows.

He and Zain took up much of the couch with their big frames.

"Oh, gross. Is that all you think about?" Jordan took the recliner chair.

They were all in their civilian clothes, having left work to meet at Brodie's house.

Declan leaned against the doorframe, while Mac was putting coffee on in the kitchen.

Myles, who was spread out on the loveseat, barked a laugh. "Forgive them, Jordan. That's how they were programed."

"Hey, I resent that. Not too long ago, you were with us. You were the one who decided to go fall in love with Roxxy." Zain snorted. He looked over at Jordan. "Don't believe Mister Goodie Shoes. He used to be the leader of the pack."

Jordan giggled, rolling her eyes.

Brodie knelt on the floor in front of his coffee

table, placing his laptop on top of it. With the entire team over, his living room would be a little snug.

Opening his computer, he went into a program he had that was a gift from a friend. Excitement filled him. This was the first time he got to play with this new toy that Bryce Hayes, who had served with Brodie in the Army, had given him. His father owned a technological conglomerate, and Bryce started a division for military-grade tech that was earning him a pretty penny.

Brodie was one of the lucky bastards to be able to test it out first. Bryce was wanting to sell it to the local police divisions to help the war on crime.

"Yo, I said we were able to put that device thing where you needed us to," Iker repeated. "Are you going to give me a prize or something?"

"And for that, you get a gold sticker," Brodie joked. His fingers moved along the keyboard. "Hold a second, I'll explain."

"What does that do anyway?" Zain asked, his smile disappearing. Apparently, he wasn't listening to Brodie. "Cruz came home and almost caught me in his damn bushes."

"I told you to let me go," Jordan chimed in. She pushed her dark hair behind her ear. "I'm way smaller than you and would have been able to hide much easier in those bushes."

"That shit was hilarious." Iker chuckled.

"What you placed on his house was sort of like a bug, only more sophisticated. It is one hundred percent undetectable. Even if Cruz were to sweep his house for bugs, it would be undetectable."

"So you wanted to hear what his conversations were?" Declan asked.

"This is enhanced. It will pick up all signals to and from the house. I can see what he watched on television, the games he plays on his cell, text messages, and telephone calls. I can even slip into his computer without him knowing and see what he's working on. I now have full access to everything electronic in his house."

"Shit," Myles cursed. "That is something you got there."

"Well, before Brodie goes into more details of his findings, I want a report of what the three of you found out," Mac said, entering into the room.

All joking was put aside.

All eyes turned to the trio who were to find out more information on Cruz.

"First of all, let me say that Cruz leads one boring life," Iker said.

Brodie's gaze flicked to the computer screen, waiting for the rest of the information to download. His hands were itching to delve into what was waiting for him. Computers were a natural gift to him. Growing up, he had built his first one by the age of thirteen and was a whiz when it came to programming. His parents had enrolled him in a coding program by fourteen, and then it just blossomed.

In the Army, he had been an Army Intelligence Officer. He was in charge of commanding and coordinating military intelligence soldiers, assessed risks, and worked to neutralize threats.

The information he provided saved the lives of the soldiers fighting.

Now he used his gifts to help the best SWAT team in the land.

"He's a man of routine. Up early, runs, home, shower, work, then returns home," Zain chimed in.

"He did surprise us and went to the grocery store on day three." Jordan snickered.

"We didn't find anything else than what Brodie had already discovered about him." Iker propped his socked-covered feet on Brodie's table.

Brodie stared hard at the two large feet then

flicked his gaze to the owner. Iker wiggled his toes then dropped them to the floor.

A ding on the screen captured Brodie's attention. He slid on his earphones and clicked on the first file. While the team continued on with the conversation, he began going through all the files. Some he discarded immediately. Others he set aside, but then he came across one that made him pause. A phone call. One that spooked Cruz. He listened then held up a hand.

All conversation paused, and eyes fell to him.

"Got something," Brodie said. He pulled the earphones off and rested them on his neck. "Listen to this. It came through around three this morning."

He hit a button to allow the recording to play.

"Hello," Cruz answered the call, sleep filling his voice.

"I got the information you asked for," a gravelly voice came onto the line.

"You shouldn't be calling me on this—"

"Do you want it or not?" the voice snapped.

"I do." Cruz's voice was hard and clear. He must have fully woken up. "Just tell me where she—"

"Not on the phone. It's probably being traced."

"By who? No one knows nothing. I'm sure of that," Cruz replied.

"Meet me at Neon Nights tonight at ten."

"Fine."

The call disconnected.

"Who the hell is the 'she' Cruz is talking about?" Declan asked.

Everyone shook their heads.

"In the three days we watched him, nothing. No visitors. He didn't go anywhere." Zain scratched his head.

"Family. Did we look into his family?" Mac asked.

Brodie's fingers flew across his keyboard as he pulled up another report that he had on Cruz.

"Raised by his single mother. Siblings, a brother and sister. Brother was shot and killed at a gas station when he was twenty years old. Looked like he was at the wrong place at the wrong time. Cruz was about fifteen at the time. That was what was credited in him wanting to become a police officer," Brodie read aloud.

"Makes sense to me on why he became a cop. Someone killed my brother and got away with it, I'd go after them," Myles said.

"The killers of his brother were found, tried, and sentenced to life in prison," Brodie murmured. He closed that screen and opened another one. He had been through the family before but wanted to look at it again. He started running checks on all known family members. "I didn't go further into his family. Just checked him out. Doing it now."

"Whoever the 'she' is, has to be the reason he's turning on us," Jordan remarked. It didn't go unnoticed how she said 'us'.

A red flag appeared as soon as Brodie clicked on Cruz's sister, Lupa Cruz.

"Shit," he cursed.

"What did you find?" Mac barked, his patience appearing to be wearing thin.

"Lupa Cruz, younger sister of Officer Diego Cruz, was reported missing four years ago." Brodie scanned the report, running a trembling hand along the side of his face. "His sister had a drug history. A few arrests for possession. Nothing that stuck. All small amounts. Last seen with boyfriend, Pablo Seco, known member of the Demon Lords."

"Any death records?" Declan asked.

Brodie shook his head. He went deeper in his search, thankful he had the experience of researching things quick.

"A few reports of Cruz hiring private investigators to find her. A few potential sightings of her. No wonder there isn't a death certificate. She's still alive somewhere."

Brodie rested his hands on the table and eyed his sergeants.

"It would appear we're heading down to Neon Nights," Zain's low voice broke the silence.

Tension was thick in the air. If everything Cruz did was to save his sister, then it sort of made sense.

Brodie ran a hand along his face again.

Cruz could have asked for help. If he thought his sister was involved deep with the gang and was trouble, he could have gone to Vice, Gang or, hell even SWAT.

"Why wouldn't he say something?" Jordan asked, looking around. "He has the resources."

"If they have his sister, they want something. I'm willing to bet they are using her against him," Mac said. He folded his arms in front of his chest. The sergeant had a hard glint in his eyes.

Brodie knew that expression.

It seemed SWAT would be going down to the seedy bar.

Brodie's cell sounded. He glanced down and saw it was Ronnie calling.

"I got to take this." Brodie snatched his phone from the table and slid his finger across the screen. "Hey, babe."

Scoffs was heard behind him, but he ignored it.

He already knew he was in for a ball-busting when he returned. He flipped them off and walked into the kitchen.

"I'm not interrupting you, am I?" Ronnie's husky voice greeted him. She was working second shift today and wouldn't be getting off until close to midnight.

"Nah, me and the team are over here working on some things." He missed her already. His mother's assumption was still ringing in his ears. Maybe what he felt for Ronnie was more. She was always on his mind, he couldn't keep his hands from her. It was more than a passing fancy. He'd never craved a woman like he did her.

"Well, I don't want to keep you long. I just wanted to hear the sound of your voice while I took my break." She giggled.

"You got me, baby." He leaned against the counter, staring at the floor. His heart did a weird dance. A nervousness filled him as if he were a young teen talking to his crush on the phone for the first time. This was all new for him, opening himself to a woman.

"About dinner with the family, I found someone who could cater at the last minute. I won't have time to do all the cooking. But I found someone who wouldn't be too expensive."

"Whatever you want to do, I'm good with that. I'll get the booze," he offered. He had given her one of his credit cards so she wouldn't have to pay for anything.

His woman was stubborn and at first wouldn't take it.

Brodie could be very persuasive and was able to convince her to take it.

"That would be perfect." She paused. Only a slight hitch in her breath could be heard.

"What's wrong?" he asked

"Nothing. I'm just excited and nervous. What if your parents don't like me, or—"

"I sort of already told them," he admitted.

"What?" She gave a laugh.

"I couldn't help it. They would have figured something out. They were already suspicious." He chuckled.

"That's fine. At least that Band-Aid has been ripped off."

"It'll be okay. I promise."

"Here, I got to go. Now I'm hungry. One minute I'm nauseated and don't want to see food, the next

I'm scarfing everything down that's not bolted to the table." She sighed.

"Have a great break."

They disconnected the call, and he was left staring at the phone.

The words 'I love you' were on the tip of his tongue.

Sensing a commotion at the doorway, he saw his teammates crowding it.

"Something you want to tell us?" Myles held up the sonogram Ronnie had given Brodie. He had placed it on the nightstand beside his bed.

Guess he was telling his team tonight.

He stood erect and slid his phone into his back pocket. He faced his teammates as he would a firing squad.

"My girlfriend and I are expecting," he said, a grin spreading onto his face.

"Girlfriend?" Myles laughed.

The team rushed into the kitchen, all talking at once.

"When did you start seeing someone?" Declan asked.

"Who the hell would allow you to impregnant her?" Iker muttered, rolling his eyes. The big man was all teeth, grinning.

"Back up, back up," Brodie shouted.

Jordan hopped up on his counter while the others backed away slightly.

His team was as close as family, and he truly saw them all as brothers and sister.

Brodie plucked his child's picture from Myles' hands. He had memorized every part of it. He looked around until his gaze landed on Mac. His sergeant had relaxed enough to even grace them with one of his rare smiles.

"Mac, I meant to chat with you." Brodie grew nervous, not knowing how his sergeant was going to take the news.

"Spit it out, Brodie," Mac said playfully. "Who is it?"

"Ronnie."

The room fell silent. Mac's eyebrows shot up.

"Sarena's Ronnie?" Mac asked.

"Yeah, that Ronnie. We sort of hooked up and now we're expecting."

Mac stepped forward. Brodie braced himself. His sergeant rested a hand on his shoulder and met him with a hard gaze.

"Ronnie's like a sister to me and you're like a brother. You're a good man, and as long as she's happy, then I'm happy. For the both of you." Mac gave him a hard squeeze.

The tension in the room broke, and there was nothing but laughter and cheers.

It was something to break up the seriousness of the conversation they had just had in his living room.

Tonight, SWAT would be in motion.

13

Brodie pulled the baseball cap lower on his head to try to disguise himself. He and Jordan made their way through the crowd portraying a couple.

"There." Jordan pointed to a table. She was dressed like a woman out on a date. A shirt cut low, tight jeans, but she wore flats. She had joked, just in case she had to run, she wouldn't have to do it in heels.

He could respect a woman who was always prepared.

"Perfect." He stretched his arm around her shoulders and guided her over to it.

The rest of the team were spread out. Zain had gone in ahead of them and took a seat at the bar. Mac and Declan were over at the pool area. Iker and

Myles were left outside to keep eyes on the building. They were each outfitted with their communicators while dressed in civilian clothing.

They had canvassed the building, and all of them had memorized all exits. The bar was crowded, even for a Friday.

It was the perfect place for a public meeting.

No one would be paying them any attention.

Brodie pulled out a chair for Jordan, who gave him a coy smile. He held back a smirk.

This girl was good.

He knew she had done some undercover work in Atlanta and it showed.

"Hi, I'm Jane. What can I get for you?" the waitress came over. She looked haggard and worn out. The fake smile she presented was strained.

"Jack and Coke for me," Jordan replied.

"I'll have the same," Brodie said without thinking. His gaze was too busy roaming around the area.

"Be right back." Jane spun around on her heel and disappeared into the thick crowd.

"See anything?" Jordan asked. She tossed her dark hair over her shoulder and leaned in.

"Nope."

"Nothing over here either," Zain murmured.

Mac and Declan replied the same. Tension was

high amongst the team. They had to blend in and be inconspicuous. They couldn't allow Cruz to see them. He would know they were onto him.

Jane returned with their drinks. Not that either of them planned to drink them. They couldn't risk it, with the seriousness of the situation at hand.

They both took fake sips before turning to each other. Somehow, they'd got chosen to be on a pretend date.

"So tell me about yourself," Brodie joked.

Jordan's eyes twinkled. "Oh, well, let me see. I'm a Taurus. I like long walks on the beach and love to shoot things. You go next."

She petted his hand and leaned in closer with a wide grin on her face.

"Is that what you posted on your Tinder profile?" Iker's voice came over their coms.

Brodie laughed.

"Fuck you, Iker," Jordan murmured.

"Ah, doll. You can't do that. You've been officially adopted by me, and us fucking would be frowned upon," Iker came back.

Brodie snorted.

"All right, you two," Mac threatened. "Leave her be, Iker. We don't want to chance them getting made."

The coms went silent again.

"As I was about to say before I got so rudely interrupted..." Brodie grinned. He leaned his arm back along Jordan's chair, his gaze falling on a familiar figure. His smile disappeared. "Eyes up, fellas. Twelve o'clock."

Cruz had entered the building. He seemed out of place, a button-down shirt, jeans. A cold hard expression on his face. He maneuvered his way over toward the crowded bar at the opposite end from Zain.

Zain immediately swung around, putting his back to Cruz.

"Copy that," Mac and Declan responded quietly.

"Anyone with him?" Jordan turned, scanning the bar as if searching for someone.

"He's solo," Brodie said.

"He ordered a drink," Zain murmured. "Looks like his party hasn't arrived yet."

"Whoever it is, when they leave, Myles and Iker, I want you to snag him," Mac ordered.

"Copy that," Myles replied.

Brodie tried to keep his muscles relaxed as he and Jordan continued a small conversation to sell the act. Between the music and chatter, it was getting harder to hear.

"Heads-up. Someone just slid in next to him," Declan said.

Looked like the show was finally on.

"They are on the move, headed your way, Brodie and Jordan," Mac informed the group.

Brodie kept his head down and moved closer to Jordan. She, too, kept her face away from Cruz's view. From the outside it would seem they were a couple in a heated moment.

"They are seated. Four tables from you."

Brodie glanced up and found Cruz's back to him. He breathed a sigh of relief. He wasn't sure what was being said, but the newcomer didn't seem too pleased with Cruz.

He didn't recognize the guy. He appeared late twenties, early thirties, Caucasian, dark hair, slender build.

Cruz pounded his fist on the table.

Things appeared to be getting hot and heated.

Brodie drew comfort in knowing that he had two guns on him and a knife strapped to his ankle. His partner for the night was also carrying.

No member of the team would go into an unknown situation unarmed.

"That's all you have for me?" Cruz cursed, pushing up from his seat.

Mac immediately rattled off what the guy was wearing for Myles and Iker to seize him so they could have a chat with him.

The guy stood from the table, tucking an envelope into his jeans. He reached for Cruz's abandoned drink, knocking it back before setting the glass down.

"Thanks for the drink," he said. The guy turned and made his way through the crowd, leaving Cruz cursing.

Brodie grabbed Jordan's head and brought it close to his. He didn't want to chance Cruz seeing them.

"Myles and Iker, heads-up. The suspect is on the move, heading out the front door," Declan said.

"All right, love birds. Cruz is on the move. Myles and Iker, you better act now."

"Roger that." Iker's voice was hard and cold. They must have their eyes on the man.

Brodie and Jordan separated, breathing a sigh of relief.

"This was easy," Brodie murmured. He didn't know what he expected, but they would get the information they needed from the stranger.

"Yes, it was, and your cologne isn't as stifling as Zain's." Jordan laughed.

"I heard that, and there's nothing wrong with my cologne," Zain huffed defensively.

"Only that you bathed in it." Jordan snorted.

"We got him." Myles growled.

"Let's go, children." Mac's voice sliced through the air.

Brodie and Jordan stood, heading for the front of the bar. Brodie lost sight of his other teammates, but Jordan remained near him. They stayed close, managing to get through the crowd.

"Gipson."

Brodie paused at the sound of his name being called. He turned and found Cruz staring at him.

Shit.

He blinked and acted surprised. "Cruz, what are you doing here?"

"Are you shitting me?" Mac's exasperation came through the coms.

Brodie didn't respond, not wanting to alert Cruz.

A presence appeared at his side. He glanced down and found Jordan standing next to him.

"Out for a drink." Cruz moved closer to him, a new glass in his hand. He must have double-backed into the bar unseen. Cruz's attention landed on Jordan. "Officer Knight. Out with your teammate? I thought fraternization was frowned upon by the higher-ups?"

"There's nothing to it. Coworkers go out for drinks all the time." Brodie folded his arms against his chest, trying to keep himself from punching Cruz in the face. "What are you trying to say?"

"I don't know. You don't live in this area—"

"I do." Jordan stepped in front of Brodie. "Is this not a free country? A friend mentioned this place to me, so I asked Brodie to come with me. Got a problem with that?"

Jordan was tense, and her right hand was balled up into a fist. She may be small, but she was as fierce as a lioness protecting her cubs.

"You don't need to explain anything to him." Brodie rested a hand on her shoulder. He spun his baseball cap around so the bill was now in the back.

"She's cute. Now I see why SWAT picked her." Cruz took a sip of his drink.

Brodie moved Jordan out of his way, his gaze narrowed on Cruz. "Be very careful of what you say next, Cruz."

"Am I supposed to be scared of you?" Cruz expelled a laugh. They were drawing the attention of patrons around them. "A big bad SWAT officer."

"Walk away, Gipson," Declan's voice sounded in the com.

But Brodie wasn't listening. The ass was not going to talk ill of Jordan. He didn't give a shit who he was.

"I'm not going to tell you again," Brodie warned.

"Fine. I'll say what the entire precinct is thinking. You hired her because she's a woman. Are you and your team planning to run a train—"

Cruz didn't get to finish what he was saying. Brodie's fist plowed straight into his mouth. Cruz flew back into the crowd. Screams went up in the air as he disappeared somewhere on the floor in the midst of the onlookers' feet.

"Let's go, Gipson," Jordan barked. She grabbed his arm and yanked him behind her.

"Someone please tell me Brodie punched that fucker in the face," Iker ground out.

"Confirmed," Jordan said.

They made their way out of the bar, finding Zain standing at the mouth an alley.

"This way." Brodie ignored the deep pulse of his knuckles and headed into the dark alley.

"I DIDN'T DO NOTHING," their captive proclaimed.

Myles and Iker had him pinned against a dark car that was parked behind the bar. Mac, Declan, and Zain stood near them, glaring at the screamer.

"Who are you?"

Jordan remained near the mouth of the alley as a spotter.

"Don't worry about who we are," Mac retorted, stepping forward to stand in front of the guy. "Tell me your name."

"Why should I?" His words ended in a shriek. He glared at Myles. "What the fuck, man?"

"Answer his question," Myles threatened.

"Jack!" he hollered.

Brodie bit back a chuckle. His friend was a little bloodthirsty.

"What do you want to know?"

"What were you doing in the bar?" Declan asked.

"Minding my own damn business...ow!" He yelled. He tried pulling away from Iker and Myles. He glared at Iker who grinned back at him.

"Keep being a smart-ass and I'll break this fucking arm," Iker threatened.

If possible, Jack lost all coloring in his face. Iker may joke around, but he was quite scary when he wanted to be. Jack swallowed hard and turned back to face the two sergeants.

"Now I'm going to ask you another question. Why were you meeting with Diego Cruz?" Mac asked. This time he was directly in front of Jack.

Brodie folded his arms, opening and closing his hand. He grimaced, feeling the skin burn. He was sure it was going to be purple and blue come morning.

"Aw, fuck. Are y'all Narcs?" His eyes were wide and frantic.

No one answered.

"Okay, okay." Jack continued, "Fuck, they're going to kill me anyway for the information I gave him."

"What was that?" Brodie asked, rolling his eyes. They would be here all night with the way Jack was answering the questions.

"If I tell you, will you put me in protective custody?" Jack swung around and looked at Mac.

"Who said we were cops?" Mac asked.

"Fuck," Jack swore. He stopped struggling against Myles and Iker, apparently defeated. "Fine. He wanted to know the whereabouts of some woman."

"What's her name?" Dec demanded. Apparently, he was losing control of his patience as well.

"Um…Lupa."

Brodie's gaze met Mac's.

Now they were getting somewhere.

"Where is she?" Mac asked.

"She's Demon Lords property, and I like I told Diego, there's no taking her back. She has a debt to work off, and they will get it from her."

The air grew tense. It was like an unspoken taunt.

SWAT was the best at what they did, and if someone needed rescuing, they were the team to do it.

14

"God, why?" Ronnie groaned. She rested her hands on the toilet seat and prayed that the wave of nausea would pass. It was late, and the second she got home, she had raced to the bathroom.

She had been doing well with only throwing up a few times. Tonight, she didn't know if it was something she ate at work or if it was the pregnancy.

Flushing the toilet, she stood and moved to her sink, turning the faucet on. She leaned down, cupping her hands to gather water. She brought it to her lips and sucked it in to try to rinse out her mouth. The sour taste was not pleasant.

"At least I made it," she muttered. She picked up her bottle of Listerine and rinsed her mouth out, preferring the mint flavor to vomit. Peeling out of her scrubs, she dropped them on the floor and walked over to the shower.

She opened the drawer of her vanity and took out her shower cap to cover her hair. Once the water was a tolerable temperature, she got in.

"This has been one crazy day." She had started her shift off working in the Intensive Care Unit before having to float to the Emergency Department. They were short, and multiple traumas had come in.

The gang violence in the city was on the rise again. Many gunshot wounds, stabbings, and even victims of a huge car wreck on the highway came in tonight. Ronnie had never run to the time clock so fast when it was time for her to leave.

The warm water trailed down her body. She stood underneath it, allowing it to pound on her shoulders. Her hand slid down and skimmed along her little pudge.

She smiled, trying to imagine what her baby was going to look like. Thoughts of the baby always brought a warm sensation through her body and helped pushed down the stressful shifts at the hospital.

"Tomorrow, Mommy's family will be meeting Daddy's family." She grinned, unable to contain her excitement. Her parents and siblings were suspicious about coming to her home. She'd finally spilled to them that she was seeing someone. It had been a long time since she had introduced someone to her family. Her previous relationship lasted less than a year. He was a nice guy, but it felt forced to her.

Ronnie wanted to find someone where everything was natural between her and him.

You have that with Brodie.

Grabbing her loofah, she lathered it up with her shower gel and began washing her tired body.

If she had to list everything she would want in a man, Brodie would check off practically every box.

She was going to have to protect her heart. Everything was going perfect, and she didn't want to jinx anything. Luck hadn't been on her side in the past when it came to love. This time, she just prayed things with Brodie would go further.

"Well, the cart is already before the horse." She chuckled, running her soapy hand along the swell of her belly.

She quickly finished bathing and rinsed off. A few minutes later, she was wrapped up in her warm thick towel and laid across her bed. Her gaze landed on her e-reader that was fully charged and her cell phone.

She hadn't heard from Brodie since she had called him on her lunch period. She was missing him something fierce and had decided to call him.

Now that heaviness was back in her heart.

She needed to hear his voice.

Hope I'm not turning into a clingy pregnant woman, she laughed.

Before she could even pick up the phone, it rang.

Giggling, she snatched it up. "Hello?"

"God, you sound sexy as hell," Brodie breathed.

Ronnie giggled, lying back on her pillows. *Look at that. Think him up, and he calls.*

If only he'd shown up at her door.

Would that have been too much to ask?

"And I'm not even trying," she bragged. She rolled over to her side, thankful the nausea had moved on. It would not be sexy if she started throwing up while on the phone with him.

"You wouldn't even need to."

"Long night?" she asked. Glancing at the clock, she saw it was going on one in the morning. She wasn't sure how long she had been in the bathroom.

"Yeah, I wasn't sure you were up. Guess I was taking a chance. I'm just now seeing what time it is." He laughed.

"That's okay. I'm still up."

'Is something wrong?" he asked, concern lining his voice.

"Oh, just the things that comes along with pregnancy." She groaned. She bit her lip, unsure if he would want to hear about her visit to the porcelain throne.

"Like what? Is there something you need?"

Ronnie smiled. Of course he was worried. She was going to have to get used to the fact that she was not as alone as she thought she would be.

"Let's just say the second I walked through the door, my tummy decided to evict everything I ate at work this evening," she replied with a dry chuckle.

"If you need me to, I can stop by the store and get you—"

"I'm fine. Seriously, I am. Nothing a hot shower couldn't fix."

"You sure about that?" His voice dropped low, sending a tremor through her body.

Tucking the corner of the towel to make sure it stayed secured, she wished he was there to unwrap her like an early Christmas gift.

"Oh, I don't know. It would be nice to have someone here to cuddle with. Hold me throughout the night."

"Is that so?"

"Yup," she whispered, closing her eyes.

"Well, why don't you come open your front door."

Ronnie sat straight up and scooted to the edge of the bed. She didn't want to sound too excited. She cleared her throat, her feet resting on the floor.

"Don't play with me," Ronnie warned. It would be cruel to get her hopes up and he not be there. She pushed off the bed and rushed over to her closet. She pulled out a silky robe she had and wrapped it around herself then hung her towel up in the bathroom.

"Babe, come open the door."

Ronnie took off running through her house. A giggle escaped her.

She had officially lost her mind.

Arriving at the front door, she pressed against it and tried to manage her breathing. When had she got this out of shape to be out of breath? She peered out the peephole and found him standing on the other side of the door.

Ronnie opened it, her lips curving into a smile. Brodie turned around, his gaze sweeping her body. The neighborhood was quiet, the only sound a single car passing by.

Her nipples beaded into tight buds at the chill in the atmosphere and the heat of his gaze.

He pushed his way inside, slamming the door shut behind him.

"We received a call that cuddle services were needed?" A lopsided grin appeared on his lips.

"Yes, Officer. I called." She raised her hand, easily sliding into character. If he wanted to play games, she was all for it. "I didn't even know the Columbia Police Department offered these types of services."

Ronnie backed into her home, her heart racing. The predatory gleam in his eyes had her breaths coming short and her core growing slick with need.

How could one man draw this type of response from her?

Gone was the memory of her episode in the bathroom. All she could think about was getting this man into her bed.

"Oh, yes. We aim to please and serve our community." He peeled out of his shirt and toed off his boots. The jeans went next, creating a nice little pile of clothes on the floor. He was left in his black cotton briefs that did nothing to hide the raging erection tenting the material.

"Well, I'm glad you came so fast." Ronnie

reached for the tie of her robe and undid it. The soft material drifted off, sliding down her arms.

Brodie stalked to her, scooping her into his arms, and began to make his way to her bedroom. Their laughter echoed through the air.

He carefully laid her down on her mattress, then stepped back, his eyes taking her fully in. At that moment, Ronnie felt beautiful.

He shoved off his briefs, his cock standing erect from him. Ronnie licked her lips, unconsciously staring at it.

"Don't lick you lips like that if you aren't planning to do anything with them," he growled, kneeling onto the bed.

"Oh, I have plans already, Officer Gipson." She chuckled.

Waving him over to her, she sat up on her elbows. He crawled over, but she was able to take him by surprise and pushed him down on the bed. She straddled his waist and propped her hands on the pillow either side of his head.

"Is that so?" His eyebrows rose high.

"I do," she replied haughtily, pressing her lips to his.

He relinquished control and allowed her to

explore his mouth with her tongue. She stoked his softly while the kiss deepened.

Wanting to kiss and taste every inch of him, she trailed kisses along his scruffy jawline where his beard was breaking through, down to his neck. She continued on down to his chest, to his abdomen where she traced each ridge of muscles with her tongue.

"Had I known this was what you were needing, I would have been waiting here for you when you got off work," he muttered.

She grinned, continuing on her journey.

When her mouth reached his cock, she stole a look at him. He was watching her intently, heat flaring in his eyes. Ronnie wrapped her hand around the base of his member. A strangled groan rumbled from him.

Slowly, she ran her hand along the length of him. He was soft yet hard at the same time. A lone plump vein was visible along the shaft.

"Maybe you should have been."

He choked out a laugh that was quickly silenced the second her lips curved around the mushroom head. Tracing her tongue around it, she tasted the salty precum that had beaded on the tip.

Releasing him, she stroked the tip of him with her tongue, his body jerking underneath her touch.

"Ronnie," his deep voice vibrated through his body.

Ignoring him, she fisted the base of him and guided him back into her mouth. This time she took as much as she could before withdrawing. She repeated her action, suckling him farther inside.

His groan was louder this time.

She took her time licking and sucking his glorious dick. It was one to be worshipped, and she was enjoying every minute of it.

Her body heated as she watched him. She sucked harder, loving how his eyes were now closed, his hands fisting her sheets while his breaths were shallow and rapid.

She moved up and down on him faster, using her hands in tandem. His one hand shot out, and he entwined his fingers in her hair.

That sent an electrical current straight to her core.

Pleasuring her man was turning her on in a way she never thought could happen. The apex of her thighs was slick with her desire coating her thighs.

His groans and grunts were growing louder. The girth of him seemed to expand.

Ronnie moaned, and Brodie's eyes snapped open.

"Come here," he growled, reaching for her.

He dragged her up the length of his body, positioning her over him. The tip of him nudged her slick lips, and Ronnie didn't hesitate, impaling herself with his cock.

Their simultaneous groans filled the air.

She continued until she was fully seated on him. A sigh escaped her at the familiar sensation of him spreading her wide. Her body clenched around him, eliciting a grunt from him.

Brodie settled his hands on her waist and guided her up and down on him. His hips thrust up hard, sending him deeper.

Ronnie couldn't hold back her cries of ecstasy.

His hips were on a mission.

He pulsed hot and deep inside her.

Brodie's look of determination almost did her in. Her hands clenched the pillows while she threw back her head, allowing him to control everything.

There was nothing for her to do but to hold on for the ride of her life.

"Oh God," she called out.

"Ronnie," he gasped.

His fingers slipped between her slick folds and

connected with her clit. A few strokes, and she detonated.

Her scream pierced the air. Hot white lightning raced through her body. Brodie's roar joined her as he filled her with his release.

Ronnie collapsed onto his chest, spent. Sweat coated her entire body, but she didn't care. Slight tremors still made their way through her as she lay sprawled across Brodie.

Brodie's strong arms closed around her. He, too, was out of breath, his semi-soft cock still snug inside her. She didn't want to move—ever.

She let out a sigh, her body now feeling like wet noodles.

"Babe?" Brodie's warm breath caressed her face.

"Hmmm?" She didn't even have the strength to lift her head.

"I didn't hurt you or the baby, did I?"

"Only the good kind of hurt." She chuckled.

A deep rumble vibrated his chest. "Really?"

"Yes. You can put this type of hurt on me anytime," she joked.

A cry escaped her when he flipped them over, resulting with her on her back and Brodie hovering over her.

"Is that so?" he asked, dropping a kiss on her chin.

He trailed openmouthed kisses along her jawline and down to the crook of her neck. Her head fell to the side to give him access.

Her eyes grew wide.

Was he getting hard again?

"Um, you're ready so soon?" Her question came out breathless.

Brodie leaned back and grinned at her. He entwined their fingers and raised her arms over her head. He laughed, leaning down and capturing her left breast with his lips. A moan slipped from her; she was unable to believe he was ready to go for round two already.

Ronnie cried out from the one thrust. Brodie's lips curled up into his sexy grin.

"I told you, we aim to please and serve."

15

"This is the day we've been waiting for," Mac's hard voice broke through Brodie's thoughts.

The air held a slight chill in it. According to the weatherman, it should be warming up to the seventies.

Brodie narrowed his gaze on his opponent. Jordan didn't back down. She folded her arms in front of her with a scowl on her face.

"These two fine SWAT officers will run the gauntlet. Both are in tip-top shape," Myles called out.

The entire team was present. No one would miss this. Even a few others from the precinct who were present on the training grounds came over to watch the event.

It was widely known how hard the SWAT team trained and how well they played.

Today was more on the line than newbie versus experienced.

This was woman versus man, and there was no way Brodie was going to lose to a woman.

He loved the female gender, believed they could do anything they set their minds to, but today would not be the day of one being victorious.

"You're going down, Gipson," Jordan promised.

"Oooh!" the team snickered and laughed.

Brodie bit back a laugh and raised a single eyebrow.

"Not a chance, Knight." He shook his head. He was confident in his abilities of completing the obstacle course. He'd won when he was the newbie, and he wasn't planning on losing today.

"Yo! Don't think this is going down without me," a familiar voice shouted.

Brodie looked over and took in Ash walking toward them with a wide grin on his face.

He made it to the team, fist bumping and hugging them all.

"How's father duty treating you?" Declan asked, slapping Ash on the back.

"Let's just say, I'd rather face down bad guys with

guns than hear Evan's screaming in the middle of the night." Ash was all smiles and looked good. Fatherhood definitely suited him.

Brodie felt a small twinge of jealousy but brushed it off. He didn't have long to go. Soon he would be welcoming his child with Ronnie.

"Hope it's not making you go soft," Brodie bantered when Ash made his way to him.

They hugged, laughing as they stepped away from each other.

"I could still whip your ass on this track." Ash pointed to him before making his way to the rest of the team.

Once the excitement of having their missing teammate join them settled down, Myles waved his hands to garner everyone's attention.

"Let me explain for those of you watching," Myles said.

They stood before the course that was designed based on military basic training.

It was reminiscent of his days in boot camp and having to run the obstacle until he was throwing up. His sergeants then were hard-asses and loved torture. That basic form of torture helped shape Brodie into the man he was today.

For the course, Brodie and Jordan were dressed

identical, both in long-sleeved black SWAT t-shirts, black cargo pants, and matching shitkickers.

The gauntlet wasn't for tryouts. It was designed for the experienced SWAT officer. They had to be at the top of their game and drew from military training to stay in top shape.

"These two fine SWAT officers will have to tackle the wall, cargo net crossover, balance beam, and monkey bars just to name a few," Myles explained. He spun around and faced Brodie and Jordan. "Are you ready, Officers?"

"Yes, sir," Jordan confirmed.

"Yes, sir," Brodie echoed.

"Well, all right then. Officers, get to the starting point," Mac barked.

Brodie stepped forward and offered his fist. Jordan smirked and met it with hers.

"Good luck," he offered.

"Is something you'll need." Jordan laughed, walking away.

Brodie scoffed, staring after her.

"All right now, Brodie. Show them how we do it," Myles said, coming over to him and slapping him on the back. "Make them see how great the men in green are."

"Hooah!" Brodie yelled.

"Hooah!" Myles shouted alongside him.

They followed the group over to the starting point. Brodie glanced over to the fence surrounding the course. There were a group of females shooting and cheering for Jordan. Squinting, he recognized them from the precinct. Some of them were from patrol, plus a few detectives, all showing up to support their fellow officer.

He chortled at their signs and antics to cheer her on.

"Where the hell are my signs?" he hollered over to the guys.

"I left mine at the house," Iker yelled back.

"My dog ate mine," Zain shouted, nudging Iker.

"You don't have a damn dog." Brodie laughed.

"Well, I'll be damned. Look who showed up." Declan pointed to a black unmarked sedan parking near the fence.

Captain Spook stepped from the vehicle. The hardnosed captain was a man no one on the force wanted to cross. Brodie and his fellow team members had a standing reservation on his shit list. Another man walked alongside him. Brodie paused.

Shit.

The mayor.

"I didn't do it," Brodie muttered, resting his hands on his waist.

The captain and mayor strolled across the greenery toward them.

"I was at home all night, last night." Jordan gave a strangled cough.

Brodie glanced at her and smiled.

Yup, she fits right in.

"Morning, men and ladies," Captain Spook called out.

"Morning," they all echoed.

"Don't mind us. We are just coming to observe this fine tradition of breaking in the new member." Captain Spook tittered. His features softened. He walked over to where Myles stood before his gaze landed on Ash. "Frasier, when did you return back to duty?"

"I'm not, sir. Couldn't miss out supporting my fellow teammates." Ash grinned.

Spook nodded to him as the mayor stepped forward with a short wave. Mayor Kennedy was a stocky African-American man who was the poster child for a politician. Tailored suit, clean-cut hair, and a bright smile.

Brodie didn't buy that friendly grin at all. Politicians didn't bode well with him. Brodie couldn't stand smooth-talking public figures who were like Dr. Jekyll and Mr. Hyde.

If he was here, it was for a reason.

"Good morning. Pretend as if I'm not here. It's been a while since I've been to your training facility." Mayor Kennedy glanced around. He wore a sweater over a button-down shirt, and dark slacks. "During our meeting this morning, your captain had nothing but great things to say about your team. Good luck to the two competitors."

Brodie and the others relaxed. He gave a nod to the mayor before turning his attention back to the matter at hand.

"Let the competition be fair and may the best man or woman win," Myles proclaimed. He, too, was dressed the same as Jordan and Brodie.

Myles reached for the whistle hanging around his neck. Brodie's muscles tensed, waiting for the shrill sound.

The others would jog along beside them, encouraging them as they ran the course. The competition may be between Jordan and Brodie, but this was all about teamwork.

He braced, bending at the knees to prepare to take off. He relaxed his body, ready to go. He kept his eyes straight, not looking at Jordan who he was sure was just as focused.

The whistle sounded.

Brodie sprinted toward the first obstacle.

The tires.

He blew out a deep breath, taking the tires one foot at a time. Thankfully, he was coordinated, each foot landing inside each tire before moving on to the next.

"Let's go, Gipson!" Declan shouted, jogging alongside him.

"Pick up pace, Knight!" Mac barked from the other side of Jordan.

Brodie finished the tires and raced on.

Up next, the balance beam.

He glanced over and found Jordan hanging with him.

"Push it, Knight," Ash yelled out, jogging with them.

A grunt escaped him as he ran up the plank that led to the large wood beam. Carefully, he tiptoed across. His arms went out to help him maintain his balance, and he raced across. He skated down the descending steps, not pausing.

They reached the monkey bars at the same time. He leaped into the air, swinging from bar to bar.

Falling from the last rung, he kept going, pushing himself.

Brodie didn't have to look over to see that Jordan was keeping up.

The girl has heart.

"She's keeping up with you, Gipson. Show her what Army tough means," Myles shouted.

The high wall was next.

Brodie didn't hesitate when jumping toward it. He gripped the handholds, allowing him to pull himself up. His boots pushed off on the holds as he crawled up the wall. Once at the top, he straddled it before leaping down.

He landed on the ground with a thud while Iker and Zain encouraged Jordan to get up the wall.

Shit, I'm going to feel that in the morning.

Jordan was still on the other side. He sprinted to the next circuit.

The cargo net crossover. It was a series of ropes crisscrossed that he would need to crawl over and not fall through.

Every time he ran this course, memories of his Army bootcamp came to mind. The camaraderie, the hard work, and the show of strength was something he gained from the Army, and today, as a member of SWAT, he received the same.

"Don't think you left me behind, Gipson," Jordan shouted.

Brodie jumped, looking over at her.

"It took you long enough, Knight," he taunted. He picked up speed, leaving her in his dust. He arrived at the cargo net and crawled up the wooden stairs and immediately gripped the ropes with his hands.

This took certain skill to balance on the ropes with his hands, feet, and keep his body centered where he didn't fall through the ropes.

Sweat poured down his face, dropping into his eyes. He blinked to clear his vision. After this, they had one more circuit.

"Shit," Jordan cursed.

"Don't give up, Knight," Iker and Zain hollered, arriving at the side of the nets.

"Gipson, move!" Mac shouted.

Mac, Declan, and Myles walked alongside clapping and hollering, while Zain, Iker, and Ash were cheering Jordan on.

This was why he loved SWAT so much.

Brodie tumbled down over the net and hit the ground.

"Shit," he breathed.

"Get up, Gipson. One more. You can do it!" Mac

bellowed.

Brodie pushed off the ground just when Jordan landed beside him. They took off, racing to the large tubes they would have to crawl through. Brodie arrived, dropping to his knees, and proceeded to crawl as fast as he could through the ribbed tunnels. They weren't meant for someone of his height, so he had to keep his head down.

His teammates could be heard outside the tubes giving their encouragement.

Breaking through his, he glanced over at Jordan as she emerged at the same time.

They took off toward the finish line.

It came down to speed and endurance.

Right at the last moment, Jordan had a burst of speed with a battle cry escaping her.

She pushed ahead and beat him by a hairsbreadth.

The women on the sidelines went wild, jumping and screaming.

Brodie's breathing was rapid. He braced his hands on his knees, trying to draw breath into his lungs while watching her dance in place.

He smiled.

There wasn't a sore loser bone in his body.

His sister in blue beat him fair and square.

The team surrounded her, hugging and slapping her on her back.

He shook his head. They had completely forgotten about him.

Standing erect, he walked over to the crowd and pushed his way through.

"Let me at her," he playfully growled.

Jordan spun around to face him. Her hair was damp with sweat while a wide grin was in place.

"Congratulations, sis." He held out a hand.

She took it, and he drew her in for a hug.

"Thanks, Gipson." She stepped back and jogged a few paces toward the women along the fence. "Black girls rock!"

"We all can't win." Ash patted Brodie on the back.

"Can't believe you lost to a girl," Myles joshed, ruffling his hair.

Brodie knocked his hands away. His team would never let him live this down.

"Congratulations, Officer Knight," Captain Spook said. He arrived with the mayor.

Both men were all smiles.

"I can see what the captain has been saying about your team. I wish all teams and departments were as close as you. Good job," Mayor Kennedy said.

Jordan strolled over to them.

"Thank you, sir," Mac replied.

They all echoed the same sentiment.

"Now, I'm sure you are wondering why I'm here," the mayor said.

All joking and smiles disappeared. There was always a hidden agenda when it came to the mayor.

He looked each of them in the eye. "The war on crime is getting harder to beat. Your team has been an extreme asset for the city. We thank you. But crime is on the rise, and I won't stand for it in my town so I have created a task force that I want SWAT to participate in."

"There will be more details coming as soon as everything is ironed out," Captain Spook added.

The two gave final waves before walking back to the sedan. They waited until the captain and mayor were back at the car then faced each other.

"Task force?" Zain asked quietly.

"What the fuck have I missed?" Ash asked.

"Plenty. We'll have to bring you back up to speed," Mac responded. He glanced over his shoulder, apparently waiting for the captain's car to drive off. Once it was gone, he turned back to the group.

"We're going to have to act soon. I don't know what the hell this task force is, but I don't like the sound of it."

Brodie released a grunt.

He didn't either.

16

"I just want everything to be perfect." Ronnie flew around tinkering with everything. The food had been delivered and set up in her kitchen. She double-checked the warmers to make sure they were still lit.

For the fifth time.

She was a nervous wreck.

This was the first step with Brodie, and she wanted his family to love her and hers to love him. She was already sure her family would like him. He had a career, a good head on his shoulders, and had a sense of humor that would blend in with her father and brother.

"Stop worrying." Brodie's strong arms closed

around her. He pulled her back to him and nuzzled his face into the crook of her neck.

Ronnie leaned back into his embrace, a smile playing on her lips. The feeling of his hardness pressed against her had her core clenching.

"But, I want to make sure—"

"If your family is anything like you, then I know we will get along just fine," Brodie said, his lips brushing along her skin.

Her heart fluttered at the sensation of his warm breath.

Ronnie spun around in his arms, a grin on her face. She stood on her tiptoes to wrap her arms around his neck.

"How are you so confident?" she asked.

He cupped the side of her face. Ronnie leaned it to his palm as he gently stroked her cheek with his thumb.

"Because there is no way my parents and brothers won't be as captivated with you as I am," he murmured. Brodie bent down and took her lips in the sweetest kiss.

She sagged into him, a moan slipping from her.

The doorbell sounded, breaking into her lust-driven fog.

Dammit.

Her gaze landed on his lips, and she blew out a sigh. Now was not the time to wonder if they had a few minutes to steal away for a quickie.

She looked up and smiled.

"It's going to be fine," he promised again.

Brodie entwined their fingers together and led her through the house to the front door. She was impressed by how cool and collected he was.

But then again, he was a SWAT officer and ran head-first into danger every day.

Meeting your girlfriend's parents for the first time must be a walk in the park for him.

Girlfriend.

Just the word brought a smile to her. Ronnie slid her hand down to her tummy.

Brodie opened the door revealing her parents, brother, and sister.

"Hey, y'all," Ronnie exclaimed. She released him when they walked through the door. She flew into her father's embrace. "Daddy, how are you?"

"I'm good, pumpkin." He laughed. He gave her a good squeeze before letting her go.

"Are you sure you didn't want us to bring anything? I can't fathom coming over for a gathering empty-handed," Jackie complained.

"I don't know about you, but I brought wine." Her sister, Rowan, giggled.

"Wino," her brother, Junior, muttered, shaking his head.

"I'm sure. We took care of everything," Ronnie replied.

The foyer grew silent as all eyes landed on Brodie. He had stayed back, allowing her to greet her family. She turned and tried to see him as her family probably did.

Tall, muscular. His dark hair was pushed back away from his face, but a few strands fell forward. He was dressed in a casual button-down, the sleeves folded up showcasing his forearms, and jeans.

Her sister nudged her with her elbow.

"Oh, look at me. Where are my manners?" Ronnie giggled again. She walked over to Brodie and wrapped an arm around his.

Brodie pulled her in close, tucking her possessively into his side.

She couldn't wipe the grin from her face. "Mom, Dad, Rowan, and Junior, this is Brodie Gipson. My boyfriend."

"Hello, everyone." Brodie nodded.

"Brodie, this is Ornell Sr., Jackie, Rowan, and

Junior." Ronnie waved to each member of her family.

Brodie moved forward, shaking hands with them. Their laughter filled the air, allowing Ronnie to relax.

Rowan glanced over at her and tossed her a wink.

Ronnie already knew she was in for a quizzing by her younger sister. They hadn't had a good chat in a while.

Her parents laughed at something Brodie said.

"So, this is why you've been super busy?" her sister murmured, walking over to her.

Rowan may be a few years younger than her, but they resembled each other. She, too, had deep-brown skin and long dark hair even though she kept it highlighted with bright colors. This month's color of choice appeared to be red.

"Yes and no," Ronnie said. "Work has been crazy. They've been calling us in for overtime."

"I'm so sure you're pulling in overtime with Mister Tall and Handsome." Rowan smirked. She leaned in closer. "Please tell me he has a brother."

Ronnie grinned. "He sure does. Two of them."

Rowan's eyes grew wide before turning back

toward Brodie who was chatting it up with her parents and brother.

"Come on in. Why are we standing here in the foyer?" Ronnie asked. She waved everyone into the house. She bit her lip. Her parents were the easy part. Soon, his parents would be arriving.

"I told you, everything is going to work itself out," Brodie said. He tugged her to him now they were the only two in the front of the house.

"I know." She rolled her eyes. Of course he would be right. "I'm not worried about my parents, it's yours." She softly hit him on his right pectoral muscle. It was solid and firm. "Ow."

He took her hand in his and pressed a kiss to it. Ronnie's heart stuttered, and she stared up into his clear blue eyes.

"I swore my parents to secrecy, and they are going to act just as surprised as everyone else," Brodie said.

"All right." Ronnie tried to hold back a smile, but she couldn't even be mad at him. He was too cute, and his excitement was heartwarming. "I just don't want my family finding out yours knew first."

They were interrupted by the doorbell again. Ronnie froze.

Brodie grinned and pressed a kiss to her forehead before returning to the door. Ronnie stood back as he opened it. She instantly knew the man and woman entering the house were his parents.

His father was an older image of Brodie, and his mother shared the same blue eyes.

After hugs, the woman brushed past Brodie and went straight to Ronnie.

"You must be Ronnie," she exclaimed. She wrapped Ronnie up in a tight hug. "I'm Teri, and this here is my husband, Heath. Our other sons are still outside on the porch."

Ronnie smiled. One look into Teri's friendly gaze, and she relaxed.

"Welcome to my home, Mr. and Mrs. Gipson," she said.

"Oh, please. You can call me Heath." Brodie's father reached out and tugged her in for a big hug.

Ronnie was all smiles when she stepped back. "What are they doing out there?"

"Not sure. Zayden spotted a car with a man parked across the street. I reckon those boys of mine are checking it out." Heath ushered Ronnie and Teri toward the living room. "I'm sure they won't be long. I'm starving."

Ronnie led them inside to meet with her family, but curiosity was blossoming in her chest.

What was going on outside?

"DID YOU GET THE LICENSE PLATE?" Brodie asked Zayden as they carried dishes into the kitchen. He hadn't had a chance to ask his brother once they had entered the house when he'd arrived.

"Yeah, I took a picture of the car. I'll text it to you," his brother replied.

The gathering was going well. Their two families were getting along perfectly. When his family arrived, a dark sedan had been parked across the street.

As soon as he and his brothers focused their attention on it, the car suddenly took off down the road. Brodie was unable to see who was inside the vehicle, but it left him feeling uneasy.

There was a lot going on in the city with the gangs, and knowing he and his team were about to be right in the middle of it, he had to take certain precautions.

It was more than just him and his parents.

Now he had Ronnie and their unborn child to think about.

When he got a moment, Brodie was going to run

the tags. It just didn't sit right with him that someone could potentially be following him or watching Ronnie's house.

His brother, Zayden, was a sergeant with the K9 Unit of Columbia Police Department. He was the eldest of the Gipson brothers. He had joined the police academy right out of college and had worked with the K9 unit for the last six years. He was always an animal lover, and it was no surprise to any of them that he'd joined this particular division. His partner, Duchess, was a German Shepherd who was like an extension of the family.

She had been invited to the gathering, too, and was lying in the corner of the dining room.

"Thanks," Brodie said. He tossed some of the empty containers into the trash before heading over to the sink to wash his hands.

"So you and Ronnie?" Zayden set the empty plates on the counter near him. He leaned against it, staring at Brodie. His brother didn't miss anything.

"Yeah."

"That's it? Just yeah?" Zayden's clear blue eyes bored into him.

Brodie shut off the water and flicked some onto his brother.

"Why? What are your spider senses telling you?"

Brodie laughed, drying his hands on a few paper towels.

His brother was never patient. Even growing up, he couldn't never wait for anything. There were plenty of years around Christmas they would all get in trouble because of Zayden trying to figure out what presents were his and what was under the tree.

"Not sure. I think it's more than y'all just wanting the family to meet."

"What are you pansies in here talking about?" Anders entered the kitchen.

The Gipson brothers were all tall, muscular, and had the same blue eyes they had inherited from their mother. It was the only thing they received from her; all of their features were their father.

Anders may be the middle child, but he was the biggest of them. Thanks to working as a firefighter, he was pure muscle. He kept his hair a little longer than Zayden and Brodie.

"Trying to find the motive of today's gathering." Zayden shrugged.

"Motive?" Anders laughed. He came over and slapped Brodie on the shoulder. "Can he ever turn it off?"

"Apparently not." Brodie grinned, knowing his brother would not let it rest until he got answers.

That's what made him one of the best cops on the force. "Anyway, I was sent in here to see what was taking you so long. Ronnie is asking for the chocolate cake to be brought in there."

"And she picked you to come in here after us?" Zayden asked, his eyebrows rising high.

"Well, I might have volunteered when she said cake." Anders grinned. It was no secret that he had a sweet tooth. He worked out enough that he could indulge in the sweets he loved.

Brodie shook his head at his brothers. They were close, and he couldn't believe he hadn't told them yet.

He wouldn't.

He had already blabbed to his parents.

"Cake is over there."

They went back into the dining room where everything was going well. Dinner had gone well, too. Laughter, great conversation, and delicious food was just what they all needed.

Anders was on cake duty, volunteering to cut it.

"You outdid yourself, sis." Rowan groaned, taking a bite of her slice of cake.

"This is one of my favorite places to order food. We get them to cater at work for special occasions," Ronnie said.

"We do, too," Anders said, having passed out the last slice. He took his seat at the table. "The fire station is always ordering from this same restaurant."

Brodie sat next to Ronnie and took her hand in his. He lifted it to his lips and pressed a kiss to it. Ronnie's lips curved up into a small smile. She gave a slight nod.

"Can I have everyone's attention?" Brodie cleared his throat.

He hadn't released Ronnie's hand. They threaded their fingers together. The room fell quiet. He glanced around the room and took in the twinkle in his mother's eyes.

She was in love with Ronnie.

Every chance she got to pull him to the side, she gushed nonstop about Ronnie.

All eyes fell on him. He glanced over at Ronnie who smiled at him. She blew him a kiss.

"I'm sure you're wondering why we wanted to get everyone together today," he began and sat back and figured he'd better just blurt it out. He didn't have a fancy way with words. "Ronnie and I are expecting."

The room exploded with laughter and screams.

He leaned over and pressed a kiss to Ronnie's

lips before she was pulled away by her mother and sister.

He laughed, settling back in his chair. The men in the room were all smiles.

"I think I saw a few beers in the fridge. This calls for a drink," Ornell Sr. announced. He pushed back from the table and disappeared into the kitchen. "Junior, come help."

"Sure, Pop." Junior strolled behind their father.

Ronnie had been sure her brother would find her stash she kept in the kitchen. There was plenty for them to choose from.

"I knew you were hiding something," Rowan screeched, hugging her sister tight.

Brodie glanced over at his father who smiled and nodded to him.

Everything was just as he'd said.

It would be all right.

The women were already gushing about gender reveals, shopping, and plans for the spare bedroom in Ronnie's house.

His gaze swept the room and went over to the living room. Night had fallen, but outside the window, lights flashed. The echoes of a door slamming broke the silence.

What the hell was that?

His smile disappeared from his lips. He stood up immediately. Two other chairs scraped along the floor, and he didn't have to look to know who was behind him.

"Duchess," Zayden commanded, calling for the German Shepherd.

Conversation stilled.

Brodie stalked to the front door with his brothers behind him. He peered out the window. His breath was snatched from his throat at the sight that met him.

A few figures boldly stood out on the lawn.

It wasn't the fact that they were standing on Ronnie's grass. It was the weapons in their hands pointed at the house.

17

"What's going on?" Ronnie looked at Heath. Her heart pounded. Something was wrong. Brodie and his brothers, along with Duchess, had stalked out of the dining room. She stood from the table, but Heath held his hand up.

"I'm sure whatever it is, my boys will take care of it," he said, pushing back from the table. He stood, his head turning to the front of the house where the Gipson brothers had disappeared.

"It's probably nothing," Teri murmured. She moved over to her husband with concern on her face.

That didn't help Ronnie's anxiety creeping into her chest.

"I thought we were celebrating?" Her father and

brother were all smiles returning to the room. They froze at the silence. Senior's smile disappeared when their eyes connected. "What's wrong?"

"I don't know. Something caused Brodie and his brothers to head to the front door." Ronnie brushed past her mother and Teri.

Rowan was instantly behind her as they walked into the living room. Brodie, Anders, and Zayden were deep in conversation with Duchess sitting patiently by them. "Brodie?"

He looked over at her. Whatever he and his brothers were discussing must have been intense. The three of them had the same expression.

Pissed off.

"I don't want you to freak out." Brodie walked over to her.

"I'm already there," she replied.

He rested his hands on her shoulders and pressed a kiss to her forehead. She was comforted by the warm feel of him next to her.

"I want you and your family to stay away from the windows," he murmured.

"What?"

"Go back into the dining room—"

"What is going on?" Her voice shook. Her hands balled his shirt up into a tight grip. Fear spread through her like she'd never know before. Her gaze flickered over to Anders and Zayden. She wasn't sure why, but the sight of Zayden with his gun in his hand with the dog posed next to him shook her.

He stalked over to the front door again and peered out the window.

She glanced back to Brodie whose mouth was set in a firm line. "Tell me."

"Look, there are some not so nice men standing out on your front lawn. I want you to take my phone and call Mac—"

"But, Brodie—"

"But nothing. I need you to do what I say." He squeezed her shoulders, his expression softening slightly. "Call Mac."

He handed her his cellphone, unlocking it with his thumb. Walking over to his brothers, he left her standing there with her mouth agape. He was giving instructions like a drill sergeant. Brodie was always laid back with a smile on his face. She'd never seen him like this. There was no joking. A seriousness had come over him, snatching the breath from her.

This wasn't her everyday Brodie. Now she saw the other side of him. This was who he was when he was out protecting the streets and facing danger.

He was a bad-ass SWAT officer.

With the hard glint in his eye, those men better think twice about confronting her man.

"Check out the back door and make sure it's secure," Brodie instructed.

"Sure thing," Anders said, with not a smile on his face. He marched past Ronnie and Rowan, heading into the dining room toward the kitchen.

"Come on, sis. I'm sure he knows what he's doing." Rowan tugged on her arm, snapping Ronnie out of her shock.

She followed behind her sister and found Mac listed in Brodie's contacts. She hit his name and placed her ear to the phone.

"Gipson, I thought you would be busy tonight?" Mac's familiar voice came on the line.

Even though it was hard, it was soothing to Ronnie. She was used to his granite persona but had seen the softer side of him with Sarena.

"Mac, it's Ronnie," she said. Ronnie hated how her voice shook. Brodie was calm and collected while she was a mess on the inside.

"Where's Brodie?" he asked, completely falling into the role of SWAT sergeant.

"He's in the front of my house with his brothers. He said something about three men outside on my front lawn and for me to call you." She blew out a deep breath. She leaned back against the wall and felt all eyes on her. She stared down at her feet, unable to meet their gazes.

"You did good. I'm on the way," he said.

Ronnie was sure Mac would break every speeding law there was to get here. She didn't live far from him and Sarena.

"I'm scared, Mac. I don't like the sound of this," she admitted.

Her sister took her free hand and entwined their fingers. Ronnie glanced over at Rowan whose eyes were wide with concern. Ronnie observed the room and found her parents and brothers sitting at the table. Her brother had already opened the bourbon and poured him and her father a drink. Heath and Teri were standing against the other wall. The room was silent while she spoke with Mac.

What had been a joyous occasion had turned solemn.

"You just told me that Brodie's brothers are there with him, so that's a plus. Just tell Brodie don't do anything stupid."

Ronnie drew in a strangled breath. She leaned over to see if Brodie was still in the house.

"Brodie," she called out.

"Yeah?"

"Mac said don't do anything stupid."

That earned some chuckles around the room.

"Tell him to get his ass here now," Brodie replied, his voice clipped.

"He said to get your ass here," she passed on the message.

"Sit tight, Ronnie. Do exactly what he says," Mac ordered.

She rolled her eyes at him.

He just couldn't stop being so bossy. "And Ronnie?"

"Yeah?"

"Congratulations."

"He told you?" she exclaimed softly. She couldn't believe it. Brodie was worse than a woman when it came to keeping secrets, apparently.

"No, Sarena told me."

"Oh." She should have known that Sarena wouldn't have been able to keep a secret. "Thanks, Mac."

"Don't worry. We're on our way."

The line went dead. Ronnie took the phone away from her ear and stared down at the device.

Who was the 'we'?

She was sure she already knew.

Knowing the guys, when one was in trouble, they all showed up.

"Is Sergeant MacArthur on the way?" Heath asked.

Ronnie jerked her head in a nod.

The Gipson relaxed slightly. "Well then, if the sergeant is on the way, I'm sure they all are coming."

"But who would be outside? Ronnie hasn't done anything to anyone?" Jackie asked. She reached for her husband's glass and downed the rest of his drink.

"I don't know, Momma," Ronnie replied. She couldn't think of anything that would warrant sending men to her house after her.

"It's not Ronnie." Heath walked over to the table and snatched up an empty glass. He poured himself a healthy bit of the dark liquor before continuing. "Brodie called the other day warning me and his brothers that some things were heating up at work."

"Like what?" Senior asked.

"Not sure exactly. He told us to watch our backs."

"The news has been filled about the gang war that is going on," Junior said. He looked around the table. "The police and the gangs are at war. The gangs are at war with each other, too. It's been a mess. Shootings, killings, and robberies have been on the rise."

"That is true. At least I can speak from experience at the hospital. Our emergency room has been bombarded lately." Ronnie squeezed Rowan's hand then released her. The hospital was offering overtime to help with the rise in admissions.

"But I'm sure the news doesn't cover everything," Jackie said.

"They don't." Teri blew out a deep breath. She tucked her blonde hair behind one ear and took a seat at the table. "I worry every day for all of my boys. One who runs into burning buildings, the other two chasing bad guys."

The tension in the room was palpable.

The sound of the front door drew Ronnie's attention. She moved to the doorway, her heart seeming to lodge in her throat watching Brodie step outside.

***

"BEAUTIFUL WEATHER WE'RE HAVING," Brodie announced, stepping onto the small porch.

The dark night sky was littered with a few stars. He had turned on the light to the porch before exiting the house. There was no point in standing inside. He needed to know who the hell was in the yard and what they wanted.

Zayden and Duchess trailed out the door behind him. The German Shepherd was well-trained. Her ears were erect, and her eyes were locked on the figures standing on the lawn.

"You Officer Gipson?" This one held a shotgun. He stepped forward, casually resting the weapon on his shoulder.

The three men were of average height, dressed in dark clothing. Brodie scanned the street and took in the SUVs parked haphazardly on the road. There may be only three men standing in front of him and Zayden, but there were more in the vehicles.

He was sure of it.

"Who wants to know?" Brodie asked.

Duchess growled low, as if giving her only warning. It would take one command from Zayden and she'd dart straight toward the targets.

The door opened, and Brodie didn't dare take his eyes off the men before them to see who it was. He just prayed Ronnie had followed his instructions, called Mac, and stayed safe inside. He couldn't worry about her safety with armed men standing on her property.

"All clear in the back," Anders murmured low.

"Junior's going to keep an eye out the kitchen window to make sure there are no surprises."

Brodie gave a slight nod to acknowledge his brother.

"A friend." The thugs chuckled, glancing at each other. Neither appeared to be bothered by the large German Shepherd growling even louder.

"I don't have any friends," Brodie snarled. He edged down the first step. He wasn't afraid of them at all. He had his Glock concealed in the back of his jeans and a pistol strapped to his ankle. Anders always carried, and Zayden sure as hell did. "What the hell are you doing here and what do you want?"

"Too bad you don't have friends." The leader stopped smiling. "Consider this a friendly warning."

"Of what?" Brodie's fingers itched to reach for his weapon, but doing so could be disastrous. There was no way in hell he could risk Ronnie's house getting shot up with their families inside.

"We've heard you been digging into some business that has nothing to do with you."

"Is that so?" Brodie folded his arms in front of his chest. He narrowed his eyes on the three. He wasn't going to confirm anything with them. He wanted them to talk and spill something unknowingly. "And what business is that?"

"He playing dumb, Spade," the bigger thug to the right muttered. He, too, held a shotgun, but he kept it trained on Brodie and his brothers.

"I say we light this little house up right now and get it over with." The man on the other side grinned.

Brodie had the strong urge to slam his fist into his face. There was no way he was going to let them start shooting up the house. Not with his family inside.

"I say you get in your vehicles and get the hell out of here," Zayden warned.

Duchess barked. Her low growls and whines continued. The poor girl was ready for action.

The ringleader held up his hand and shook his head.

"I'm sure Officer Gipson knows exactly what I'm talking about," he said. "Stop looking into Demon Lords' business. The girl is none of your concern."

Brodie kept his face neutral. So there was something about Cruz's sister.

Where in the hell was Mac?

"Well, see here's the thing, fellas." Brodie scratched the back of his head. "I've been known to be a little hardheaded and don't take too kindly to threats."

"We are really good with teaching lessons," the

leader sneered. "You don't want to tangle with the people who you—"

"I couldn't give a fuck about your little threats," Brodie cut him off.

Engines sounded as vehicles flew down the road. Brodie knew without looking who it was. Mac put out the call, and his teammates would be there.

The calvary had arrived.

It was about damn time.

Mac slammed the door of his truck. Declan came from the other side of his. Iker, Zain, Jordan, Myles, and even Ash stepped out of their rides. They blocked in the SUVs on the street. Even if the gang-bangers tried to make a run for it, their trucks would be pinned.

His team made one bad-ass vision. Dressed in all black with their badges around their necks.

The three gangsters found themselves surrounded.

"Is there a problem here?" Mac snarled. The expression on his face was one that would make the toughest son of a bitch turn tail and leave.

He, Declan, and Ash stood behind the three men, their weapons trained on them.

"Nope. No problem at all, Officer," the leader

said. He faced Brodie with a hard gaze. "We were just having a friendly conversation."

"Well then, we arrived just in time," Iker said.

He, Zain, Jordan, and Myles strolled by the other SUVs with their weapons raised.

"CPD. Hands on your head and step out of the vehicles," Zain ordered. The doors didn't open at first. "I'm going to say it one more time. Get the fuck out of the truck."

Seconds later, the doors opened, and men stepped out with their hands in the air.

Blue and white lights lit up the night sky as patrol cars flew down the street. They even brought the paddy wagon. Brodie grinned at his team. Called for one and the entire damn precinct showed up.

"Drop your weapons on the ground," Declan commanded the three.

They shared a look amongst them but did as they were told.

"On your knees with your hands on your head."

Duchess's barking and growls filled the air along with shouts and orders being thrown around.

"Heel, Duchess," Zayden instructed. The dog instantly went quiet.

"We'll be out of jail by morning," the leader murmured.

"Don't count on it, asshole." Brodie sniffed. He rested his hands on his waist, watching the scene unfold before him.

Six other men were apprehended and were being led to the wagon.

A patrol man came and placed the handcuffs on the three gangsters kneeling on the grass.

This was far too close to home.

Everyone he cared about was in that house. Had the thugs just fired upon them, someone could have been hurt, or killed.

18

"Love you," Ronnie mumbled, squeezing her father tighter.

He pulled back and stepped toward Brodie with his hand outstretched.

"Protect my little girl," Senior said.

"Always." Brodie shook his hand.

The police had finally taken the gangsters away and towed their vehicles, leaving her street quiet again. It was enough excitement to last forever. Her neighbors all came outside to see what the ruckus was. It was a little embarrassing, but Ronnie would get over it.

At least no one got hurt and the cops handled everything.

Now she was left with a house full of SWAT officers. A few were sprawled in the living room while someone was in the kitchen.

"Come on, Senior. It's been a long day, and I'm ready to go home." Her mother came over to her and wrapped her up in a tight embrace. "He's certainly a keeper, baby."

Ronnie smiled and returned the hug. "Thanks, Ma."

Her parents gave one last wave to everyone before walking out the door. Her brother and sister were standing on the driveway by her parents' car. The four of them had carpooled, her siblings having met at their parents' house.

Ronnie leaned against the open door and gave them a wave.

"I think we're going to head out, too." Teri stood from the couch and grabbed her purse.

"You call me if you need anything," Heath offered. He trailed behind Teri as she made her way to the front door. He patted each of his sons on the back in passing.

"Thank you for a wonderful meal. Your family is lovely," Teri said. A wide grin stretched across her face.

Ronnie laughed, being pulled in for another strong hug. She was smitten with Brodie's family.

Now after meeting them, she could see where he got his good looks and personality from.

"I'm going to follow them home and make sure they get there safely," Anders said, giving Brodie a manly hug. He stopped in front of Ronnie and hugged her also. He was like Brodie, dwarfing her with his height. "You watch out for my brother."

Ronnie stepped back and nodded. A lump formed in her throat. She wasn't sure what it meant, but she was sure she'd figure it out.

"Of course," she murmured.

He strode out of the house behind his parents. Brodie tugged her to him, wrapping an arm around her. They watched his parents and Anders walk over to their cars. Once they were in and driving away, he shut the door.

His body was tense, and she sensed there was a reason why his teammates were still there. Not that she minded, but the team had never been to her house. She'd been over Mac and Sarena's plenty of times and was familiar with them all.

Even Zayden and Duchess were still there.

"There's something you need to tell me?" she asked softly, looking up at him. Before they went back to their guests, she needed to know what was going on.

Brodie blew out a deep breath and tunneled his hand through his hair.

"I had hoped I wouldn't have to share work shit with you, but since it's made its way to you, there is a lot I have to tell you," he said.

"This has to do with that gang that kidnapped Sarena?" she asked. Fear crept into her chest.

From what Sarena had shared with her, this gang, the Demon Lords, were no joke. They had planned to sell Sarena into sex slavery. Her friend's description of the women who had been held against their will gave Ronnie nightmares for days. Lucky enough, Mac and the guys had been able to rescue her with Declan shooting and killing the leader.

"Yes, and I promise you they will not come anywhere near you," he vowed.

This was the most serious she had ever seen Brodie. She nodded, believing him. The stories she heard from them were impressive and at times hard to believe. They all sounded like something she'd see in movies.

"Come on. Let's go in the living room with the others."

They entered the living room where the entire team and Zayden and Duchess waited. Mac pushed off the wall where he was leaning and walked over to her and Brodie.

"You good?" he asked her.

"Just a little shaken up," she said. It wasn't every day she looked out her window and saw men with guns pointed at her home.

Brodie's arm tightened around her.

"So I'm taking it from the warning I got from my brother, you crazy sons of bitches are tangling with the Demon Lords again?" Zayden asked. He sat on the floor next to Duchess. The German Shepherd lay next to him with her head resting on his legs. Not too long ago, the dog was growling and barking trying to attack, now she was acting like a docile house dog.

Her living room once appeared roomy. Now it was snug with all of the members of Columbia's finest chilling there.

Brodie motioned for them to take the last seat on the couch. He pulled her onto his lap and wrapped an arm around her, resting his hand on her belly. She glanced at him and found his blue eyes on her. His hand spanned their child as if to protect it.

"Not sure how much your brother has shared with you, but anything discussed tonight is something we expect you to keep silent on," Mac began.

"Of course." Zayden nodded.

"There's been information leaked to the Demon Lords. Things they shouldn't know," Declan said.

"Shit," Zayden cursed.

"Things that shouldn't be easily accessible to just anyone. Confidential shit, and they've been a step ahead of us," Iker interjected. He walked in, carrying a plate of food. The team had made themselves at home. "And your little brother cracked who it is."

"It's an inside job?" Zayden's gaze flicked to Brodie.

"Yeah, and when we dug for a motive, we found one hell of one," Brodie said. His deep voice rumbled against her back. He tightened his grip on her.

"Have you confronted who it is?" Zayden looked around the room.

Ronnie was wondering the same thing. Her romantic suspense books she loved reading had nothing on the information she was hearing tonight.

Who needed books?

She was in the middle of an action-packed romance.

"The officer's sister is Demon Lords' property, and he's trying to pay off her debt to free her."

Ronnie stiffened.

Dear God. That poor woman.

Ronnie covered Brodie's hand with hers. She couldn't even imagine what the woman was going through.

But the cop giving away secrets, he must be desperate. Leaking information could get someone killed.

Every time she had taken care of the members of SWAT in the hospital, was that a result of his treachery?

"We all know what that means," Jordan, the only female member of the team, spoke up.

Ronnie hadn't really got to know her yet. Sarena had mentioned to her that the guys now had a woman on the team. Taking one look at Jordan, Ronnie could see she could easily hang with the boys with no problem.

"They are probably prostituting her out," Jordan said. "We are going to need to move in fast. She's not going to last much longer if they've had her for as long as we dug up."

"If you need help, you know the K9 unit will be down for whatever," Zayden offered.

Duchess raised her head and gave a yip as if to agree.

"Brodie, you may want to have Ronnie stay with

you for a few days. I don't like that the gang knows about her," Mac said.

Ronnie stiffened. Her gaze flew from Mac to Brodie who jerked his head in a nod.

"Wait, what do I have to do with anything?" she asked, confused. She didn't do anything, but a small voice in the back of her head told her to remember her BFF's situation. It wasn't about what Sarena did, but who she was involved with.

"Sorry to break it to you, Ronnie, but you will be guilty by association," Myles informed her.

Ain't that some shit.

"It sucks, Ronnie," Ash said. "They are going to know you're Brodie's woman—"

"Actually, they may not," Brodie interjected, cutting Ash off.

The room grew silent. Ronnie turned to him, still confused.

"Why wouldn't they?" Declan asked.

"They didn't see Ronnie. I wouldn't let her come to the door when those asshats were out in the yard," Brodie said.

"Remember the other day when we went to the Neon Nights, Cruz thought we were there on a date." Jordan snorted. The woman's lip curled up with disgust. "Let's just say he's lucky Brodie punched him before I got a chance."

Ronnie's eyes grew wide. She tried to imagine the woman beating up a fellow cop but had a hard time visualizing it. She was no taller than Ronnie.

"If we let him continue thinking that, then maybe that will keep Ronnie off the gang's radar," Zain suggested. He, too, had made himself a plate of food from the leftovers that were in the kitchen.

"They're onto something," Declan said. "If Cruz thinks Brodie and Jordan are together, then who are we to say any different. If he sics the Demon Lords on Jordan, then we know she will be able to handle herself."

Brodie nudged her to get her attention. "You okay with this plan?"

"Of course. I would hate to put Jordan in danger."

"Don't worry, Ronnie. They can come for me if they want." Jordan's cynical chuckle sent a chill down Ronnie's spine.

Oh, yeah. Jordan fit right in with the guys.

Brodie brought her close to him, his lips brushing her ear. "Pack a bag. You're going to be staying with me."

IT WAS late by the time Brodie and Ronnie arrived at his place. Ronnie appeared dead on her feet. He'd escorted her to the master bathroom where they had taken a shower.

Even with his cock fully erect, he didn't have it in his heart to take her in the shower. She tried to seduce him, but those little dark areas under her eyes held him back.

"I can't believe you turned me down," she mumbled, resting her forehead on his chest.

He ran the large soft towel along her body to dry her off.

"You are tired." He joked. He just needed to take care of her. Something on the inside of him had him in pure protective mode. It didn't sit right with him that the Demon Lords sent their flunkies to her house.

That was entirely too close.

He didn't just have him to worry about anymore. He had a woman and an unborn child to think of. Fear like he had never know had been weighing heavy in his chest.

"I am not." She leaned her head back to meet his

gaze. She'd had to fight to keep her eyes open in the shower as the warm water pounded on them.

She was one stubborn woman.

He wrapped the towel around her, tucking it in so it would stay in place.

"Come on, woman. Let me put you in the bed." He bent down and scooped her up into his arms.

"Hey, I can walk." She sniffed. Her arm came around his neck, and she nuzzled her face in the crook of his neck.

"Humor me." He chuckled. He entered the room and marched straight for the bed. He sat her down on the edge of the mattress and went over to his dresser. Taking a t-shirt out, he headed back to her and removed the towel.

"I can dress myself," she mumbled as he brought the shirt over her head.

Brodie didn't know why, but the urge to take care of her and keep her near him was strong. He pulled back the covers and assisted her in. He removed the towel from around his waist and tossed it on the chair in the corner. He walked around to the other side of the bed and crawled in. He laid back against the pillows and slid Ronnie's soft body to his.

His cock was aching with need, but it was going to have to wait. Tonight, he just needed to hold her.

They fit together perfectly. Already her eyes were closed and her breathing was slowing. He reached behind him and hit the light, basking them in darkness.

She rolled over to face him, her warm breath fluttering across his skin. He smiled and held her close.

The emotions filling him left him speechless.

In just a short amount of time, his life had changed.

He had everything he ever wanted and would be damned if it were taken from him.

He would do any and everything in his power to ensure Ronnie and their child remained safe.

The Demon Lords sending someone to her home was a direct threat. One that he wouldn't take lightly.

Now, he was going to have to pull out all the stops to ensure that the gang paid for all of their crimes.

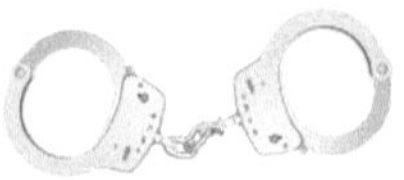

Brodie opened his locker and took his ballistics vest off and hung it up. He was beyond tired. His body ached in ways he had forgotten it could. They had been out on two calls already today.

They had a meeting with the captain about the task force the mayor was putting together. He just wanted to grab his shit and go home, but he couldn't.

Duty called.

He pulled his chain with his badge over his head so it could rest on his chest. He didn't need all of his gear on for a stupid meeting.

"I wonder what the captain is going to say," Myles muttered.

It was late afternoon and change of shift. The

men's locker room was filled with those cops coming on and those getting off.

"Hopefully, we won't have to participate. We're busy enough," Zain said from behind Brodie.

"If we get called out for one more hostage situation, I'm going to take someone hostage myself," Iker teased, opening his locker.

They all chuckled. The case they had been working that morning was in conjunction with the FBI. A teen had been abducted in Tennessee, and her captors had dragged her to South Carolina. Due to the girl being a minor and they'd cross state lines, the FBI was involved and called in the local SWAT team for the extraction.

A familiar voice grabbed Brodie's attention. He looked up and saw Cruz walking past their aisle laughing at something Reeves was saying.

Brodie swung his locker shut and headed in his direction.

He was pretty certain the Demon Lords had followed him to Ronnie's house.

"Shit," Myles cursed.

Doors banged behind him, and footsteps could be heard following him.

Brodie turned the corner to find Cruz and Reeves standing in front of their lockers.

"How's the nose, Cruz?" Brodie asked, leaning onto the wall. He narrowed his gaze on the traitor. His knuckles had been slightly bruised but were already healing.

Cruz faced him with a scowl. "You son of a bitch."

Brodie's feet carried him over before he had a chance to think. He slammed into Cruz and grabbed him by his shirt. Cruz pushed back but was no match for Brodie who pinned him against the row of lockers.

"I'm a son of a bitch?" Brodie said, his face close to Cruz's.

"Throwing cheap punches then leave? You're a fucking coward." Cruz tried to break Brodie's hold. "Out with your little girlfriend. Soon the whole precinct will know you're fucking Knight."

"That's none of your business," Brodie ground out, not denying the accusation. Just as they planned, they would play that card. Hopefully, it would keep heat off of Ronnie.

"Hey, cool it." Reeves tried to pull Brodie off his partner, but he was snatched back by Myles and Iker. They dragged him away.

"This has nothing to do with you," Myles barked.

"The hell it doesn't. He's my partner," Reeves shouted. "Leave him alone."

"Ain't nothing to see here." Zain motioned for the other police officers in the locker room to get out.

They adverted their eyes and headed out of the room.

"What the hell is going on?" Mac demanded.

He and Declan arrived with twin scowls on their faces.

"You're lucky I left," Brodie bit out, tightening his grip on Cruz's uniform.

"You SWAT think you're the shit, but let me tell you—"

"Tell us what? You fucking traitor," Brodie sneered.

Images of those thugs standing outside Ronnie's house came to mind.

Memories of the shootout when they were rescuing Aspen flooded him, Ash's kidnapping, and the men sent to kill Myles.

All because of this asshole.

"You don't know what the hell you're talking about," Cruz snarled. His dark eyes narrowed on Brodie while he tried to peel Brodie off him.

"We don't?" Declan smirked. He moved to stand

beside Brodie with dark fury rolling in on his face. "We know all about your little secrets, Cruz."

Cruz paled. His Adam's apple bobbed up a few times as he tried to swallow.

"All of your deception. Does your partner even know?" Brodie badgered him, slamming him into the lockers. His temper was two seconds from blowing. He wasn't going to be satisfied until his fist landed a few times in the smug mole's face. "Putting out contracts on fellow officers."

"What the hell are y'all talking about?" Reeves asked, fighting against Myles and Iker's hold.

"Do you want to tell him or do we?" Declan asked.

Mac came to stand on the other side of Brodie. The sergeant had murder in his eyes. Brodie was sure Mac was thinking the same thing he had been.

Everything they had been through lately was because of the information this mole was leaking to the dangerous gang.

"Listen. It's not as it seems." Cruz held his hands up, the fight leaving him.

Brodie released him and took a step back.

Cruz straightened his uniform shirt and looked around. "You guys don't know what I've been going through."

All eyes were on him.

Zain had ensured all the other men in the locker room had left. Brodie already knew someone would blab to the captain that some shit was going down, and they only had a short amount of time before Spook showed himself.

"We don't know what you've been going through? Is that what you just said?" Brodie bit out through clenched teeth. He couldn't believe this piece of shit. His hands balled into tight fists. He wanted to punch him in the face again. "You could have got people killed and you're worried about what you're going through?"

"I can explain," Cruz pleaded.

"Oh, you're going to do more than explain," Iker scoffed. He narrowed his gaze on Cruz. "And if I hear one lie, I promise you, I will beat the truth out of you."

"Talk," Mac ordered, pointing to Cruz. "Zain, door."

"On it." Zain walked away out of sight.

"Not here," Cruz said, his shoulders slumped. His hand trembled as he ran it through his dark hair. "We can't speak here."

Brodie didn't take his eyes off Cruz. He didn't trust him as far as he could throw him. It just boggled Brodie's mind that the guy wouldn't ask for help at work. If he was truly trying to save his sister, he had many resources he could have called on.

Even being an ass, no one would have turned their back on him to save a woman in trouble.

"What is going on, Diego?" Reeves asked.

Myles and Iker released him. The younger cop walked over to his partner with concern on his face.

"There's a lot of shit going down, and I didn't tell anyone. I've done some fucked-up stuff." Cruz shook his head.

"Fucked-up?" Myles exploded. His expression darkened.

Brodie had half a mind to switch spots with the big man.

"What is it? You could have come to me," Reeves said.

"Not here. I don't know who is listening." Cruz's eyes grew wide. He looked around the area, but it was only them in the room.

Brodie's eyes flicked to Mac whose attention was still locked on Cruz. The sergeant didn't believe Cruz either.

"We are going to have a long chat. Today." Declan folded his arms in front of his chest.

"We got trouble. Captain is on his way in here." Zain arrived at the group.

The door flew open, slamming against the wall. Brodie braced himself for the captain's arrival to where they were.

"What in the hell is going on in here?" Spook's voice boomed.

No one said a word. Brodie slid his hands into his pockets and kept his lips closed.

This was not the time to bring in the captain. They could handle this shit themselves. Brodie glanced over at Myles who was still staring at Cruz.

"Nothing at all, sir," Reeves mumbled.

"Is that so?" Spook narrowed his gaze on all of them. "You must think I'm an idiot. When I hear that my SWAT team kicked everyone out of the—"

"We asked if we could have the room nicely," Zain said innocently.

The captain's expression was cold enough to freeze lava.

Brodie closed his eyes briefly. Was Zain trying to get them all busted down to traffic duty?

"Shut up, Roman!" Spook shouted. He walked around them all, meeting their gazes with a hard glare. "Now someone tell me what in the hell is going on in here?"

Spook stopped in front of Brodie, but he kept his eyes averted. Brodie looked straight ahead as if he was back in the Army and his drill sergeant was stopping in front of him to assess him.

"I expect more from my SWAT team and from patrol. You are to work together, not against each other," Spook seethed, his anger almost palpable. He may be a big supporter of his men and women who carried a shield, but one wrong move, and you'd be on his shit list.

That was somewhere none of them wanted to be, and SWAT always teetered on that fine line.

"We were just working some shit out," Reeves said.

"Is that so?" Spook focused on Reeves. "I know SWAT won't say shit. They are too close and stubborn as hell. I'm sure you'll tell me what is going on in here."

The captain knew their team well. They didn't rat each other out, and when one was in trouble, they all were in trouble.

"It's nothing, sir. Just personal." Reeves blew out a deep breath and met the captain's gaze.

Spook moved on to Cruz. "What do you got to say?"

"Same as Reeves, sir. Just personal shit." Cruz swallowed hard but met the captain's cold glare.

The tension in the air was stifling.

Spook strode through them again before pausing at the end of the locker row. He turned back and rested his hands on his hips.

"I better see all of you in the task force meeting in fifteen minutes, SWAT. Don't be late." He spun around on his heel and stalked out of the room.

No one moved or breathed until the door shut.

"We'll come and find you, Cruz," Mac promised. He stepped closer to the mole, his gaze hard and his voice low. "Then no one will stop us from getting what we need."

RONNIE LEANED against the nursing station counter and blew out a deep breath. Tonight was one for the books. They had three patients code on them, one didn't make it, while the other two were now in intensive care.

According to a few cops who had come in with two of the patients, there was a huge gang fight at a club that led to the emergent admissions.

"Ronnie, you're up for the next admission. A

squad is on the way. ETA, five minutes," Tania called from behind the desk.

"Okay." Ronnie sighed. "Do we know what it is?"

"Stabbing."

At least it wasn't a trauma.

Those patients took up a lot of resources in the hospital. Radiology would hold bringing other patients down, and an operating room was reserved, just in case the patient needed their services. Even security arrived in the department to ensure nothing crazy jumped off.

"Bed three is available. He can go in there," Tania said.

"Thanks." Ronnie headed over to the room where her new patient would be assessed. She peeked in and discovered there wasn't a bed in the area. Looking around, she saw Monica coming from another room.

"Hey, Monica!" Ronnie waved the nursing assistant over.

"Hey, Ronnie. Tania just told me we're getting a patient in three."

Monica appeared about as tired as Ronnie felt. They were taking a beating, and Ronnie couldn't wait for the change of shift. She would attack the oncoming nurses as soon as they arrived and force them to take her patients.

"Yeah, and there's no bed in there." Ronnie was irritated. The previous patient who had been in this room had been admitted to the hospital and taken up to the instant unit.

But where was the bed?

"I know where one is." Monica spun around on her heel and jogged toward the doorway that led to radiology.

Ronnie grabbed everything else she would need for assessing the patient when he arrived. She would get details from the EMTs. Since it wasn't deemed a trauma, she wouldn't get a full report until they delivered the patient.

Within minutes, Ronnie and Monica had the room prepared for the patient and the EMTs came bursting through the doors of the ED with a man strapped to their stretcher.

"Hey, Ronnie." Eric grinned, pushing the cart.

He and Liam rolled the patient over to the room.

"What do you have for me?" she asked, eyeing the patient.

He was a young white male with a ton of tattoos covering his body. His torn shirt was covered in blood, as were his jeans.

"A stabbing." Liam shook his head. He handed her a clipboard with his paperwork on it.

Ronnie scanned it, catching the patient's name, a summary of what happened, and his vitals while in the ambulance.

Jack Broomer. Twenty-three years old. No medical history. His blood pressure that was documented from the EMTs was slightly elevated, but that would be expected with pain.

"I don't need a hospital. I'm fine," Jack muttered.

Ronnie looked at him, and from the blood, the bruised face, and no shoes on his feet, he wasn't in shape to go anywhere.

"Good, then you can go straight to jail," a voice countered.

Ronnie glanced over and found a patrolman standing beside them.

Just great.

"How is it I'm getting arrested, but I'm the one beat up and stabbed?" the guy argued.

"Everyone at the fight is going to jail. We'll let the courts figure everything out," the officer replied.

"This is bullshit," the prisoner mumbled. He flopped down on the stretcher and closed his eyes.

"Let's get him in the room so the doctors can come look him over," Ronnie directed.

"Will do." Eric chuckled.

He and Liam rolled the cart in next to the bed Monica had brought.

"Are you handcuffing him?" Ronnie asked the cop. Her gaze dropped down to his nameplate.

Officer Jones looked as if he would rather be anywhere else but the hospital emergency department.

"Yup. Can't risk him running. Once he checks out, me and my partner will be running him in." Officer Jones moved to stand at the door.

"Ronnie, you helping or standing around blabbing?" Liam joked.

Monica was with them preparing to pull the patient over to the other bed.

Ronnie smiled and shrugged. "Sorry, guys. I can't pull patients."

She hadn't told anyone at work, and now that she'd shared the news with her family, she didn't care who knew.

She slid her hand down to rest it on her slight baby bump that was hidden beneath her scrubs.

"Wait, you're pregnant?" Monica screeched.

Ronnie nodded, grinning from ear to ear.

"Congratulations, Ronnie," Eric said.

"Don't worry, we can pull him over. I was just

teasing." Liam smiled. "But that's awesome, Ronnie. Congrats."

Monica rushed over to her and took her in a tight hug.

"That is so awesome, Ronnie." Monica laughed.

They moved out of the way to allow the guys to get the patient situated in the hospital bed.

"Who's the lucky guy?" Eric pushed their cart out of the room.

She handed Liam back their clipboard and took off the sheet of paper that she was to keep.

"Wouldn't you like to know." Ronnie couldn't contain her smile. She spun on her heel and entered the room. She stowed the paper away in her pocket.

Monica grabbed the blood pressure machine and dragged it in the room behind her. She began hooking it up to Jack to obtain his vitals. He didn't open his eyes while she worked.

"Don't leave us hanging." Liam laughed.

Ronnie glanced over at Monica who was smiling at her. Ronnie waltzed back over to the door to allow Monica to finish.

"Well, I have a boyfriend now. He's a cop." Her cheeks hurt from grinning so much.

"Really?" Eric's eyebrows flew up. He folded his

arms in front of him. "And does this cop have a name?"

"I don't want my business out in the streets," Ronnie teased.

Eric and Liam burst out in laughter at her silliness. Even Officer Jones's lip curled up in the corner.

"Really?" Liam snorted.

"Okay." Ronnie rolled her eyes. "His name is Brodie Gipson."

"SWAT?" Officer Jones turned to look at her now.

She nodded, Liam letting out a whistle.

"You got yourself a bad-ass." He chuckled.

"What? He's a big marshmallow." She giggled. Yeah, he was a bad-ass. The stories the guys shared with her and the girls made them all cringe. It was like a walk in the park for them while the women tried their hardest not to show they were scared knowing the guys were running head-first into danger.

"He's a good man. I remembered when he first joined the force when he came home from the Army," Jones said.

She smiled at him, proud of her man.

"Vitals done," Monica said.

"Duty calls." Ronnie waved to Eric and Liam and went back into the room. Before the physicians came to check out the patient, she would need to see what they were dealing with and look him over briefly. "All right, Jack. I need to assess the wound."

"But the paramedics patched it up," he whined. He opened his eyes and proceeded to roll them.

Ronnie blew out a deep breath and prayed for strength in dealing with this patient. She was riding high on being able to finally share with her coworkers that she was pregnant.

Nothing was going to ruin her day.

20

"It ain't no surprise the mayor is putting together a task force," Iker muttered. "Where the hell was this when we were getting our asses handed to us?"

"It's coming up on election season, and you know what that means," Myles said.

They walked through the door that led to the parking lot.

Night had fallen. Brodie glanced down at his watch. Ronnie would be at work at this time. She was on the evening shift and would be getting off around eleven thirty. A small smile played on his lips at the brief thought of his woman. Maybe once he was done with the guys, he would swing by and pick her up from the hospital and take her home.

He was beat, and there was nothing like wrapping Ronnie up in his arms and lying together. He was man enough to admit he loved cuddling with his sexy girlfriend.

He wanted to get lost in her body tonight. His cock twitched at the thought of sinking deep into her.

That always guaranteed to take the stress from him.

An hour and a half of their lives would be lost forever. Apparently, the mayor was coming down on the chief of police who was currently getting in the captain's ass about the gang violence and how they were going to fight back.

The solution was to combine the efforts of the gang unit, narcotics, SWAT, and the K9 units to win the war on crime.

They would reclaim their streets.

"Yup, and the mayor has to show that he's actually doing something for the community." Brodie grunted. He had known there was an ultimate reason the mayor had shown up at their challenge. There was always an agenda, and now SWAT was going to be right in the middle of it.

Brodie followed behind Zain and Iker. They walked over to Iker's oversized pickup truck. Brodie felt his phone buzz and glanced down at it. Declan's name came across the screen.

"Yo, what's up?" Brodie answered. He was dead tired, and there was no end in sight for them tonight. They had vowed to grab Cruz. There was no way in hell they were letting him slip away. They needed to get to the bottom of everything.

"Cruz just clocked out. This is going down tonight," Declan replied.

Brodie tapped Iker on the shoulder. Iker and Zain immediately quieted, their gazes landing on him. They grew still waiting for Brodie to get off the phone.

Jordan and Myles exited the building behind a few other patrolmen who had been included in the meeting.

"Looks like we'll be carpooling," Brodie responded.

"We're on our way." Declan cut the call.

"Cruz is heading out now," Brodie informed them.

"Well, all right then. Two vehicles it is," Iker said. A dangerous gleam appeared in his eyes.

Brodie smirked, recognizing it.

Iker loved the hunt of the suspects and got a thrill out of it just like they all did. "I'm driving."

"Seriously. Why do you get to drive all the time?" Jordan asked, coming to stand by them.

"Well, first of all, Officer Knight." Iker grinned at her.

Iker and Zain teased her unmercifully as if she was truly their little sister. Brodie laughed at her dramatic eye roll.

"Only you can fit in that small vehicle of yours."

"It's a sleek—"

"Seriously, Jordan. Just get in the damn truck," Zain cut her off, pointing to Iker's ride.

"Can I drive?" Her eyes grew big with hope as she stared at the oversized truck on huge wheels.

"Hell no. We'll come back for your car later." Iker shook his head. He opened the back door for her. "No one drives Betsy girl but me."

"Men," Jordan muttered. She moved and hopped in.

"You riding with them or Mac and Dec?" Myles asked.

"I'll take my chances with them." Brodie motioned to Iker's truck.

"All right." Myles saluted and backed away.

Mac and Declan stepped from the building and headed toward Mac's truck.

They piled into Iker's Betsy. Brodie sat in the

back with Jordan while Zain took shotgun. Iker cut the engine on, and they waited for Cruz to come out of the building.

"Anyone know which car this bitch-ass drives?" Zain asked, not holding any punches.

The tension was high in the cab. It wasn't every day a cop turned on his own. Brodie leaned back in his seat and sent a quick text to Myles asking him.

"It's a car," Jordan murmured. "A dark one. I saw him pull in the other day but didn't pay attention to it."

"Well, I see about five dark cars," Iker joked.

"Ass." Jordan leaned forward and slapped him on the shoulder.

"Now, now, children," Brodie said. His phone buzzed with the reply from Myles. "Black Acura."

"There he goes," Zain said.

The cab fell silent as they watched Cruz walk briskly toward his vehicle. The headlights turned on, and he drove out of his parking spot.

"Here we go." Iker threw the truck into drive and drove forward.

Mac's truck moved at the same time, and Iker fell in line with him. They pulled out onto the street.

Iker's phone rang. He hit the 'accept' button, and

the call went to the hands-free, allowing everyone to hear the call.

"Yeah," Iker answered.

"There's an abandoned gas station not too far from here," Mac's hard voice filled the air.

"Yup. I know exactly which one you're talking about," Iker said.

"I don't care how we get him there, but we're chatting tonight with the fucker," Mac growled.

"Roger that, Sergeant," Zain replied.

Brodie's muscles grew tight. They trailed behind Mac's truck. There wasn't much traffic on the road. The destination was familiar to Brodie. It was about two miles away.

Iker's engine revved up as he pushed down on the gas. The truck sped forward and pulled up in the left lane to keep Cruz from getting over. Mac's truck was behind his car.

They had him trapped.

"Stay on him," Mac shouted.

"Oh, don't worry. He ain't going nowhere," Iker answered coldly.

Jordan chuckled, looking out the window. Brodie leaned over to glance out the glass, and he could see Cruz was panicking.

His hands were tight on the steering wheel.

They continued to put pressure on him, making him turn at the light to force him down the road where the abandoned gas station was located.

Cruz blew his horn, sticking up a middle finger.

"Um, Iker. Cruz just put up his middle finger," Jordan shared.

"Son of a bitch," Iker cursed. He expertly guided the truck close to Cruz. The gas station was coming up fast. They were speeding down the road. "If that fucker scratches my paint, I'm personally going to take it out on his hide."

Iker swerved just in time, causing Cruz to drive into the gas station. It was a run-down building. The gas pumps were no longer there. It had closed years ago, and the city had never done anything with the space. The old store was boarded up, and only the streetlights provided light.

Mac pulled in behind Cruz, blocking his car.

He wouldn't be able to go anywhere without banging into one of their trucks and risk damaging his car. They flew out of the truck, slamming the doors behind them. Mac, Declan, and Myles stepped from Mac's truck. They walked over to Cruz's Acura. He exited his car with his hands held up in the air.

"So what the fuck is this?" Cruz snapped.

"Don't play dumb," Mac said with fury in his eyes. "We said our talk wasn't over."

They surrounded him, forcing him to lean back against his car. He glanced around, meeting all of their gazes.

"They are going to kill her if I talk with you." Cruz's shoulders drooped.

"Who is they?" Declan asked.

"The fucking Demon Lords. Who the hell do you think?" Cruz spit out. He ran a hand through his hair.

"You better start talking now," Myles ordered. His voice dropped low. "And why you put a hit out on me."

Cruz visibly paled. He swallowed a few times before nodding.

"I know that was fucked up, and believe me, I didn't want to do that." His voice trembled with fear. "You have to believe me. I may not like y'all, but it isn't worth killing you over, but I had no choice. If I ever want to help free my sister, I have to do what they say."

"Who made you take out the contract on Myles?" Brodie asked. That was the one thing he couldn't find in all of his digging.

Who the hell was running the Demon Lords now that House was in prison?

The organization had been falling apart, and some factions of it were doing whatever the hell they wanted. A gang the size of the Demon Lords was even more dangerous without some form of leadership.

"Viktor Huff."

The silence was deafening.

Brodie glanced around at his team.

Viktor Huff was the head of the gang, but he was in prison. How was he still running the gang from behind bars?

"But why Myles?" Jordan asked.

They would have to catch her up on what happened the night Viktor was taken into custody. It was the night he had kidnapped Ash and was going to kill him. SWAT had been able to locate their teammate and take down the gangster.

Myles, Declan, and Mac were the ones who had found Ash.

Iker, Zain, and Brodie had been knee deep in a shootout with the gangsters in the building.

"He was there when we took down Viktor. Is he planning to kill all of us?" Mac stepped forward, crowding Cruz's space.

Cruz hesitated before nodding. "Myles was the first."

"But how did he know it was me?" Myles asked.

Cruz swallowed hard. "I gave him the identities of all of you. Anything they wanted to know, I gave it to them. He knows all about you, your women... everything I could dig up on you."

Growls went up in the air.

"You son of a bitch," Myles bit out through clenched teeth.

"I didn't have a choice," Cruz emphasized. "They are pimping my sister out, she's strung out on drugs. She was one of Viktor's personal pets. They are threatening to kill her if I don't do as they say."

"Why didn't you ask for help?" Declan questioned. It was the million dollar question they all wanted to know. "Something like this, anyone with a badge at the fucking precinct would be willing to help you."

"Because if I did, they would find out and then hurt her." Cruz fell back against his car. He looked like a man who had been rejected his entire life. It was as if the fight had left him. "It started off with just general information, then it morphed into more. I knew it could cost me my job, but I didn't have a choice."

"How do you even know she's still alive?" Jordan asked softly.

Cruz paused, glancing away.

The wind blew gently. A slight chill was in the air, reminding Brodie it was getting late. He glanced around and took in the area. No cars had passed in a long while.

"They send me videos of her. She's not right in her head. Drugged out, barely able to move some days." He feverishly wiped the tears trailing down his cheeks. "I'd do anything to save my sister."

Brodie didn't bring up that videos of her weren't a true proof of life. They could be recorded at any time and shared. The man appeared like he'd been to hell and back, and Brodie didn't want to cause any more pain.

If the thought of rescuing his sister was going to keep him going, then they would do their damnedest to try to rescue her.

"How is he getting messages through to you?" Zain asked, folding his arms in front of him.

It would take one call from their captain to the warden to have the gangster's room searched and privileges taken away. It was common knowledge that prisoners had cell phones and other communication devices smuggled inside the jails.

It appeared like they would have to put pressure on the gangster. SWAT was going to have to teach him yet another lesson.

"One of his goons," Cruz replied.

"Here's what you are going to do," Mac said. His voice dropped eerily low. It sent a chill down Brodie's spine. "You are going to give us all of the information and contacts that you have."

"We will give you new information to pass on to them," Brodie added.

Nods went around. They would take advantage of this aspect. If they could feed the wrong information to Huff, then it would give them time.

"Why would you help me?" Cruz asked, viewing them.

"It's not you we're helping. We're helping your sister," Declan said.

"Are you almost done?" Jack whined.

"Don't tell me you're scared of a little needle?" Ronnie eyed his tattoos. She reached over and cleared up the papers from the gauze the resident had used cleaning off Jack's wound. She tossed them in the trash, trying to clean up as they went.

"A stabbing one, yes." Jack grimaced.

"It won't be too much longer," Raj murmured. His hands were steady, threading the needle through Jack's skin.

Rajesh Bakshi was a senior trauma resident who would soon be moving on in his training. She had worked with him for a few years in the ED and the ICUs. He was a handsome physician who had come all the way from India to study in America. All of the nurses were crazy over his smooth brown skin, short spiked hair, and dimples. He had impressed Ronnie with his skills when they had first met. That was saying much because it took a lot for nurses to be impressed by residents. Most came in cocky but were shitty physicians.

Rajesh was special. He truly cared for his patients and was one hell of a surgeon.

"You done with these?" Ronnie grabbed the lidocaine vials lying on the bed.

"Yup." Raj continued to sew up their patient while she finished tidying up his workspace. "So, you do know Rajesh is a good strong name."

Ronnie dropped the used medication vials in the red hazard bin on the wall. She spun around and grinned.

He looked up at her, trying to appear innocent.

"Really? You, too?" Ever since she'd told Monica and the EMTs, she'd had to share her news with the entire emergency department staff. News of her pregnancy was spreading like wildfire.

"I'm just saying, if you are having a boy, Rajesh is a good name. It means ruler of kings." He sat back, admiring his handiwork.

"Well, I will share that with the baby's father." Ronnie walked over to the door where

Officer Jones still stood watching guard. "It should be a few more minutes. The doctor is finishing up."

"Good." Jones nodded.

"I'm going to order a gram of ampicillin IM." Raj stood, walked over to the sharps container, and dropped the needle in the hazard box.

"Yes, Doctor," Ronnie replied in a sweet tone.

"Don't patronize me." Raj chuckled. He hated when the nurses treated him differently.

Ronnie just hoped that when he finished his training, he wouldn't change. He was a good guy and was going to go far in his field.

"Put the order in and I'll grab it," she said, waving him out of the room once he'd finished washing his hands at the sink. "I'll finish up here."

"Yes, Nurse Ronnie." Raj saluted her and disappeared out the door.

Ronnie seized a couple of new gauzes and quickly covered the wound up. She applied tape to hold them in place.

Jack's wrist closest to her was shackled with handcuffs. She hated to admit she was quite used to patients being handcuffed. Working in the ED meant all walks of life came through the door needing medical attention.

"I'll be right back. The doctor wants you to get an antibiotic then you will be able to go," she said.

"It's not like I'm free to go home." Jack snickered. He reached up with his free hand and scratched his head.

Tossing the rest of the trash in the garbage, she left the room and headed toward the medication room.

There was a line at the medication room. A few nurses stood around chatting, waiting for their turn.

"Look who it is." Jason, one of the other nurses, grinned at her. "Now we know why you are walking around with a glow to you."

"Hey, Jason. How are you?" she asked. Glow? She honestly didn't feel any different, but if he wanted to tell her she had a glow, she'd take it.

"How are you feeling?" he asked.

"Good. Morning sickness catches me off guard here and there." She groaned.

"My wife had it bad. I think her first hour of each day was spent with her head in the porcelain bowl."

Ronnie grimaced. She was thankful it only hit her once in a while. That would be downright torturous. "I pray mine doesn't get that bad. Guess I shouldn't complain."

"Hey, guys." Tabbi opened the door and stepped

out with her hands full with a couple of IV bags. "Let me move out your way."

"Hey, Tabbi," Ronnie and Jason echoed.

Jason entered the area and shut the door behind him. According to the hospital, they had to have a door for the medication room to help prevent the nurses from getting distracted.

A few minutes later, Jason was done. Ronnie went in and logged on the computer that sat on top of the Pyxis machine that dispensed the medications. She pulled up Jack's chart and saw the script for the medication he'd ordered.

She logged in to the Pyxis and removed the antibiotic vial. Slamming it shut, she logged out and moved over to the preparation counter. She followed the instructions on reconstituting the power substance and drew it up in a syringe. Grabbing the proper needle, she headed out of the room and back to Jack.

She swung by the nurses' station and picked up his discharge papers. At the ED, they just fixed them up and sent them on their way.

"As soon as I give him this, he's all good to go." Ronnie flashed the medication and papers in her hand.

"Perfect. It's about time for the end of my shift," Jones muttered, following her into the room.

"A shot?" Jack whined.

"Seriously? You have a ton of tattoos. How are you afraid of this one little needle?" she asked. She put the needle on the end of the syringe and walked over to him. Taking an alcohol swab from her uniform pocket, she tossed it on the bed along with the needle and papers.

"Tattoos don't hurt."

"Bullshit," Jones chimed in. "The one on my shoulder hurt like a motherfucker."

Ronnie donned gloves and tore open the alcohol pad. She cleaned off Jack's shoulder and administered the shot.

"See. That was it." She laughed at the grimace on Jack's face while covering it with a Band-Aid.

"It burns," he moaned.

"Just for a second. It will go away." She dispensed her items and took her gloves off. She snagged the papers and went over his instructions. "Any questions?"

Jack shook his head.

Ronnie paused.

Was that a scream?

She met Jones' gaze.

"What the hell was that?" Jones muttered. He strode over to the door and released a curse.

A pop sounded that strangely reminded Ronnie of gunfire.

"What is going on—? " Her words ended on a scream.

Jones fell back, holding his chest. A large red stain spread across his blue uniform shirt.

"Oh shit. They're coming for me." Jack tugged at the handcuffs. "You got to let me out."

"What?" Ronnie shook, hearing a scuffle outside the room.

Two large men appeared in the doorway with guns aimed at her and Jack.

Ronnie froze in place, her heart pounding. The guns looked huge and were certainly deadly.

"You heard him. Get him out of the cuffs." The tall, beefy thug growled. His dirty brown hair was long and shaggy.

One glance at him, and she assumed those muscles were developed in jail.

"I don't have the keys." Ronnie gulped.

Beefy motioned to Jones on the floor. "Check him for the keys."

Ronnie hesitated.

"Now," the other one ground out. He was just as

scary as Beefy. He was dark-skinned with a bald head. His eyes were menacing and locked on her.

Ronnie jerked as if she had been electrified. She scurried over to Jones who groaned slightly. She reached on his utility belt and found a set of keys. She moved over to Jack and tried a few of them. Her hands trembled with the thugs watching her.

Finally, the key slid in and she was able to turn it, releasing Jack. Ronnie stepped back into the corner of the room. An alarm went off in the corridor.

"Get up," Beefy ordered. "He wants you."

"Ah, come on. I didn't do anything." Jack groaned. He held on to his side and swung his legs off the edge of the bed.

"Stop your fucking whining. The cops will be on their way," Baldy snapped. "Now let's go."

"He's just going to kill me anyway." Jack sniffed. He stood to his feet, swaying slightly.

"That ain't my problem." Beefy shrugged.

"We don't make decisions. We're just the muscle." Baldy's laugh was low and threatening.

Ronnie tried to keep quiet in the hopes they would forget about her.

"Come on." Baldy stepped into the room with his gun aimed at Jack.

"We need to take her with us." Jack pointed

to her.

Ronnie's heart sank.

"Wait? What?" She gasped. "No, no, no."

She shook her head feverishly. Why would they need her?

"We don't need her. Let's go—"

"She's the girlfriend of one of the SWAT officers," Jack blurted off. "If I bring her to him, then my ass could possibly be saved."

Beefy and Baldy looked at her for a moment.

Tears blurred her vision.

"Really? Well, I'll be damned." Beefy snorted, moving to her.

"No. Please leave me be." She tried to dodge his hands, but he wrapped an arm around her and lifted her from the floor. She cried out, kicking the air.

Baldy kept a hand on Jack and pushed him out of the room, keeping his gun trained on him. They exited the room, Ronnie's gaze sweeping the emergency room.

The department was under siege.

"Please. Don't take me," she cried out.

"Shut up before I make you," Beefy snarled.

Ronnie closed her eyes, imagining Brodie's warm smile and the strength of his embrace. She prayed she would be able to see and feel him again.

Looked like her day was ruined after all.

BRODIE LEANED back against Iker's truck while listening to Cruz share with them the information he knew. The gas station proved to be a safe place to remain without the fear of someone overhearing the conversation.

Cruz had been talking for an hour straight. Brodie had his phone out, taking notes on it. So far, they had the name of Viktor's second hand that had been running the operation while he was in prison.

Sergio Cabal.

It was amazing the intel that Cruz knew.

What a waste.

He could have used this to help put away some criminals.

"That's all I know." Cruz held his hands up.

"You're going to make contact with Sergio. Set up a meeting," Mac ordered.

"'That's not how it works," Cruz whined.

"We're going to make it work. You're going to have some vital information that you want to give him." Mac stepped closer to Cruz.

He could be one mean son of a bitch, and Brodie was certainly glad he was on the same team as Mac.

Brodie's phone rang, as did the entire squad's. He glanced down and saw it was dispatch sending out an alert.

Fuck.

Mac answered his phone. "MacArthur."

The tension in the air heightened. All eyes were on Mac. Not a person spoke a word. They were all standing by, waiting on their orders.

Brodie stood to his full height.

Something didn't sit right with him.

Mac turned and faced him with his phone pressed to his ear.

The bottom of Brodie's stomach threatened to give way. He met Mac's gaze, needing to know what he was hearing.

"Roger that. On the way," Mac said, finally breaking his silence. He looked around at the team who had subconsciously moved closer. "Five armed men stormed into General Hospital's emergency department."

"No." Brodie shook his head. Not the hospital where Ronnie worked. He searched his memory to try to remember if she'd told him where she would be working tonight.

"They went after a gangbanger who had been rushed to the hospital with a stab wound. He and the nurse caring for him were abducted," Mac continued.

"Who was the nurse?" Brodie demanded to know. He slid a hand along his face and turned on Cruz. "What else are you not telling us?"

He flew toward Cruz, but strong arms snatched him up.

Myles and Iker detained him.

"We don't know if it's her," Myles said.

Brodie struggled against their hold.

"How do we know he's not lying to us? Setting us up?" Brodie snarled.

"What are you talking about?" Cruz backed away, holding his hands up.

"You said that you told them everything about us? Our women. Our families," Brodie said.

"I don't get it. You're fucking..." Cruz paused his words at the sounds of growls echoing through the air. "I mean, sleeping with Knight."

"Call her, Brodie," Zain suggested.

Brodie shrugged Myles and Iker off him and reached for his cellphone. He took it back out of his pocket. He hit Ronnie's number and held it up to his ear. It went to voicemail.

Her sweet, sultry voice announced she was unavailable at the moment. He squeezed his eyes shut at the sound of her words washing over him.

Mac's phone rang again.

"Shit." Brodie ended the call and hit her name once more. Just like before, the call went to voicemail. He hit it a third time, begging God for her to answer.

"Brodie, hang up." Mac's voice was quiet.

Brodie flicked his gaze to Mac. His head instantly shook recognizing the facial expression on his sergeant's face. Mac held his phone up before putting it in his pocket.

"No. It can't be," Brodie shouted.

Mac strode to him and gripped his shoulder. "That was Sarena. It's Ronnie. The hospital just confirmed it."

Brodie locked his legs together, his knees weakening. There was no way in hell he would fall to his knees in front of his team. He blinked back the tears that threatened to fall.

"Look at me." Mac's voice was cold and calculating.

Brodie blinked, clearing his vision, and returned Mac's gaze.

"We're going to get our gear and we're going to

find her."

"We won't rest until she's safe in your arms," Declan vowed.

Brodie looked around and found his entire squad surrounding him.

"You got that fucking right," Iker chimed in.

Fear unlike any he had ever known filled Brodie's chest, but the fact that his brothers and sister were standing by his side meant a lot.

Brodie jerked his head in a nod. His gaze landed on Cruz.

"If I hear that you had anything to do with her kidnapping, there will be no one to stop me from hunting you down," Brodie threatened.

He turned around and stalked toward Iker's truck. Jordan fell in step with him.

"So you and Knight aren't together?" Cruz shouted.

"Shut the fuck up and go home!" Mac ordered.

They arrived at Iker's truck. Brodie rested his hand on the door handle and paused at the slight touch of a hand on his forearm.

"We're going to get her back," Jordan assured him.

Her eyes held a dangerous glint that was soothing to his frantic soul.

22

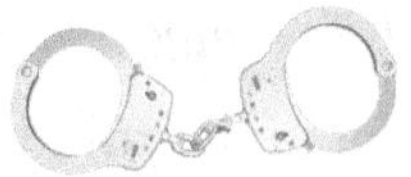

Ronnie tried to will her heart from racing. Her breaths were coming fast, and she was sure she was two seconds from a full-blown panic attack.

Her face was covered with a dark mask. Her hands were tied behind her back. Her body swayed back and forth with the vehicle's movement.

Biting her lip, she tried to hold back from crying. It wouldn't help her right now.

Praying was the only thing she could do.

Brodie would save her.

Without a doubt, he would.

There would be nothing to stop him from coming after her.

Memories of the night those thugs showed up at

her house came to mind. He was like a different person, and she knew that version of Brodie would come for her.

The van slowed to a halt.

Ronnie inhaled sharply.

Don't worry, girl. The guys will save you.

She repeated that in her mind.

Mac wouldn't let her down either. She would be safe. She only had to bide her time and pray they could find her.

The doors opened and shut from the front of the vehicle. The two thugs' voice carried outside. Ronnie strained to hear what they were saying, but their words were muffled. She wasn't sure how many men were with them. At the hospital, it seemed as if a small militia had moved in on the ED. In the van, it was only her and Jack in the back. The second they were tossed inside of the truck, dark cloth bags went over their heads, keeping them from seeing anything.

"Shit, we're here," Jack muttered.

"You know you are a real asshole, right?" Ronnie snapped.

"Yeah, well, if it's worth anything, I'm sorry," he said. "I had to do something to save my ass."

"You did hear that I'm pregnant, right?"

She couldn't believe that he would have a pregnant woman kidnapped to save his ass.

That was lower than low.

Hell wasn't good enough for him.

"It's either you or me."

"Are you kidding me?" She gasped. Rage like she had never known filled her. With the material over her head, she couldn't glare at him.

How dare he?

He was slime, and Ronnie hoped he would get what he deserved.

The door on the side of the vehicle nearest Ronnie swung open. Her pulse quickened with the unknown.

"Come on," a gruff voice ordered.

Rough hands latched on to her arm and dragged her from the van. She stumbled out and tried to right herself but fell into a hard body. Her captor gripped her tight and pulled her up straight.

"Ow," she yelped. "You don't have to be so rough. I can't see."

"Shut up," he snarled.

"Why do I have to be blindfolded?" Jack's whiny voice echoed through the air.

"Shut the hell up before I knock your ass out!" the other goon growled.

Ronnie was unable to distinguish between Beefy's and Baldy's voices. The one holding on to her arm guided her along. The sounds of nature met her, and it sent a chill down her spine. She lost track of how long they had been driving. The scent of the fresh air met her. She breathed it in and became a little worried.

How far away were they from the city? Her feet met gravel and dirt, and her fear increased.

"Where are you taking me?" Ronnie demanded. She got nothing but a snort and a firmer grip on her arm. She continued walking next to him, and soon her feet were no longer on even ground. High grass brushed along her legs. The ground was uneven, and she stumbled a few times. Walking with her arms behind her back and blindfolded was proving to be a challenge.

Where the hell were they taking them?

A shrill whistle went up. The guy next to her replied back with the same sound. The ground morphed into rocks again, and it made it easier for Ronnie to continue along.

"It's about time you all made it back," a new voice said.

"It took us a little longer than we thought," the thug next to her replied.

"Who's the broad?"

"Jack seemed to think she would be worth something." Her escort scoffed.

"Hmm...we'll see. You sure you weren't followed?"

"Positive," the other kidnapper said. "What do you think we are? Fresh meat?"

"Just can never be too careful, that's all."

The sound of a door creaking open greeted Ronnie's ears.

"Watch your step, ma'am," the newcomer advised.

The guy holding on to her arm paused, allowing her to step up into the building. They walked through the building until she was guided down into a chair.

"Don't move."

The cloth was removed from her head leaving her to stare into the eyes of Beefy. Ronnie blinked and took in the dark wood-planked walls. A single window with bars on it was the only outlet from the room except the door. There was a cot located in the corner and a desk. It housed only the bare minimum. Ronnie's gaze landed on the toilet in the other corner.

Looked like she wouldn't need to leave for any reason.

Beefy removed the handcuffs from her wrists.

"What are you doing with me?" she asked.

He stood straight and snickered. "Not sure yet. Waiting to find out."

That answer sent a shiver down her spine.

Ronnie gulped.

He headed toward the door.

"You're just going to leave me here?" she shrieked. She looked around and determined that this must be her prison until they decided what to do with her.

"Yup." He disappeared through the door, shutting it behind him.

The sound of a click met her ears.

Great. She was locked into a room alone.

It could be worse.

Blowing out a deep breath, she stood and walked toward the window. She stared out of it, finding it was completely dark outside. There was no lighting and no clues as to where they had taken her.

Ronnie turned and glanced over at the cot. She made her way there and kicked off her shoes. If she was going to be there a while she might as well get comfy.

Surprisingly, the sheets smelled halfway decent. She'd half expected them to be stale and moldy. Who would have thought the modern-day gangsters did laundry and prepared a bed for guests.

Settling down on the bed, she scooted over to the corner and leaned back against the wall.

Now the wait would begin.

Soon, she was confident Brodie and his team would be storming the building and rescuing her.

She couldn't lose hope.

They would come for her.

RONNIE JERKED awake from the sound of the door opening. Lifting her head off the wall, she blinked watching Baldy and Beefy come into the room. They stood near the door while a Hispanic gentleman who appeared to be in his early forties entered behind them. He was dressed in slacks, a button-down shirt, and a blazer. His dark hair was slicked back away from his face.

He was definitely someone who looked to be in charge.

Ronnie pushed herself up higher on the bed, not taking her eyes off him.

"So this is her?" he asked.

"She has a name," Ronnie said. She would have to put up a brave front. Desperate times called for desperate measures. She was going to have to find some way to ensure she protected her baby and herself until her knight in shining armor arrived.

"She is feisty. Lovely." He slid his hands into his pants pocket, staring at her. "Where are my manners? My name is Sergio Cabal."

"Ronnie Floyd," she replied.

"Ms. Floyd, I had a very interesting conversation with Jack a little while ago, and he shared some information about you," Sergio began. He walked over to the chair and motioned to it. "Do you mind?"

Ronnie's eyebrows shot up. A gangster with manners?

Who knew?

"By all means." Ronnie nodded.

Sergio moved the chair toward the middle of the small room and took a seat. He crossed his leg over the other and appeared to be relaxed as if they were about to have a normal conversation.

"As I was saying, Jack shared some information with me. Now it contradicts what I've been told."

"What does what he told you have do with me?" she asked wearily.

Sergio may seem as if he was relaxed, but there was a darkness to his eyes that left Ronnie feeling uneasy. Her gaze dropped down to a spot on her crisp white shirt.

Was that blood?

Her gaze flicked back up to Sergio's.

"Well, Ms. Floyd, that would depend on how you answer the questions I have for you." Sergio's lips curled up into a sinister grin.

The bottom of her stomach gave way. She swallowed hard to keep the contents of it down.

Ronnie didn't like the sound of this.

"What does that mean?" She was afraid to ask, but she had to know. Why would they be speaking about her?

"Your answers determine whether our buddy Jack lives or dies," he answered matter-of-factly.

"What?" Ronnie gasped. Her hand flew to her mouth at the thought that she would be the cause of someone's death. "I don't know anything."

"Oh, quite contrary. From what Jack tells me, you are the exact person I need to ask," he replied.

Ronnie racked her brain to try to figure out what she would know that they would need. Was it about

Jack? Her? She just didn't understand what they would want to know from her.

"What is your relationship with Officer Brodie Gipson?" Sergio asked. He grew quiet, his dark eyes locked on her.

Ronnie was floored by the question.

Beefy and Baldy stood braced as if she were going to try to escape from them. They could both crush her with one hand.

"Brodie? He's my boyfriend," she answered. That was the truth. Why were they questioning her relationship?

"What of his relationship with a Jordan Knight?" Sergio asked.

What was going on? Ronnie grew even more puzzled by the line of questioning. In all of the books she had read and movies she had watched, this wasn't anything like them.

She was thinking he was going to ask her about Jack and what he had talked about in the hospital.

But her love life?

What was going on?

Was she being punked?

"Jordan is on his team. She's new." That was common knowledge. As of right now, nothing he was asking would put Brodie in danger.

"So there is no romantic connection between them?" he asked.

"Why are you asking these types of questions?"

She would have never imagined that questioning from a gangster would have centered around her love life and gossip.

"When doing research on the team of men that one is going to kill, we want to know about all of their relationships and entanglements."

Ice slid through Ronnie's veins, chilling her to the core.

Team of men that one is going to kill.

Oh God. What was going on?

"See, when men are warned over and over to stay out of business that is none of their concern and they don't learn, we need to kick it up a notch. Comprendé?" Sergio snarled. He didn't wait for her to answer. "My boss wants to eradicate them, and we will. It is because of them that he is in prison. This little SWAT team has been a thorn in the Demon Lords' side for a while now, and I will be the one to take care of them."

"Where are you getting your information from?" Ronnie's voice was hollow. Who would have told him that?

"It would seem my informant had his information wrong and he will pay for that." Sergio stood from his chair and walked over to her.

She cowered away from him.

A smirk appeared on his face. "And according to Jack, you are pregnant with Officer Gipson's child, no?"

Ronnie swallowed hard and nodded.

Fear had taken a hold of her and rendered her speechless. Her vision blurred with unshed tears as the mounting situation weighed on her.

Brodie could die trying to save her.

Hell, she could die waiting on him.

"Then I'm guaranteed without a doubt that Gipson will come for you." Sergio spun around on his heel and left the room with Beefy and Baldy trailing behind him.

The door shut again, and the click sounded as if a cannon had gone off.

She fell back against the wall, the tears finally spilling.

Ronnie bit her lip to keep the sobs from escaping her. Pulling her knees up to her chest, she wrapped her arms around them and held on for dear life.

What had the guys gotten themselves into where this gang wanted them all dead?

She thought of the team she had gotten to know

over the years and knew without a doubt they would come for her. They were strong and resilient.

Ronnie couldn't lose faith in them. They would move Heaven or Hell to get to her.

Brodie, she knew, would be leading the way.

23

"The van observed leaving the hospital was reported stolen. The last known location of the vehicle was here." Mac tapped on a map of the area.

The team was gathered in the conference room at the station. They hadn't been called in yet for an extraction, but they were damn ready.

The manhunt had begun for those who had taken Ronnie.

Brodie folded his arms in front of him. It was hard for him to concentrate. It had been over twelve hours since Ronnie was taken from her job, and the leads were now pouring in.

"It remained there for approximately one hour before leaving. Remains of a vehicle fitting the similar make and model was found scored and charred five miles away, here." Declan pointed to the map. "Ronnie's cellphone pings lined up with the van's locations. We know she was in it."

Brodie heard them but he wasn't there. All he could think about was Ronnie.

Was she unharmed?

Scared?

Alive?

A sour taste came to his mouth. He hadn't been able to sleep at all.

Thank goodness, there were no bodies found when the van was discovered.

No ransom demands. No communication with the kidnappers at all. The news was filled with the hostile event at the hospital. The shooting of a police officer and abduction of a patient and a nurse was the headline of the day. He couldn't even walk past a television without seeing Ronnie's face splashed across the screen.

Desperate, Brodie sent a text to Bryce asking for any help he could give. His friend responded immediately, promising he would send Brodie something he could use. Brodie knew Bryce would come through.

He always did.

The Demon Lords hated every single one of

them who wore SWAT across their chests. They would have to take extreme precautions going into their turf.

"What's taking them so long? If we know the last location before the truck was ditched, why aren't we storming in?" Iker muttered.

The entire team was already decked out in their gear. Tension was high in the room as they all waited.

Brodie rubbed the back of his neck. He promised when he got his Ronnie back in his arms, he was going to lock her away so she would remain safe. If one hair was harmed on her head, he would lose his shit.

He'd tear the Demon Lords apart with his bare hands if he had to.

"We don't have to wait. What if we just happen to be in the area?" Zain suggested.

Grunts went around the room in agreement.

Brodie stared down at the map.

Zain was right.

The location was about forty minutes away.

If they just happened to be in the area, it would cut down on time.

'Gipson!" Mac barked.

Brodie blinked and raised his head, meeting the

hard gaze of his sergeant.

"Are you good?" Mac asked.

Brodie glanced around the room, finding his team's attention on him.

"Yeah." He cleared his throat. "I'm good."

"Why would they take her?" Jordan asked. She leaned back against the wall with a deep scowl on her face. The woman appeared just as fierce as the rest of the team in her all-black.

"That's the million dollar question," Myles murmured. "Brodie and you never denied that you were a couple, so if Cruz was feeding them information on our families and people we are involved with, there would be no connection."

"Look who the fucking patient was." Mac held up the department tablet. He hit the mug shot to make it bigger.

The room grew quiet.

Shit.

Their boy Jack from the bar.

Brodie tensed staring at the photo. Guilt filled him. They should have found a reason to run the son of a bitch in.

Had this been done, Ronnie wouldn't have been in the middle of this war.

Brodie cleared his throat; it was suddenly

constricting. His heart was racing, and breathing was growing more difficult.

"Brodie." Myles grabbed him by his shoulder and spun him around. He met the gaze of his teammate.

"Don't blame yourself. We know what you're thinking." Myles' grip on Brodie tightened.

"There's no way we would have known," Iker said. He came to stand by Brodie, a hard glint in his eyes.

It never failed to amaze Brodie how close they were. They each could read the other.

"We should have run him in," Iker said. "I'm sure we could have come up with charges or something, but we were all focused on the information he had to give us."

Brodie nodded, unable to speak. He glanced around the room and saw nothing but determination on his entire team's faces.

"We'll find them," Zain's voice broke the tense silence.

"Let's ride out," Mac said.

"There's nothing stopping us from doing a ride around." Declan nodded in agreement.

"Let's roll," Jordan ordered, walking over to the

door. She opened it and motioned for them to follow her.

"You heard her," Myles said. He gave Brodie one last squeeze before heading out behind Jordan.

They exited the room and followed their sister.

Brodie pushed down the darkness and rage that he always held back. In the Army, he had done and seen things that he would never want to admit to anyone. Uncle Sam had made him become someone he never thought he would ever be.

Now, that darkness was resurfacing.

Brodie was focused on one thing.

Getting his woman back.

His team surrounded him while they walked through the precinct. All conversations ceased, and the focus in the room was them as they crossed the bullpen.

They exited through the back doors where the BEAR was parked. Zain jogged to the front of the vehicle while Myles opened the back door.

"SWAT!" a harsh voice shouted.

They paused and turned to see Captain Spook walking out the door. The older man had a scowl on his face, and that couldn't be good.

"Shit." Zain came to stand with them.

They all stood braced, unsure of what the captain was going to say.

"Where the hell are you going?" Spook demanded, stopping in front of them. "There is a manhunt going down right now, and we need you on standby."

"We can't stand by, sir," Brodie said, finally finding his voice. It came out flat with an edge. He faced the captain, not giving any fucks. They were leaving, and there was nothing the captain could do short of shaking them all to keep them in place.

"And why is that, Gipson?" Spook's frosty gaze landed on him.

"Because the woman abducted is mine and pregnant with my child," Brodie growled. His hands balled up into tight fists with the admission.

"Son of a bitch," Spook swore. He rested his hands on his waist and looked at the entire group. "I take it you all are going with him?"

Nods went around. That was a question that shouldn't even have to be asked. The captain knew how SWAT rolled.

Always together.

"What happened this time?" Spook asked.

"There's some shit going on that we haven't

brought to your attention, sir." Mac stepped forward, always the one to take responsibility for the team.

"Why am I not surprised?" Spook muttered. "If there was something I needed to know, you should have come to me, MacArthur. How many times have I—"

"There's a mole in the department," Mac cut him off.

Spook held Mac's gaze for a moment. He glanced away before blowing out a deep breath.

"I know. IAB has been in my ass for months. When you return you are going to tell me everything you know," Spook ordered. He met each of their gazes. "Am I clear?"

"Yes, sir," they echoed.

"I'm bringing in backup on this case," Spook said.

Curses went around in the air.

The captain held up his hand to silence them. "You all will need help on this one. The area that's being reported where the hostages are kept is a thick wooded area. It's a vast piece of land that will take more than just you."

Brodie glanced over and met the curious gaze of Myles.

Who the hell would he be bringing in for their backup?

SWAT was the backup.

Their attention was drawn to five police cruisers and SUVs driving into the parking lot. Brodie's attention was drawn to the SUV first in line.

K9 Unit was splashed on the side of the vehicle.

The dark SUV rolled up near them and pulled to a stop. The driver's door opened, and Zayden stepped out. Duchess's bark was muffled, but she made her presence known.

Zayden marched over to them. His unit came to stand behind him. Each man gave Brodie a nod. He was sure his brother had already brought his team up to speed. Zayden's team members were fierce, highly decorated, and all former military. Brodie knew each of them and trusted they always had his brother's back.

"Zayden called in offering his team to back you up," Spook said.

"As soon as I saw it was Ronnie, there's no way I'm standing down," Zayden said, not taking his eyes off Brodie. Words didn't have to be said aloud between the brothers.

She is family.

Zayden would help move Hell and Earth to help

ensure Brodie's woman was returned safe and sound. Brodie knew this as much as if it were him being held hostage.

"Well, hot damn. It's going to be a party now." Iker rubbed his hands. "SWAT and the K9 Unit get to kick ass together."

"Mac will take lead on this one. I'm sure he has more details than I do," Spook said, commanding the air.

All focus turned to the captain. He was in charge for a reason. Highly respected and didn't take any shit.

"I'll be in touch and will share with you updates as they come in. The detective on this case is reporting directly to me."

"We're going to canvas the area to be prepared. It's a secluded area and we don't trust the last maps. They're a few years old, and I'm sure with the gang taking over the area, things have changed," Mac stated. He turned to the K9 Unit. "I hope you got your gear with you, we're rolling out now."

"We're always ready." Zayden's devilish grin spread across his face.

Duchess barked again along with the other dogs in the vehicles. His team murmured their agreement.

"Well, all right then. It's settled. Good luck." Spook gave them a salute before spinning around on his heel and heading back to the building.

They all eyed him, waiting for him to disappear inside. Once he was gone, Zayden moved over to Brodie.

They shared a manly hug. Zayden patted him on the back. He rested his hand on Brodie's shoulder once they pulled away.

"We're going to get her back," Zayden declared.

His words were comforting to Brodie. Zayden had always been Brodie's idol growing up.

Hell, both his brothers were someone he looked up to. They always allowed him to tag along with him when they were younger. They always got into shit together, and always bailed each other out.

There was one thing Brodie knew for certain.

His elder brother always kept his promises.

Brodie's phone buzzed in his pocket. He took it out and saw Bryce's name across the screen. He hit the 'answer' button, and Bryce's face appeared on his screen.

"Brodie," Bryce greeted him. From the sight of the ocean behind him, his friend must be out on his yacht. Bryce was filthy rich, and there was no telling what part of the world he was in.

"Tell me you got me something good," Brodie replied.

"Oh, you know I do." Bryce gave him his infamous killer-watt smile.

Brodie nodded, swearing to himself that he owed his longtime friend if whatever he had helped rescue Ronnie.

"Appreciate it."

"I'm sorry about your woman." Bryce's smile disappeared. "A package should be arriving to you now. It's something I'm sure you are going to have fun with."

Brodie took in the dark luxury sedan approaching. It parked, and a tall, leggy redhead stepped from car. She was dressed in a black pantsuit. When their eyes connected, she tilted her head slightly in a greeting then moved over to the trunk and opened it.

"Who the hell is that?" Iker muttered, his attention on the woman.

"I take it this is your delivery woman?" Brodie's eyebrows rose high. He flipped the phone to where Bryce would be able to see the newcomer.

"Yeah."

Brodie nodded, excitement lining his face like a kid on Christmas morning. "The perks of being rich."

Brodie walked over to the car.

"Hello, Officer Gipson." The redhead smiled. She waved a hand toward the trunk before stepping to the side. "Compliments from Mr. Hayes."

Brodie arrived and took in the large box waiting for him.

"What is it?" he asked.

"It's a stealth drone. One unlike you have ever seen. Once it's up in the air, it is practically invisible and silent. From the intel I've gathered, you will need this," Bryce said.

Brodie wasn't going to ask his friend what intel he had. The guy was a technological genius. He could hack into any system with his eyes closed.

"You remember how to fly one of those?" Bryce asked.

Brodie snorted. When they were deployed, they had used plenty of drones for recon missions.

"Hell yeah. It's like riding a bike." Brodie eyed the box. He couldn't wait to get it out and up in the air. "I owe you, man."

"Nah, all you have to do is get your girl back home safe and invite me to the wedding." Bryce chuckled, sliding on a pair of dark Aviator sunglasses.

Brodie's gaze flew back to the phone.

"Done."

RONNIE PACED THE ROOM. Being locked away for hours had her anxiety levels through the roof. If not for her watch, she wouldn't know how much time had passed. Her phone was long gone, so there was no way she could even reach out for help.

"Come on, Brodie," she murmured. She ran a hand along her small bump and closed her eyes. The connection she had with her child brought tears to her eyes. She had to live for her baby.

Brodie's baby.

They both deserved to hear the first cry, change the poopy diapers, have countless sleepless nights. Ronnie wanted to be able to hold her baby in her arms and sniff his little neck.

Brodie wouldn't let her and their child down.

Her stomach chose that moment to make itself known. The small breakfast they had given her earlier that morning had worn off.

Ronnie moved over to the window, and the only thing she could see were trees. That wouldn't give her a clue as to where they were.

Leaning against the windowsill, she wondered

what the gangsters had in store for her. Was she going to be bait?

It seemed as if Sergio wanted Brodie and the guys to come for her.

Suddenly, it dawned on her.

She was the bait in the trap for Brodie and his men.

Sergio wanted them to come. He and his gang wanted Brodie and the rest of the SWAT team to die.

"Oh God." She whimpered. There was no way she could get a message to Brodie to warn him. He and the guys were going to head straight into a trap.

Ronnie turned her head at the sound of the door being unlocked. She stood to her full height and faced the opening door.

Beefy walked into the room with a bag from a fast-food joint and a drink.

"Here's your dinner." He smirked.

"How do you know what I like?" she grated out.

"Does it even matter? You're lucky Sergio is as lenient as he is," Beefy remarked.

Ronnie shut up and took the bag and drink from him. He was right. They could have left her here to starve. Pregnant or not.

"What are you going to do with me?" she asked.

"Not for me to decide. Sergio will issue and order when he's ready." Beefy chuckled, eyeing her.

Ronnie's skin crawled at the lust that appeared in his eyes. She automatically took a step back.

"Too bad Sergio ordered you to be left untouched. We could have a little fun while waiting for your boyfriend to show up."

"No thanks." Ronnie shook her head. Fear crept up inside her with the realization that they were in the room alone.

He towered over her and was all muscle. There was no way she'd be able to fight him off even if she tried.

"I like when my women put up a struggle." His eyes darkened, his gaze running along her body again. He licked his lips like a lion about to pounce on its prey. "I could take a little taste. No one would know."

"No," Ronnie whimpered. She took another step away from him, her body trembling. She eyed the open door and wondered if she could make it.

"Go ahead."

Ronnie's gaze flicked back to him. A devilish grin spread across his face. This was fun for him. One look into his eyes, and Ronnie knew the sick bastard got off on torturing women.

"Go ahead. Try it."

"Titus."

Beefy stiffened and glanced over his shoulder. Baldy stood in the doorway, watching them. "He said she was to remain untouched."

"But where is the fun in that? We normally get to try out the merchandise," Titus replied. "All I need is a good—"

"Get out of here before Sergio finds you in here," Baldy ordered.

"I'll be back for you." Titus, formerly Beefy, tossed her a wink.

Ronnie swallowed her bile that threatened to erupt. He turned around and stalked out the door.

Baldy gave her a nod and shut the door. The lock sounded, and it was then Ronnie was able to breathe a sigh of relief.

24

"See anything yet?" Zayden asked.

Duchess sat next to her handler's feet. The bond between Zayden and Duchess was unbreakable. They had been a team for a few years, and she was just like another member of the Gipson family.

It felt good to be working with his brother. If he could have anyone working this with him and his SWAT brothers, it would be Zayden and his men.

Brodie shook his head. He had just sent up the drone to the skies. They were a few miles away from a compound that was tucked away from the general public on private ground.

Bryce had sent along a laptop that was fully equipped to display the feed the drone was picking up. They needed to scout out the area and see what security measures were in place before charging in.

It had been a while since he had flown a drone, and the thing he had to remember was this one was more expensive than the common one bought in stores. Bryce wasn't lying when he said the drone was a stealth machine. The engine was completely silent, and once it was in the air, it basically disappeared from sight.

"I need rich friends like yours." Iker leaned against the car.

"Yeah, what you need?" Brodie muttered, concentrating on the land that was on display thanks to the aircraft.

"I don't know. Maybe to attend some yacht parties I hear Bryce throws." Iker chuckled. "It's funny how you've been but never invited any of your teammates with you."

"He does throw some wild ones," Brodie murmured. Now wasn't the time he wanted to think of his friend's wild adventures. Bryce was known to party, and when he threw an event, it always went down in the books. "My next invite, you can have."

Brodie wouldn't need a party with women and booze.

There was only one woman he would want forever.

Ronnie.

"I knew I liked you better than Zain's grumpy ass." Iker slapped him on the back.

Brodie knew his friend was trying to distract him from his nightmare of what Ronnie was going through.

The rest of the team was coming up with a decisive plan on how they were going to approach.

"Shit," he muttered.

The drone flew too low, but Brodie was able to right it and allow it to hover so they could take in the sight on the screen. Sweat beaded his forehead at how close he came to being found. The drone had gotten close enough that Brodie could see the color of one of the guard's eyes. A few of them were out doing perimeter checks, not noticing they had a small hovering craft over their heads.

Zayden let loose a whistle, leaning down toward the monitor. "Look how clear everything is coming out."

"Got anything?" Mac asked, walking over to them.

He and Zayden immediately began making plans for infiltrating the area around the building.

"Yup. Here we go," Brodie said.

The building was a single-story with barred windows, men on the roof, and those walking around it. He flew the drone around, taking in all sides of the building. A garage with open doors revealed a black Mercedes parked inside with a few SUVs. They were able to see everything, and this helped them know what they were walking into. He snapped a few photos of the license plates of the vehicles so they could run them to check out the owners.

Brodie's gut told him Ronnie was inside.

They studied the layout of the area and made plans for their attack.

"The captain has the search warrant for us." Declan hung up his telephone call. "The wagon is on the way."

"Perfect." Mac stepped back from the laptop. He rested his hands on his hips, commanding the group. "Zayden, I want two groups. One team must disable the vehicles. We're going to force them into the forest. We have plenty of zip ties to hog-tie a small army."

Chuckles went around.

Declan's phone went off again. He stepped away and answered it.

"Whatever you want us to do, we will." Zayden nodded.

Brodie continued watching the screen as he guided the drone closer to the building. It flew near a window, hovering near it.

"I'll be damned," he whispered.

"Got something, Gipson?" Declan asked. He walked back over to him.

Brodie felt all eyes land on him. He squinted, looking at the screen.

Was that Ronnie?

A figure paced back and forth in front of the glass.

"I think this is where they are keeping her," he admitted, growing excited. He wasn't sure if it was her, but it gave him hope that she was left unharmed.

"I just got off the phone with Cameron from Gang Unit. He shared a little information he was able to find for us," Declan said.

The entire team surrounded him, listening for updates.

"According to Cameron, they were able to piece together who was taking over the Demon Lords while Vincent Huff rots in jail. His second-in-command is named Sergio Cabal. We are to believe that is who is inside this building. We are to apprehend him and bring him in. Alive."

"We sure about that?" Zain snickered.

"You best believe, if they raise their weapons at you, you better damn well shoot to kill," Mac growled.

The tension in the air grew. This was some serious shit. Mac wasn't lying. These gangbangers were dangerous and out for blood.

"It's either them or us."

Silence ensued around them.

"I just sent a picture of Cabal to your phones. Zayden, please forward it to your team," Declan said.

"Forwarding right now." Zayden glanced down at his cell.

The dogs standing around were getting restless. They were ready for action just as their human counterparts were.

"All right, men. North sector of the building is our target. We will restrain anyone who gets in our way and obtain the person in that room," Declan announced. "Good job, Brodie."

"Thank Bryce. It's his tech," Brodie said. His friend's technology may have just saved Ronnie's life.

"All right, I want Zain, Jordan, Myles, and Declan as our Team Bravo," Mac said.

"Dax, Lane, and Arlo, you're with Bravo," Zayden ordered.

Team Bravo moved together and started going over their approach to the building.

"Everyone else will be Team Alpha," Mac said. "Let's grab our gear."

Brodie flew the drone back to him. The damn thing was fast as hell, arriving within minutes. He stored it away in a side storage container in the BEAR. He joined his team in outfitting himself as if he were going to war.

Never had he ever wanted to rush into a building with guns blazing so bad. The infiltration plans were finalized. Bravo would disable the vehicles first while Alpha would infiltrate first. Bravo would follow in behind once they had neutralized all threats on the outskirts of the building.

"Patrol and the paddy wagon will be here in thirty minutes," Declan said.

Brodie slid his face mask on and pulled his helmet down snugly on his head. His heart slowed to a calm beat as it did every time before a mission. He gripped his MP5 tight, holding it to his chest.

He took in the fierce team members surrounding him and felt love for each member.

They all were here to rescue his woman, take out bad guys, and save the day.

The K9 Unit was dressed in their dark fatigues just as SWAT was. Their dogs were all prepared with their bulletproof vest and badges.

Zayden, Duchess, Rhys, and his partner, Honor, would join Brodie, Mac, and Iker to complete the Alpha team. He met the eyes of Rhys, a well-experienced officer and longtime friend of Zayden's. He was cool when hanging out, but when it came to pursing bad guys, he and Honor were a fierce duo. All the dogs were trained and must have sensed it was time to go to work.

Duchess stood next to Zayden ready to go. There was no playing or barking, she was in police dog mode.

"All right, men. Sync up your communicators," Mac ordered, shutting the door to the BEAR. He held his weapon in his hand while pulling up his face mask. "Time to hunt."

BRODIE AIMED HIS WEAPON TRUE, focusing on the men walking toward him. He was steady, watching the guards who were unaware they were about to be ambushed.

"Sector two is secured," the taller one spoke into a radio.

He placed it back on his belt and held his rifle in his hands as he and his partner drew closer to Brodie, Zayden, and Duchess. The German Shepherd crouched down low, remaining silent.

"Hold," Zayden murmured. All it would take was one order, and Duchess would spring into action.

Mac, Iker, Rhys, and Honor were silent, waiting for the perfect moment.

Brodie turned slightly and met the gaze of his sergeant. Mac motioned for the two of them to take down the guards, while Iker, Rhys, and Zayden waited. Brodie slid the strap of his weapon over his shoulder, securing it to his body. Mac put his Glock into the holster. They both stepped to the edge of the trees waiting for the perfect moment to surprise the two guards. Iker moved a few feet away, ensuring there would be no surprises. His weapon was steady in his hand while he swept the area.

"This is some bullshit. Why we have to be out in the middle of nowhere?" the shorter guard complained. "I am getting ate up by bugs."

"Quit your whining, Craig."

Brodie braced himself, still waiting. The men walked directly in front of Brodie and Mac, unaware of what was about to happen.

Brodie and Mac both sprang forward, silently taking the men by surprise.

"What the—?"

They were no match for Brodie or Mac. The men were taken down skillfully and subdued with zip ties within thirty seconds.

"Now that's what I'm talking about." Iker snickered. He kept his gun trained on the men. "Please give me a reason to pull the trigger."

Duchess whined, her eyes on the men lying on the ground. Zayden held on to her collar to keep her from rushing toward the criminals.

"You're dead men," the tall one seethed. He struggled on the ground before growing still once Mac put a knee in his back. "Mr. Cabal won't like—"

"I don't give a shit what your boss likes." Mac pressed his knee harder into the man's back.

"Want some duct tape to shut them up?" Rhys asked. He held a roll in his hand.

Mac took it from him and tore off a piece.

"I like the way you think." Iker snorted.

"Never leave home without it." Rhys chuckled.

"You can't do this—" A piece of tape went over his mouth, shutting him up.

Brodie knelt on the ground next to Craig. His eyes were wide with fear and locked on the two dogs growling near him.

"Now, you are going to tell me exactly what I need to know," Brodie began. He grabbed the back of the Craig's shirt to force him to meet his gaze. If he had to beat the information out of the guard, he would.

"I don't know nothing," Craig cried out.

The tall guard glared at Craig, muttering something behind the tape. Craig's gaze flicked to his partner.

"Don't look at him. He can't save you." Brodie tightened his hold on the shirt. "I want to know who is in this building."

"I'm loving this new side of Brodie." Iker snickered. He placed his gun in his holster.

Mac elbowed him to shut him up.

"I told you, I don't know nothing," Craig repeated.

"Zayden," Brodie calmly called for his elder brother.

There was no need to look at Zayden. There was a bond between the two brothers. The three of them always could sense what the other needed if one was in trouble.

"Duchess," Zayden's voice was low and chilling.

Duchess crept forward, brandishing her canines, her attention on Craig.

"Wait! Wait. I might know something," he cried out. He tried to wiggle way from Brodie, but he wasn't going anywhere.

"Now either you talk with me, or you get to have a conversation with my brother and his friendly little dog here," Brodie threatened.

"Friendly my ass. Those dogs will murder me." Craig's voice shook.

"I say we let them have you," Mac muttered. The sergeant folded his arms in front of his chest and narrowed his gaze on the criminal.

"I agree. We don't need them," Iker said.

Craig shrieked, trying to scoot away from Duchess. Any other day, Brodie would have joked around, but not this day.

"He wouldn't be a good nutritional meal for them." Rhys snickered, leaning down to pat the fierce-looking Belgian Malinois. She was a rich fawn, her ears black, standing up at attention. "Only the best for Honor. She's in prime shape."

"I'll talk with you," Craig said, looking at Brodie. "Just keep those damn dogs away from me."

"Like I asked before, who is in the building?" Brodie asked. They didn't have long, and he was sure the guards had checkpoints and were going to miss their next one. This would only give a short window for them to infiltrate the building before all hell broke loose.

"Our boss, other guards, and some bitch—"

Brodie's fist slammed into the side of Craig's head. Duchess and Honor continued to growl and paw at the ground.

There was no way in hell this punk was going to call his woman that name in his presence.

"What you do that for?" Craig cried out.

"Don't call her a fucking bitch again," Brodie warned. He ignored the throbbing pain in his fist. "Now tell me. Where is the woman being kept?"

"She's in a room in the back of the building." Craig rested his head on the ground. He released a curse and blew out a deep breath. "They've been keeping her locked in there until the boss is ready for her."

Brodie knew it. It had been Ronnie in the room the drone had flown near. He paused.

Until the boss is ready for her?

"What the fuck does that mean?" Brodie and Mac echoed at the same time.

Mac stood and walked over to them.

"Why did they take her?" Iker asked, all joking put aside.

"I don't know. The dude they picked up at the hospital said the woman was one of the SWAT's women," Craig confessed. "They got it out bad for SWAT."

The other guard muttered something incomprehensible behind the tape and shook his head.

"We've got confirmation of Ronnie's whereabouts. It's the north sector of the building," Mac informed the other team.

Brodie stood from his position on the ground. They were still hidden in the woods, and no one had picked up their location yet.

"We're going to get her," Zayden murmured. He turned back to Duchess. "Duchess. Heel."

She immediately stopped her growling and sat at his side.

"Honor," Rhys called his partner's name. "Down, girl."

The Malinois lay down, but her attention was still on the males on the ground. Both dogs appeared to be disappointed that their handlers wouldn't let them pounce on the criminals lying before them.

Brodie glanced around at his team and gave the nod. It was his way of thanking them for being here.

"All vehicles have been disabled," Declan's voice was clear in the com links. "Team Alpha, are you in position?"

"We are. Stay sharp. We have intel they may be expecting us," Mac replied.

"Do I even want to know how you're getting your intel?" Myles asked.

"Let's just say we're going to get the job done today," Brodie said.

It was time for all games to come to an end.

"All right, men. Just as we planned, we're going in hot," Mac stated.

Brodie's gaze landed on Zayden. His brother gave him a nod and pulled his weapon from its sheath. Just his presence comforted Brodie.

It was time to go get his woman.

25

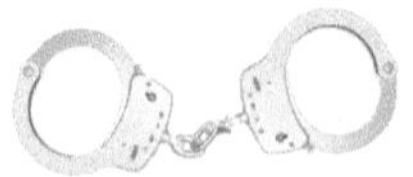

Ronnie didn't know what was going on, but the noise raging outside her door was concerning. Her gut was screaming that something was going down.

With all her years as a nurse, she'd learned to trust her instincts.

She pushed off the wall and skated across the bed. Standing, she slid her shoes on. There was no way she would be caught off guard and be without shoes.

"What the hell is going on?" she muttered. Ronnie moved to the window and peeked outside.

Nothing.

The door flew open with a bang. Ronnie spun around, her heart all but leaping into her throat.

Baldy stood at the door, a scowl embedded on his face.

"Let's go," he said.

"What is going on?" she stammered, frozen in place. If they moved her, there was no telling if she would ever see Brodie or her family again.

"That's none of your concern. Mr. Cabal wants you by his side. Now." He stalked into the room, determination on his face. He snatched her arm and pulled her along behind him.

"Okay," she cried out.

His grip was crushing as he dragged her from the room. They moved swiftly down a hallway until they came into a general area. Television monitors were mounted around with a young man sitting in front of them. His desk was a mess with papers strewn all around it.

"Craig and Damien, come in," he demanded into a radio.

She recognized him as the other voice when she had first arrived.

"Chad, any word?" Baldy asked.

"Look, Mike. Something is going on. That's now two teams not responding for check-ins. Something's wrong." The guy turned around in his swivel chair.

Ronnie glanced at Mike and wouldn't have

pegged him for a Mike. Baldy was a name that seemed to suit him better.

"Shit. I bet they are here to rescue her. We need to go," Mike said.

"I've already put out the alert. Rendezvous at the backup location?" Chad pushed back from the desk and stood. He pulled a duffle bag from beneath his desk and stuffed things in it.

"Yup." Mike tugged her behind him as he spun around.

"Why don't you just let me go," she said. It was her only hope that they would just leave her so they could save their own asses. "If you let me go, then they won't pursue you."

"You don't know your boyfriend and his little band of police officers." He snorted. He whirled around and faced her with a sneer on his face. "There's no way they are letting anyone leave in one piece."

"That's not true," she retorted.

Mike wasn't listening to her. He continued to drag her behind him. Brodie and his team weren't killing machines. They were to protect and serve the community. SWAT was a highly respected group. They didn't go around just killing bad guys with no repercussions.

"Yeah? Then why was our former boss, Silas, shot dead?" He turned on her again with a growl.

Ronnie saw the fury in his eyes and bit back her first response.

He deserved it.

Silas kidnapped Sarena and had planned to kill Mac.

Ronnie had no sympathy for the dead gangster. He accepted the life of crime and all the risk that came with it.

They entered another room, and this one had Ronnie's eyes widening. It was as if she'd been thrown into a movie. There were rows of barely dressed women working at stations with suspicious-looking piles of white powder.

Oh God.

Cocaine.

It was well-know that the Demon Lords were into some heavy things, but Ronnie never thought she would be a witness to it firsthand.

None of the women met her gaze. They all appeared battered, bruised, and exhausted. They were probably women who were trafficked off the streets. Ronnie's heart went out to them. They stood at the tables dividing, weighing, then packaging the product.

A couple of large men with guns stood in the corner watching the workers. Ronnie eyed them, taking in the teardrop tattoos on their faces.

"Code Silver," Mike announced.

The two instantly cut their conversation short and moved around the room shouting at the women.

"You heard him. Code Silver," one ground out.

The women flew into a frenzy, scooping the powder up and putting it in larger bags.

Ronnie assumed it was code for pack everything up and run.

"Hey," Ronnie cried out when Mike yanked on her arm.

He towed her from the room, and they went down another hallway and came upon a set of double doors that were at the end. He pushed them open and dragged her in.

Sergio stood at a desk packing a letter duffle bag. Titus was across the room closing a safe that was on the wall.

"Are they here?" Sergio zipped the bag and reached into the drawer, pulling out a gun.

Ronnie swallowed hard, her arm aching worse from Baldy—Mike's—grip.

"Chad can't confirm, but a few of the teams that

are supposed to be circulating the perimeter aren't answering," Mike replied.

"They are here. I know it." Sergio tucked the gun into the shoulder holster. "We need to move now."

"Boss, you didn't answer me. Do I get to have her when we get to the new location?" Titus narrowed his gaze on her.

Ronnie's skin crawled at the look. There was plain hunger in his eyes. He was all but licking his chops at the sight of her. She bit back a whimper and sent up a prayer that they were right and Brodie and the guys were there.

"When the mission is done, she's all yours." Sergio picked up his bag and stalked toward her.

She stood her ground, meeting his stare.

There was no way Brodie and the guys were going to fail.

She knew it deep in her bones they were going to rescue her.

"You won't get away with this," she said.

Sergio stopped in front of her with a devilish grin on his face.

"Is that so?" he asked. "Who's going to stop me when all of SWAT dies in this here building?"

"What are you talking about?" Ronnie's heart stuttered.

"Not so cocky now, are we?" A dry laugh escaped from him.

He reached out to touch her hair, but she took a step back. Mike squeezed her, eliciting a gasp from her.

"The second they step inside this building, it is rigged to blow. Your little boyfriend and his compadres will die trying to rescue you. Then my boss will be satisfied. Once our job is complete, Titus can have some fun with you."

Sergio brushed past her, leaving her to stand with her mouth gaping.

"Only a matter of time, baby." Titus rubbed his hands together.

"I'll die before I let you touch me," she snarled.

"You might get your wish." Mike pushed her toward the door, releasing her. "Now let's go."

Titus' laugh sent chills down her spine. He moved in behind her, and the distinct feeling of a gun pressing into her lower back had her stiffening.

Ronnie followed Mike out of the office. She was kept in between the two gangsters while Sergio was waiting with two more men she'd never seen before. One was a thin black man with a low-cut fade while the other was light-skinned but had bright-red hair that was an obvious dye job. They had to be more muscle. They held guns and had fierce scowls on their faces.

"Three units are down. We need to move now," Mike ordered.

The men nodded and brought their guns up and began leading the way. Sergio walked in front of her. They steps were brisk as they made their way through the building. They exited through a set of doors and arrived in a garage filled with multiple cars and SUVs.

Come on, Brodie baby. Where are you?

Her stomach flipped at the sight of the vehicles. If they got her into one of them and left, there was no telling if she'd ever see Brodie or her family again.

Her vision blurred with tears.

"What the fuck?" Mike strode forward, stopping near a black Suburban. He knelt by the tires. "How are all the tires slashed?"

"Brad and Red, check the others," Sergio said.

It was apparent which one was named Red. It was fitting since his hair was scarlet.

Sergio pushed back his dark hair from his face and glanced at Ronnie. "This won't stop us. Put us behind, but not keep us from leaving. Always have a backup plan."

Hope blossomed in her chest.

Curses went around in the air as they checked the tires on all of the vehicles in the garage. Ronnie bit back a smile.

"They're all slashed. We need to move to the hanger," Brad declared.

"Brad and Red, you're in the front. We move now." Sergio snapped his fingers.

The two newcomers moved to the back corner of the garage. They knelt and lifted a grate. They climbed down a ladder, disappearing from sight.

Shit.

How would the guys find her?

"Let's go." Titus pressed the barrel of the gun into her back. He rested a hand on her shoulder and guided her over to Sergio and Mike.

Sergio was next to climb down.

"Wait a minute," she gasped, trying to stall, but Titus pushed her toward the hole in the ground.

The gun dug into her back. "Down."

Not having a choice, she turned and made her way down the ladder. It put her in an underground tunnel that was dark and barely lit. There were distant lights built into the wall that were low and allowed slight visibility. She eased around, stepping off the last rung and finding Sergio waiting for her.

"We have been waiting for a long time for this." He chuckled. "SWAT will be no more after today."

Titus appeared at her side while Mike was the last to climb down the ladder. He replaced the grate, covering over their little escape tunnel.

"It won't take us long to get to the other side," Brad said.

He and Red forged ahead down the narrow tunnel. They had to walk in a single-file line.

"I'm liking the scenery from the back." Titus chuckled.

Ronnie wrapped her arms around herself and continued on. She didn't want to let on that his words bothered her. The walls of the tunnel were exposed earth. The ceiling was secured with wooden planks, and she wasn't sure how safe it was.

It would be her luck that it would come crashing down around them and she'd die from suffocating in an underground tunnel.

Not how she'd imagined her death.

"Cut it out, Titus," Mike grumbled. "We have more pressing things on our mind now."

"I know. I'm just admiring the rewards for my hard work." He snickered.

"Any word from Craig?" Sergio asked.

Titus drew silent.

"I'll check in with him." Red pulled a radio off his belt. "Craig. Come in."

Silence was the response.

"Craig. Come in," Red repeated.

Ronnie smiled, continuing on their trek underground.

Her boys in blue were there.

***

BRODIE DUCKED behind a tree as the bullets whizzed by. The building must have had cameras on the outside and picked up their presence.

Raising his MP5, he quickly snuck a peek from around the tree and caught sight of where the shooter was.

Brodie looked across at his brother who was behind another tree; he motioned that he had a clear shot.

He was going to take him out.

Zayden gave the nod.

With trained precision, he leaned around the tree, aimed, and fired two quick shots, taking out the shooter.

That was one thing when dealing with gangsters. They were trained in the tactics of battle like SWAT.

They were erratic shooters, and that made them even more dangerous. They could hurt anyone.

"Move," Mac ordered, brushing past him.

Brodie followed the command and spun around the tree and took off behind his sergeant. Zayden, Rhys, and the dogs were right behind him. They crept toward the building in a single-file line.

Brodie's gaze swept the area, his gun moving with him as if it were an extension of him. They made it to the door and pressed their bodies against the building.

"We're in position to go through the front," Mac proclaimed into the coms.

"We're a little tied up in the back," Declan responded. "Go in without us. Find Ronnie. She's not out here."

Brodie met Mac's eyes. They must have figured out they were there and started clearing out the building.

"We're going in," Brodie growled.

He pushed down the doubt and fear that they were too late. If they'd relocated Ronnie, there was no telling if she were still alive or if he would ever see her again. A sharp pain whizzed through his chest.

The baby.

Tightening his grip on his weapon, Brodie knew he had to keep a level head.

"I've got your six," Zayden said.

"We're going in," Mac shared with the rest of the teams.

"Well, all right. Let's get this party started," Rhys muttered.

Mac aimed his weapon at the door handle, a shot ringing out.

"Go," Mac shouted.

Brodie flew past him, kicking the door open. He rushed inside ready to save his woman.

They cleared the first rooms, scooting through the building. They entered the room where he was certain the drugs were getting packaged. White powder was on almost every surface. That was room was cleared.

They kept going.

Brodie burst into a small room with a cot, a toilet, and a desk. Zayden went in with him. Duchess trotted over to the bed and pawed at the sheets.

"What is she doing?" Brodie asked, walking around the tiny space.

"She smells something familiar," Zayden responded.

Brodie strode over to the cot and took notice of a

blue fabric lying on the bed. He snatched it up, and his heart came to a screaming halt.

It was a nursing uniform jacket.

Ronnie had been here.

"This is Ronnie's," he bit out. There was no other reason this coat would be sitting here. He'd seen her wear similar ones and if not this same one.

"Give it here." Zayden held out his hand.

Brodie tossed it to him.

Zayden knelt next to Duchess. "Smell this, girl. It's Ronnie's. You remember her, right?"

Duchess yipped as if to answer. She grew excited sniffing the material and danced in place. Zayden tossed it to the bed and stood.

Anger pulsed through Brodie's veins.

He was too late.

"We're going to find her. They don't have that much of a head start on us." Zayden's voice snapped Brodie out of his thoughts.

"Brodie, where are you?" Mac came in through the com link. They had split up in pairs to check out the rooms in this hallway.

"I'm in the last room. I found where they had been keeping her." Brodie walked to the door where he met Mac.

"I don't like the feeling of this," Mac admitted,

shaking his head. "They cleared this building out too fast."

Brodie paused.

Mac was right. The entire building was somehow empty, and if the other team ran into heat and she wasn't out there, where was Ronnie?

"We need to keep moving. I'm not getting a good feeling about this," Rhys said. Honor was whining next to him.

"Me neither. Let's head out toward the garage. Maybe we can meet the others outside," Zayden suggested.

"Yeah, let's get out of here," Brodie agreed.

They went down the hallway and turned the corner. They were traveling through the building blind. There hadn't been any blueprints that they could pull up and study. Duchess ran to the front of the group, her nose to the floor. Zayden held on to her leash, giving her more leeway. They followed her, but it was Honor's bark that drew them to a halt.

"What is it, girl?" Rhys asked. His K9 partner was pawing at a ventilation grate in the wall and sniffed it one last time before sitting next to it. "Shit."

Rhys and Zayden shared a look.

"What is she signaling?" Mac asked.

"Explosives," Rhys replied while rubbing her head. "Good girl."

A loud explosion rocked the building. Brodie staggered from the force.

"Run!" Zayden shouted.

They took off running, unable to go back the way they'd come. The building trembled again with another explosion. They burst through a set of doors that led them into the garage filled with cars, vans, and SUVs.

"The doors," Brodie snapped. Sweat poured down his face as he ran over to the first bay door. There was no switch along the wall to trigger the doors to open. Releasing a curse, he gripped the handle and pulled.

Nothing.

"They're locked," Rhys shouted over the roar of the building going up in flames.

"Check the vehicles. Let's see if the keys are in them," Brodie suggested.

It was their last chance.

The building shook again, leaving Brodie feeling desperate. He righted his footing and ran over to a black Suburban. Brodie hopped into the driver's seat and immediately looked for keys to the SUV. He searched every compartment and came up empty-handed.

Fuck.

These modern start engines could not be hot-wired. It wasn't like the good ol' days where they could tear out wires under the dashboard and get a car started. The newer model vehicles ran off computer systems and signals.

Shit.

There was no way no way out of the garage, and they damn sure couldn't run back into a burning building that could fall down around them at any moment.

Brodie stepped out of the truck and met Mac's hard gaze.

They had to figure out how to get out of there. It was only a matter of time before the garage went boom.

26

"No!" Ronnie cried out.

She rushed toward Sergio who held his phone in his hand. She was snatched up by Titus who barked a hefty laugh at her pain. She kicked and screamed, trying to break his hold on her. Smoke trailed across the sky as the building exploded before her eyes. Tears rushed down her face while she watched part of the building she had been held captive in crumble.

They were in the woods about a half a mile away. The tunnel led them to a secluded area that held another structure housing two other large SUVs.

"Your lover is dead," Sergio sniped. He walked over to her and gripped her chin, forcing her to look in the direction of the building. "SWAT will be no more. They should have learned before, but now, because of me, they are dead and I will reap the rewards."

It was sickening how these gangsters took joy in killing the police. They were criminals and deserved everything the police had done to them. How could people be so corrupt, cold, and uncaring?

"You are a monster. They are the good guys," she cried out, struggling against Titus's hold. Her heart was breaking into little pieces. Not only was her man in there, but so was Sarena's, Aspen's, and Roxxy's.

Men who she had grown to know in the past couple of years who were good men.

Strong, stubborn, with hearts of gold.

They couldn't be gone.

Ronnie refused to believe it.

"A monster?" Sergio smirked. His grip on her face tightened, and he turned her to look at him. "You haven't seen anything yet. Soon, we will take out all men and women who wear a badge. This city belongs to the Demon Lords."

"No," she whimpered. There was no way that the entire team was gone. She believed in the system, and if the gang thought they could take out the entire police department, they had another think coming. It would be impossible for them to take out an entire city's defense system.

"Don't believe me?" Sergio challenged, apparently seeing the doubt on her face. "I'm going to prove it. I have big plans, and my boss has been very happy with me. Once we break him out of prison, all hell will rain down, and we will control this city."

"There's no way that will happen." Ronnie sniffed and wiped her face. She grew angry at how this man before her believed his delusions.

"You better be nice to me," he threatened, stepping closer to her. He looked her up and down, a menacing grin overcoming his face. "I promised you to Titus, but I can take that back. He's just one man. I could get a lot of money for you. Especially with you being pregnant. Some of our clients would pay more to have their way with a pregnant bitch."

Ronnie shrank back, shaking her head. She didn't want to think of what he spoke of. She knew sex trafficking was big and many women went missing. It had been all over the news. The police had special task forces searching for women and children.

Ronnie swallowed hard.

"Ah, you are seeing it my way now." Sergio chuckled.

"We need to go," Mike said. "They will be waiting for us."

"Oh, not yet. We need to watch the finale." Sergio chuckled again. He held up his smart phone and tapped a button on the screen.

Boom!

Ronnie's gaze flicked to the scene, and she watched with horror as the garage exploded. Her vision blurred with the tears she could no longer control. A sob escaped her.

Brodie.

Sergio stood proud watching the destruction he'd caused. A wide grin was on his face as he took a few pictures of the sight. Ronnie shook her head in disbelief.

"Let's go." Titus tugged on her arm and towed her behind him.

They made it to the garage and entered through the main door on the side. Titus opened the back door of a dark Tahoe and tossed her in the back. He sat next to her while Sergio got into the passenger side while Red and Brad walked over to the white truck.

"Red and Brad, you're leading the way," Mike called out before hopping into the driver's seat. He hit the button, starting the ignition.

Ronnie scooted away from Titus and sat as close to the door as possible.

"Don't try anything," Titus snarled. He reached across and pulled her away from it.

"Get off me." She jerked her arm away from him.

"You're saying that now." He wagged his eyebrows at her.

She swallowed back the bile that threatened to come up.

The garage doors opened.

Ronnie's heart raced.

Red drove his vehicle out first with Mike driving out of the garage behind them. The truck rocked, rolling over the uneven gravel road.

Ronnie drew in a deep breath. She was going to survive this. She slid her hand down to her slight bump and knew she had to. Brodie would want her to make it so their child could live. She glanced over at Titus who had yet to take his eyes off her. He was grinning like a child who had a secret stash of candy.

Her stomach turned at the thought that she would 'belong' to this idiot. She had two choices, him or being sold off.

Neither were appealing.

The truck lurched to a halt.

"What the hell?" Mike muttered.

"Why is he stopping?" Sergio asked, sitting forward to try to see what was going on.

Ronnie glanced around, and something moved in the woods.

Hope blossomed in her chest.

The sounds of gunfire echoed outside the truck. The white truck rocked side to side from being hit.

"Son of a bitch!" Mike cursed. He yanked on the steering wheel and drove around the white truck. He sped past, but then their truck swayed.

"They're taking out the tires," Sergio shouted over the roaring of the engine.

Mike's curses flooded the air as he tried to drive away, but their vehicle was slowing down, unable to ride on the rims.

Ronnie couldn't contain her excitement.

Looked as if her prayers were being answered.

"THERE'S ONLY two in the white truck," Zayden shouted.

Brodie's breaths were coming fast. They had been trapped in the garage until they had come upon the grate on the ground. They would have almost missed it had Mac not checked the last vehicle and took notice of such a large opening that stood out on the floor. Drain grates in garages were normal to have to send water down into the sewers, but not man-sized openings.

They had quickly jumped down into the underground tunnel and sprinted through it.

Minutes later, the ground shook with the last explosion.

They burst out a door that led them deep into the woods.

The sounds of engines drew their attention.

Brodie's gut told him Ronnie was in one of the SUVs they'd watched pull out of the hidden garage. They couldn't risk hitting her with a bullet, so the decision was instantly made to take out the tires.

The black truck sped around the white one.

Brodie raised his gun and fired, hitting the back tire while Mac went for the front. The truck continued to speed off, trying to ride on the tires that began tearing, and soon they were on the rims.

Two men got out of the white truck and took off running in the woods.

"Zayden," Brodie called out, motioning over to the runners.

His brother and Rhys instantly sprang into motion.

"Honor!" Rhys shouted.

"Duchess," Zayden snapped.

Honor and Duchess barked and danced around, excited. Zayden and Rhys released them, giving orders to attack.

The dogs raced after the men with Rhys and Zayden trailing behind them.

"Brodie, you're with me." Mac motioned for him to follow.

Brodie jerked his head in a nod. He could trust his brother checking out the other truck and apprehending the runners.

The black truck soon drew to a halt. The driver got out of the vehicle and brandished a weapon. He fired aimlessly in Mac and Brodie's direction.

They dove behind trees.

"His aim is for shit," Mac muttered. He replaced the magazine in his MP5 and gave Brodie a nod. They had practiced these drills plenty of times, and Brodie could perform them in his sleep.

"She's got to be in that truck," Brodie said. His gut was rarely wrong, and it was screaming that Ronnie was close. He had to get to her. She was his entire world, and their future was growing in her belly.

"We're going to get her," Mac said. "Come on. Let's end this."

Mac spun around the tree and led. Brodie was right behind him with his weapon drawn up. He rested his finger on the trigger ready to pull it at a moment's notice. A bullet whizzed past him, but Brodie was focused.

His gaze landed on the shooter.

Had he touched Ronnie?

Brodie pulled the trigger.

The man cried out, Brodie's bullet hitting his thigh. He went down on one knee with a roar. The doors on the other side of the SUV opened.

"Brodie!"

Ronnie.

She flew out the door and made it to the back of the truck until hands grabbed her back.

A growl erupted from Brodie at the sight of his woman crying for him. She didn't appear harmed—

An invisible force slammed into Brodie's chest. His body jerked back, the air snatched from his lungs.

Bullets crashed into his ballistics vest.

His body flew back with pain spreading through him.

Shit.

"Gipson!" Mac shouted, firing his weapon at the driver.

Brodie rolled over to his side just in time to see the driver's body hit the ground.

"You good?" Mac asked.

Brodie pushed up off the ground and stumbled. The sight of Ronnie had distracted him from the active shooter.

"Yeah, they have her." Adrenaline rushing through his veins, he ignored the screaming pain in his chest. Even with the vest slowing down the bullets, it didn't take away the force of the projectiles hitting him. He was going to be black and blue come morning, but he couldn't care less.

He had to get his woman.

Raising his weapon, he dashed toward the truck.

"Stay behind me," Mac ordered.

"Like hell I am," Brodie bit out. He moved to the edge of the truck and grimaced. With his gun raised, he peeked around it. He assessed the vehicle and found it empty. "Clear."

His voice was strained, but he was going to continue on if it killed him.

"Stop right there!" a voice called out.

With the amount of trees surrounding them, Brodie couldn't pinpoint where it was coming from.

"CPD!" Mac shouted. "Release the woman to us. Now."

"Fuck you, Sergeant MacArthur," the voice countered.

Brodie aimed his weapon, not chancing them shooting. Mac remained at his side while they slowly crept into the woods. They were out in the middle of nowhere and were at a disadvantage. They would be sitting ducks to the men holding Ronnie hostage.

"Two men," Brodie murmured.

"Easy odds," Mac replied confidently. "And who the fuck is that?"

"It has to be Sergio," Brodie replied. "Whoever that was putting their hands on Ronnie is mine."

"Roger that."

"Not sure how you survived back there." Sergio appeared from behind a tree with a gun in his hand. The cocky son of a bitch had the nerve to be grinning. "I left you a little gift."

"You shouldn't have," Mac replied.

"You should be dead. All of you," Sergio shouted, the smile disappearing. "We're going to wipe every single police officer out. The Demon Lords will rule this town."

"Keep dreaming, fucker," Mac snapped.

"Where is she?" Brodie demanded, his weapon

trained on the gangster. There wasn't a chance in hell the gang would ever be successful. All he wanted right now was his woman.

"Brodie!" Ronnie cried out from somewhere in the distance.

Her yelp followed, and he moved before he even thought about it.

"I wouldn't do that, Officer Gipson." Sergio shook his head. "If you want her alive and in one piece, you better stay right where you fucking are."

Brodie came to a halt. Desperation was growing in him. The need to charge forward and get his woman was overtaking him.

A bark sounded behind him. Without turning, Brodie knew backup had arrived.

"Am I late for the party?" Zayden asked. He and Duchess stood at Brodie's side. He held on to Duchess's leash. The German Shepherd barked and growled, dashing forward but was brought up by her leash.

"I'd say you were just in time," Brodie responded. It was well known criminals gave up when the K9 officers arrived. The threat of being bit by the dogs made most give up immediately.

"Release that mutt and I'll shoot it." Sergio's

voice shook as he backed away slightly, waving his gun again.

"Then we'll fill you up with bullets for shooting a fellow officer," Mac snarled.

The dogs that wore a badge were no different than their human counterparts. They were loyal and helped ensure their handlers were protected.

Sergio must have thought twice about it. He turned and ran off in the woods.

"Attack," Zayden ordered, releasing Duchess from her leash.

She raced after Sergio. Zayden ran after her with his gun drawn.

Brodie and Mac followed.

Sergio never stood a chance. Duchess was on him in seconds. His screams fill the air when the German Shepherd's canines sank into his arm. Her body crashed into him, pushing him down on the ground. Zayden approached, putting his gun away. Mac continued over to help Zayden, but Brodie veered off in the direction he'd last heard Ronnie's voice.

"Ronnie!" he shouted. His heart pounded as he crept deeper into the woods away from the others.

Come on, baby. Give me a clue where you are.

He let his training take over him.

Army.

SWAT.

He had trained his entire life to save and protect others.

Never would he have thought he would use his skills to save the woman he loved.

His chest throbbed, but he ignored it. His breaths were coming faster, but he had to push through. Ronnie was depending on him.

A twig snapping sounded behind him. He turned to the sight of a large hulk coming his way. The figure rammed into Brodie, his rifle falling to the ground. He fell back into a tree with pain exploding through him.

Brodie instantly ducked a fist aimed for his head. He pushed off the tree and threw a left hook, which landed on his assailant's face. He ignored the burst of pain on his knuckles and followed it up with a right punch to the guy's chin.

"Fuck," the guy cried out. He grinned, spitting out blood, and wiped his chin with the back of his hand. "I'm going to have so much fun with her after I kill you."

Brodie's gaze flicked to Ronnie lying still on the ground. A moan escaped her, letting him know she was still alive.

This man had dared put a hand on Brodie's woman, rendering her unconscious?

Rage exploded from him.

The thug rushed him, but Brodie was able to dodge his hold. He punched his opponent in the lower back.

The guy turned around, but Brodie was ready for him. They exchanged blows. Brodie ignored all of the pain.

His woman was lying on the ground possibly hurt. What if something was wrong with the baby?

The attacker was much bigger than Brodie who was quicker. He tried to grab Brodie up, but Brodie was able to evade his reach. Brodie landed a few more punches before he kicked him in the stomach, sending him down to the ground.

Brodie was all over him, dropping punches to his face. Brodie pulled out his Glock from his thigh sheath and pressed it to the forehead of the gangster. He flipped off the safety. He tore the mask from his face, wanting the man to see his. There was no reasoning anymore. He had put his hands on Ronnie, and because of that, he deserved to die.

"You're going to pull the trigger, Officer?" he snarled, staring up into Brodie's eyes. He grinned, his teeth coated in blood. "You're no different than us, hiding behind that badge. You cops are the worst."

"Don't try me," Brodie growled.

"Do it then."

"Brodie," Ronnie's weak voice sounded behind him. "Don't."

"They took you from me." He didn't look over at her but pressed the barrel harder into the forehead of the thug.

"Show her the real you," the thug sneered. He lifted his head from the ground and pushed it against the barrel.

"I'm okay. I promise I am." Her voice was weak and soft. "He's not worth it."

"You are."

27

Ronnie pushed up from the ground with her head pounding. The last thing she remembered was struggling with Titus and screaming Brodie's name.

Then a pain to the side of her face.

He must have punched her.

She had come to with Titus fighting a familiar figure. Even with a face mask on and his full gear, she would recognize Brodie.

"I'm not worth you killing a man." She grimaced, leaning back against the tree nearest her. Her gaze was locked on her man with the barrel of his gun resting on Titus's forehead.

"They took you from me," he repeated.

Ronnie's body shook at how far they had pushed

her easy-going man. It was then she realized how far he was willing to go for her and the baby.

And it scared the shit out of her.

"You going to prison won't help me and the baby," she admitted.

That seemed to snap him out of whatever zone he was in. It was then he looked up at her, and the sight of his crazed eyes gripped her heart. The horror of whatever he had lived through while she was gone was etched on his face.

She was completely and utterly in love with him.

"Please, Brodie. Don't do this." Tears trailed down her cheeks. She needed to show him that she was all right. Kneeling on the ground, she wiped the tears from her cheeks. Ronnie was sure she looked like a hot mess right now, but she couldn't care less.

Now it was time for her to save her man.

Killing Titus would take him from her.

"Gipson," Mac's harsh voice appeared. "Stand down."

Ronnie glanced away from Brodie and took in his team surrounding them. She had never been so happy to see the entire SWAT team decked out in gear with their guns drawn. All of them were there with their weapons trained on Titus.

"We're here, Brodie," Myles said softly. The big

man walked over to Brodie. He rested a hand on Brodie's shoulder. "Go to your woman. I got him."

Brodie looked around him, blinking as if seeing his team for the first time. He jerked his head in a nod and flipped a switch on his gun then slid it in the sheath on his thigh.

Titus chuckled. "Chicken."

Ronnie cringed at the sound of Brodie's fist crashing into Titus's nose.

She closed her eyes and turned her face away, and before she knew it, strong arms closed around her, lifting her from the ground. Ronnie couldn't help the sob that tore from her at the feeling of being in her man's arms again.

"Oh my God," Brodie breathed, his lips brushing her forehead. "I thought I had lost you."

Ronnie leaned into him, the sobs taking over her. She had never been so scared in her entire life. She gripped Brodie, never wanting to let him go. His hands cupped her face and tilted it up. His eyes searched it and landed on her cheek where she was sure a bruise was developing. A growl rumbled from his chest. He swooped down and took her lips in a hard kiss.

It was over before she was ready for it to be.

Brodie rested his forehead against hers.

They remained holding each other while ignoring the people milling around them.

It was as if it were just the two of them.

Brodie was the most handsome man she'd ever seen. Even with his busted lip, blood trailing down his face from a cut above his eye, he was all she would ever need.

"Ronnie Floyd, I love you so much," Brodie murmured.

Her heart leaped. She reached up and took his face in hers. His eyes opened, showing her those blue eyes she had come to love so much.

"I love you, too, Brodie Gipson." She stood up on her tiptoes and pressed a kiss to his lips. "But I don't ever want to see that side of you again. That was scary."

"You and this baby mean everything to me." He slid a hand in between them and rested it on her small bump. "You better believe I'd do anything to keep you safe."

He grimaced, pulling her to his side. It was then Ronnie took in the melee around them. She didn't know where or when all of the people had arrived. Titus was being led away in handcuffs. Polices officers were combing the area around them. The other SWAT members were off in the distance.

"Come on. I'm sure there is an ambulance around. We need the EMTs to check you out," Brodie grumbled. The corner of his mouth was strained, and the color was slowly leaving his face.

"What's wrong?" she coaxed.

Brodie shook his head, but it was apparent he was in pain. The nurse in her immediately picked up that something was indeed wrong with him even though he was trying to deny it. They continued walking, but he was slowing down and swaying.

"Mac!" she cried out.

Mac turned and narrowed his gaze on them. He immediately jogged over to them.

"I'm fine," Brodie said, but neither of them believed him.

"We need a medic!" Mac shouted. He wrapped an arm around Brodie and took his weight off of Ronnie.

Iker joined them, concern on his face.

"Hey, buddy. What's going on?" Iker asked.

Ronnie moved out the way so he could flank the other side of Brodie.

"Nothing. I think the adrenaline is wearing off." Brodie smirked.

"You need a hospital," Mac said.

"No. No hospital. I have a nurse right here."

Brodie motioned to Ronnie then promptly passed out.

BRODIE INHALED SHARPLY and then regretted it immediately. Pain stretched across his chest like wildfire. It burned, and the skin was taut. He opened his eyes and found himself in a hospital room. A rhythmic beeping filled the air. Glancing up, he took in the computer screen with his vitals and his heart rhythm displayed. He looked down and found a figure tucked into his side. She was dressed in sweats with her hair in two braids. She smelled fresh from a shower.

He wasn't sure how long he was out, but it must have been a while.

Brodie wrapped his arm around Ronnie and brought her closer to him. He leaned down and pressed a kiss to the top of her head. She stirred, a gentle moan slipping from her.

"Hey," he said softly.

Her eyelashes fluttered against her cheeks before they opened, revealing her beautiful brown eyes.

"You're awake." She smiled, sitting up higher in the bed.

"How long have I been out?" he asked. He ran his bruised-up hand along his jaw and felt the bristles of his beard coming through. It was dark outside the window, so it had to be awhile.

"Some hours." She caressed the side of his face. "How are you feeling?"

"Good as new." He chuckled. He grimaced, learning that laughing would have to wait for now.

"Whatever, Brodie Gipson. Why didn't you tell me you got shot?" She pushed off the bed and faced him with the cutest scowl on her face.

"Because it wasn't important. I had my vest on," he said. Brodie reached for her, wanting to feel her soft body against his again.

"Oh no. What do you mean it's not important? The father of my child running off and getting shot is a pretty big fucking deal."

"Ronnie. It's okay. This is part of my job—"

"Getting shot?" Her voice ended on a shriek.

"Calm down." He took her gently by the arm and guided her down to him.

She resisted at first but then relented. He wrapped his arm around her and held her close to him. He breathed in her scent, and it calmed his racing heart.

She was safe now in his arms.

Away from the bad guys.

"Brodie, I was so scared we'd never see each other again." Her voice was muffled against his chest.

"I know. I was scared, too," he admitted. The anxiety of going to war when he was deployed didn't even begin to compare to that of the fear that overtook him when she was missing. He hoped to never experience that kind of terror again. "But I wouldn't rest until you were safe back where you belong."

"You were shot twice, Brodie."

"Was I?"

She slapped his stomach, a giggle escaping her.

It was the most beautiful sound he had ever heard. That was why he had fought so hard to so he could continue to hear it. He didn't know what he would have done if something had happened to her.

"Were you checked out, too?" he asked. He slid his hand down to her small baby bump. His heart still raced at the thought that his seed had taken and his child was growing there.

"Yeah," she breathed. Her small hand came to rest on top of his. "We are good. Just a bruised cheek. Other than that, me and baby are perfectly healthy."

There was so much that Brodie wanted to say to Ronnie, but it was going to have to wait. He didn't want to have life-altering conversations in a hospital bed. These last few days had made him realize he didn't want to be apart from her.

Ever.

She was his, and he was going to put his claim on her.

"I'm glad. I was worried I wouldn't make—"

His words were cut off from the gentle press of her finger on his lips.

"Stop," Ronnie said. Her lips curled up in a soft smile. "You saved us. Me and the baby are here because of you. Do you understand?"

"Yeah."

"Now kiss me."

He grinned. His lip was cracked, but he ignored the slight pain and did what his woman demanded.

A throat clearing at the door had Brodie wishing he still had one of his guns with him. He glanced up to see Zayden and Duchess standing in the doorway and relaxed.

Today he wouldn't shoot his brother.

"Are we interrupting?" Zayden grinned.

"Yes, you are," Brodie said.

"No, you're not, Zayden. Come on in." Ronnie laughed, elbowing him in the side. Duchess ran over to Ronnie and stood up on the edge of the bed.

"Hey, girl. I heard you had a part in rescuing me, too."

Duchess barked, her tail wagging. She loved praise and was a big baby when it came to getting her head rubbed.

"I'm the one in the hospital bed and get no love?" he asked but was ignored by Duchess.

"Want a kiss from me?" Zayden laughed, walking into the room.

"You do and I'll punch you in the face." Brodie grinned.

His brother arrived at the bed and ruffled his head.

Brodie brushed his elder brother's hand away, but he was secretly happy to see Zayden. "You didn't tell Mom, did you?"

"No. Dad is aware, and Anders is out in the waiting room on the phone with him."

It was agreed upon between brothers that they wouldn't alert their mother to either of them getting shot. She already worried about them enough with both of them being a cop and Anders a firefighter. Their father understood with his military background. As long as any injuries weren't too bad, they kept it from her.

"What happened after I passed out?" Brodie leaned back against his pillows.

Ronnie's squeal from Duchess bathing her in doggie kisses had him smiling.

"Duchess," Zayden called to the dog. She immediately jumped down and rushed to his side. He took a seat in the chair near the bed with Duchess sitting at his feet. The dog was such a softy. Her tail was still wagging feverishly. It was apparent she wasn't done loving on Ronnie.

"They took in Sergio and his goon, Titus, the one whose ass you whipped."

Brodie nodded. He snagged Ronnie's hand and drew her close to him. She settled on the bed next to him, tucking herself underneath his arm just where she belonged.

"Declan and the others rounded up enough of the other gangbangers who were the last to escape. There were about ten women who had been enslaved by the gang."

Ronnie shuddered. He squeezed her tight, sure she had witnessed the horror of the women being forced to work for the gang against their will.

"Apparently, they were all reported missing from their local towns. The feds are now involved with that."

"They questioned me about an hour ago," Ronnie admitted.

"What?" He grew stiff. The feds were assholes and they—

"Mac was with me the entire time," she continued, obviously sensing the tension in his body.

Brodie gave a nod, satisfied with that. If Mac was with her, then he was sure his sergeant kept whoever the agent was in line with their questioning.

"I didn't see much, but what I did, it was horrible, and I felt so bad for those women."

There was a knock at the door. Mac and the others stood by with somber expressions.

"You mind if we borrow him for a minute?" Mac asked.

"Sure." Ronnie pressed a kiss to his cheek and slid off the bed.

"Here, I'll take Ronnie down to get some coffee," Zayden offered, standing. He picked up Duchess's leash and walked around to the edge of the bed. "I'm sure you all have business to discuss."

Ronnie turned and waved again before disappearing through the door. His team filed into the room, shutting the door behind them. Everyone was present except Ash. Brodie would have to admit he missed his brother and couldn't wait for him to rejoin the team full time again.

"Enjoy your nap, cupcake?" Iker smirked.

Brodie flipped him the bird.

Chuckles went around the room.

"Glad you're doing good, Gipson," Jordan said.

"What's two bullets to the vest?" he teased.

"Painful as shit," Declan muttered.

"Hell yeah." Zain chuckled.

"So, some shit must have gone down if we're meeting here," Brodie said, getting down to business. Any other time when a member was at the hospital, business waited until they were discharged.

"I brought the captain up to speed on everything," Mac declared.

The room grew silent. Accusing another officer of being a mole was one thing. To discover it was true and having evidence of it was another ballpark.

"What happened to Cruz?" Brodie asked.

"The captain is having him picked up now as we speak," Mac replied.

The tension in the room grew. A can of worms had officially been opened. Even if they wanted to keep it silent, the media would be bound to hear of a rogue cop being arrested. It would be splashed all over the news.

If IAB was already snooping around, and now this, their precinct would be at risk for a full investigation. There was nothing they could do for Cruz. He had made his bed and was going to have to lie in it. The fallen officer was going to have a lot on his hands with IAB and the Demon Lords.

"What about his sister?" Myles asked, looking around at the group. "What are we going to do about her?"

Silence filled the air.

"We'll give as much information as we have to missing persons and Cameron and the Gang Unit. If they find her, then we'll answer the call," Declan replied, folding his arms across his chest.

Nods of agreement went around the room.

SWAT didn't usually get involved with ongoing investigations until they were needed. Cameron and his unit were good men and were sure to find her.

"Sergio was officially booked, and the prosecutor is already lining up charges a mile long," Mac said.

Murmurs went around.

Mac held up his hand to quiet them. "But Ronnie shared some things with me that were very concerning, and I wanted to share it with her permission."

"What is it?" Brodie snapped. He hated that he

had been unconscious. He should have been there for her after the craziness earlier that day. She was probably scared and worried about him. She didn't need additional stress on her body. After this was all over, he was scooping her up and taking her far away. Just the two of them.

"She said that Sergio was spouting off that the Demon Lords will be taking out the entire police department," Mac continued. "We were to be first. Had we all been in that building, some of us may not have made it out alive."

Thank God they had separated. They had been lucky to find that underground tunnel leading away from the building or they would have died in the garage. It was no secret the gang wanted to take them out. Brodie didn't believe the gang had the power to take out the entire city's defenses, but now he was unsure.

"What else did she say?" Zain asked.

"She confirmed Viktor was still running the gang from prison, and had Sergio succeeded today, he would have gained a higher rank. She also made mention there was a plan to break Viktor out. The prison warden has been warned of this and will be increasing security around Viktor," Mac said.

"Well shit, anything else you want to lay on us?"

Iker groaned. He leaned back against the wall and slid his hands into his pockets.

"Yup. Captain did share something with us. Good news is that Officer Jones will make a full recovery," Declan shared. They had all got the report that the cop who had been with the suspect, Jack, had been shot but was still able to radio in the distress call. "One bullet hit his vest, while another one grazed his shoulder, and he'll be back to work soon."

Brodie rubbed his chest and sympathized with the other officer. He remembered riding patrol with Jones a few times when he'd first joined the force. He was a good man, kind and tough as nails. It was a shame he was injured on the job. They all knew the risk once they put on their badge each morning.

"This war with the gang is far from over," Mac said. All eyes focused back on their hard-ass sergeant. "But for now, get some rest, spend time with your families."

"Yes, sir," echoed around the room.

Everyone took their turns coming over to Brodie saying their goodbyes. Declan and Mac were the last to leave.

"What?" Brodie asked, sensing they had stayed behind for a reason.

"You are on one week's paid leave," Mac replied.

"Oh, come on, Mac. I'm fine," Brodie argued.

"This is a direct order from the captain himself. I can have him come here to tell you in person if you like," Mac offered.

Brodie rolled his eyes.

"We're already short with Ash out. I'm not—"

"It's an order," Mac repeated, cutting him off. "Ash will be back in two days. Until then, we'll be fine. Zayden and his men have volunteered to help us out."

Looked like everything was taken care of. No wonder Zayden had hightailed it out of the room to take Ronnie for coffee. He already knew Brodie was going to be put on leave.

28

"Brodie Gipson, you are supposed to be on the couch," Ronnie exclaimed. She rested her hands on her waist, tapping her foot on the floor while watching him stroll into the kitchen.

"What? I wanted another beer?" He shrugged and headed for the fridge.

It had been two days since he had been discharged from the hospital, and already he was being one of the most stubborn patients she'd ever had to deal with.

And she was loving every second of it.

There had been nothing but family stopping by since they'd left the hospital. Her family and his ensured they had a kitchen full of groceries and plenty of company. Today was the first day someone hadn't dropped by to check in on them.

"I would have gotten it for you. I'm already in here."

"There's nothing wrong with my legs. I am going out of my mind sitting in this house," Brodie grumbled. The man was not meant to be a couch potato. Everything that supposedly needed to be fixed, had been fixed. The place was immaculate. It had to be the military in him.

There was nothing else for him to do but drive her crazy.

Ronnie was taking a week off work as well. Her job had been very sympathetic with her and the kidnapping from the facility. With the events being all over the news, Ronnie had heard the hospital was putting extra measures in place for security for the staff.

Moving over to the oven, she took the lasagna out and sat it on the cooling rack on the counter.

"That smells delicious." Brodie snuck up behind her and wrapped his arms around her. He nuzzled her neck with his face, bringing her back to him.

"We can eat in about ten minutes once I put the garlic bread on," she murmured. She would never tire of the feeling of his hard muscular body against hers.

"That's not what I want to eat right now." His warm breath blew across her sensitive skin.

Ronnie had to lock her knees together to keep from falling over. Staying in the house with Brodie and not giving in to her urges was killing her. She was trying to allow him time to heal. He had been shot twice a few days ago, and she didn't want to hurt him.

"Brodie," she whimpered.

His hands rested on her belly, and it was such a turn-on for her. One slid up to cup her breast, massaging it while he nipped at her neck.

"You know you want me." He laughed.

Damn him.

He knew exactly what he was doing.

"I never said I didn't," she moaned. Her nipples were hard as diamonds, and her core grew slick with need.

"Then why are you torturing both of us." He pinched her nipple, eliciting moan from her.

"Because I don't want to hurt you," she breathed. Her hands rested on the counter, gripping it tight. Earlier that morning, she had tossed him the remote to the television, and the movement to catch it had caused him pain.

"You could never hurt me." His lips trailed hot kisses along her neck and up to her jawline. He turned her around and pressed close to her. He swooped down and captured her lips with his.

Ronnie gave in.

There was no way she could resist him any longer.

"What about dinner?" she asked, breaking the kiss.

"We can eat later." He reached over and shut off the oven, then took her hand in his and towed her behind him.

A giggle escaped her while she trailed him to his bedroom. They burst through the door, and Brodie didn't waste any time stripping the clothes off of her. His followed, joining the pile on the floor.

Ronnie found herself sprawled across the bed with her sexy police officer bracing himself over her. She stared up into his eyes and felt so much love in her heart for him.

"I love you," she murmured.

"I love you, too." He leaned down and pressed a soft kiss to her lips.

There wasn't a day they didn't share how they felt about each other. Ronnie was so damn happy she could burst. She had everything she had ever wanted in life. A sexy man who loved her and a baby on the way.

"Are you sure I won't hurt you?" she asked.

"You'll hurt me if you keep holding this from me." His hand slid down her torso and over her baby bump to reach his final destination between her legs. He teased her, his thumb brushing along her swollen clit.

A throaty moan slipped from her. She bit her lip and pushed with all of her strength and rolled with Brodie until she landed on top.

"This will work, too." Brodie laughed.

His smile was infectious, and to think she'd almost lost him had her vision blurring from unshed tears.

"Good." She rested her hands on the mattress either side of his head and leaned down, kissing him.

He allowed her to control the kiss. Her tongue slipped inside his mouth, stroking his tongue. Brodie's hands skated along her hips, up her torso, and landed at her breasts. He cupped and massaged them. Ronnie tore her lips from his, needing to feel him inside her.

She reached back and took his thick shaft in her hand and lifted herself. She nestled the tip of him at her opening. Brodie didn't take his eyes off of her while she slowly impaled herself onto him. A moan escaped her.

"Jesus," he muttered, the smile disappearing. His hands came to rest on her waist as he helped guide her up and down on him. "Ronnie."

"Brodie," she moaned.

Their bodies moved together in perfect harmony. She took everything he had to give her.

This man was meant for her.

There was no way they would find each other only to be torn apart.

Ronnie threw her head back, turning her pleasure over to the love of her life.

Soon they crested at the same time, their moans and shouts of ecstasy filling the air. Ronnie slumped down on top of Brodie, spent. Her limbs were like wet noodles. She couldn't move if she wanted to. Brodie wrapped his arm around her, shifting them sightly to tuck her into his side.

Together, they lay holding each other.

Ronnie smiled. She wasn't sure what the future held, but at the moment, she was happy with everything she had.

"Ronnie." Brodie dropped a kiss to her forehead.

"Yes, love?" she asked, her hand resting on his chest.

He tilted her chin up so they could look into each other's eyes.

"I was just thinking that I don't want to be apart from you," he said softly.

"I'm not going anywhere."

"No, what I mean is that it doesn't make sense for us to live apart."

Ronnie pushed up onto her elbow and stared at him. A small smile played on her lips.

"Are you saying you want us to move in with each other?"

"Yes. I want to be able to hold you every night. When the baby comes, I don't want us to have two separate residences. I want us to be together. If you want, we can even go find a new house."

Ronnie's eyes teared up. "Okay."

He drew her face to his and gave her the sweetest, softest kiss ever.

"Thank you."

"For what?" she asked playfully.

"For giving me everything I could have ever asked for."

"Can we open the envelope now?" Brodie asked for the hundredth time.

"I said as soon as we get to the house." Ronnie chuckled.

They were on their way home from her ultrasound and doctor's appointment. Everything was going fine, and according to Ronnie's doctor, the baby was growing on target. It had been a month since the ordeal, and Ronnie moving in with Brodie. They had agreed on a fresh start and would sell both of their homes. Currently they were living in Brodie's house until they could find the perfect home for their growing family.

It was a beautiful day with the sun shining, and Brodie couldn't be happier.

He had returned to work, and things around the precinct were tight following the arrest of Diego Cruz. The media had turned it into a circus. Just as they all knew, Cruz was the top story, and the media was not nice at all. They were painting him as a double agent for the notorious gang while carrying a badge.

"I understand telling everyone at the same time, but why can't we know what we are having?" Brodie grumbled.

"Have some patience, Brodie Gipson." Ronnie laughed. "We will be home in a few minutes."

That was entirely too long. He had been waiting for this day. He just had to know what they were having. He wanted to have everything prepared for the arrival of their bundle of joy. Not that it mattered what they were having. All Brodie wanted was a healthy baby Gipson.

The wait was killing him. He'd been on stakeouts before and that couldn't compare to this. His anxiety was through the roof. Mac and Sarena had already found out what they were having. The MacArthurs would be welcoming a baby boy.

"As soon as we get in the house, we're opening that damn envelope. I don't care who is not in the room," Brodie complained.

Ronnie barked a laugh and rested her hand on his knee.

They pulled up into the driveway, parking behind the few cars ahead of them. Their parents and siblings were invited over. Their mothers fixed lunch while they ran out to their appointment. Brodie exited the SUV and jogged over to Ronnie's side. He helped her down and entwined their fingers.

"I'm so hungry," Ronnie announced, rubbing her cute baby bump.

"Me, too." He didn't know what their mothers were cooking, but the scent outside the house was causing his stomach to rumble. Brodie slid his key in the lock of the front door and pushed it open.

Ronnie walked inside first. He slammed the door behind them.

"Let me go into the kitchen—"

"Nope. Living room." Brodie tightened his hand around hers and tugged her behind him. "Whoever is not in the living room in one minute will miss out on the news."

The guys were all sitting around in there having a heated discussion about football.

They immediately grew silent at his announcement.

"What is all the ruckus?" Teri asked, walking in with Jackie and Rowan in tow.

"We have good news?" Jackie asked.

"I've been waiting on a text or something." Rowan snickered.

"We don't even know yet," Ronnie said.

He tugged Ronnie in front of the television so everyone could see them. He was too impatient to wait a second longer.

"Baby is doing fine." Ronnie reached into her purse and took out a manilla envelope. "And the answer to the question Brodie is dying to know is right here."

"A healthy baby is all I truly want." Brodie drew her to him and dropped a kiss on her lips. He tried to snatch the envelope from her, but Ronnie was too quick.

Laughter went around the room.

"Not so fast, buddy," Ronnie teased him, dancing with the envelope.

"Put the boy out of his misery and tell us what our grandbaby is," Jackie said.

"Okay." Ronnie tore the envelope open and pulled out a sheet of paper. She scanned it with a wide smile spreading across her face. She turned it around and held it up for Brodie to see. "A boy! We're having a boy!"

Brodie snatched Ronnie up and spun her around.

A boy.

They were having a baby boy.

Their family laughed and clapped while Duchess barked, the poor dog unsure of what was going on.

He put Ronnie down and dropped a kiss on her lips.

"I love you so much," he said.

"I love you, too."

He had been waiting for this exact moment. The room quieted as he got down on one knee.

"Brodie, what are you doing?" Ronnie asked, her eyes growing wide.

Brodie drew out a small black velvet box that had been burning a hole in his pocket all morning. He nervousness grew as their family looked on. Brodie had already discussed the proposal with Ronnie's family, and they all gave their blessing.

"Ronnie Floyd, I believe I have loved you since the moment I first met you. There's never a day that I don't think about you. You make me smile, laugh, and you're the most beautiful woman I have ever met."

"Brodie." Ronnie wiped her cheeks.

"Will you marry me?" he asked.

"Yes. Yes, I will." Ronnie nodded.

Brodie slid the ring onto her finger before standing and taking her into his arms. He swooped down and covered her mouth with his. Their families converged on them with their excitement.

Brodie held Ronnie close to him. He had everything he could have hoped for.

Dear reader,

I want to start off by saying thank you for your patience with me in getting Brodie and Ronnie to you. This series is well loved, and I want to make it as perfect as I can for you.

Hope you enjoyed Dirty Justice and I promise, I won't keep you waiting too long for Dirty Trust! Iker is up next!

Don't forget to leave a review. This is how I know you want more!

love,

Peyton Banks

ABOUT THE AUTHOR

USA TODAY best selling author, Peyton Banks, is the alter ego of a city girl who is a romantic at heart. Her mornings consist of coffee and daydreaming up the next steamy romance book ideas. She loves spinning romantic tales of hot alpha males and the women they love. Make sure you check her out!

Sign up for Peyton's Newsletter to find out the latest releases, giveaways and news! Click HERE to sign up or visit her website www.peytonbanks.com !

Want to know the latest about Peyton Banks? Follow her online:

Current Free Short Story

Summer Escape

Blazing Eagle Ranch Series

Back in the Saddle

Knockin' the Boots

Roping a Cowboy

Country at Heart

Cowboy, Take Me Away

Hard to Forget

Special Weapons & Tactics Series

Dirty Tactics (Special Weapons & Tactics 1)

Dirty Ballistics (Special Weapons & Tactics 2)

Dirty Operations (Special Weapons & Tactics 3)

Dirty Alliance (Special Weapons & Tactics 4)

Dirty Justice (Special Weapons & Tactics 5)

Dirty Trust (Special Weapons & Tactics 6)

Dirty Secrets (Special Weapons & Tactics 7)

Trust & Honor Series (BWWM)

Dallas

Dalton

Interracial Romances (BWWM)

Pieces of Me

Hard Love

Retain Me

Silent Deception

The Christmas Secret

Mr. Hotness

African American Romance

Breaking The Rules

Mafia Romance Series

Unexpected Allies (The Tokhan Bratva 1)

Unexpected Chaos (The Tokhan Bratva 2) TBD

Unexpected Hero (The Tokhan Bratva 3) TBD